For Lori Wilde, who read Lucky Cowboy for me and encouraged me to write small town westerns.

BUILT LIKE A COWBOY

MEN OF STONE RIDGE

HEATHERLY BELL

PROLOGUE

*W*ell, I'm certainly glad I was sitting down when I heard *this* news. If you're at all faint of heart, you might want to do so yourself, and get the smelling salts right now. Yes, it's true. THE Winona James, famous country singer, and CMA three-time winner of the best vocalist of the year, has made Stone Ridge her home. But were that ALL I'd have to tell you, it wouldn't be that big of a deal. After all, Stone Ridge, Texas, is home to Jackson Carver, country singer, and bona fide man of Stone Ridge. Born and bred. To us, famous country singers are not as big of a deal as they would be somewhere else, like for instance, say…Kerrville.

As the head of the SORROW, I was one of the first to welcome the new young lady to our small town. We were sure happy to have her, as we certainly don't have enough single women for all of our single men, and we would like to see some marriages going on lickety-split. And though I was getting ready to launch an email-order bride service, a few in town are squeamish about the idea. I'm in agreement that we can't just let *any* woman move here and stake her claim to one of the men of Stone Ridge. But this is all to say that I more than welcomed Winona James into our quaint little female-scarcity town. She comes vetted, so good or bad, we know what we're getting.

Then I heard what she was up to, and that's when I required said smelling salts. Apparently, Miss James is here in town to acquire herself a *sperm donor*! Yep, you read that right, folks. Not a *husband*, not a *partner*, *not* a lover, all she seems to need is the seed. For shame! The few of us in the know about her plans want to ask why on *earth* she doesn't just go to one of those banks they have in big cities where all the heathen live. Like, for instance, Dallas. Well, don't you know Miss James's first ~~victim~~ target was Jackson Carver himself, her THIRD ex-husband. But when his fiancée Eve got wind of *that*, well, you can just imagine. Jackson was rumored to have said, "'No thank you, ma'am' but in more colorful language. I'll spare you the details.

Now, as if all of this isn't scandalous *enough* for us, the woman is *interviewing* men for the position of the father of her child. Butter my biscuit, because I never *imagined* the line would be so long! All I can say is, whoever the poor man is, he best find a way to keep his baby in Stone Ridge, even if he has to hog-tie the mother.

~ Beulah Hayes, President of SORROW (Society of Reasonable, Respectable, Orderly Women) and keeper of the *Men of Stone Ridge* bible, 10th edition ~

CHAPTER 1

*W*inona James was in Stone Ridge for the men, and at this point, she didn't care who knew it.

But placing an ad hadn't seemed appropriate, so this had become a word-of-mouth situation. At this rate, she could be here for a while. This was not the happiest of thoughts.

Stone Ridge was a small town on the outskirts of Hill Country and didn't even have a hair salon. When she'd asked about the closest Starbucks or Peet's, her landlord had laughed and called her "precious." She'd had to suffer with the inadequate coffee from the General Store and beg the new owner of the Shady Grind to please start serving stronger coffee. He happened to be her ex-husband, so he *knew* how dangerous life could become if she didn't get her caffeine fix.

Of course, if her plan worked well, soon she'd have to stop drinking coffee altogether or switch to decaf (horrors). But by then, she'd be happy to leave this small town, kick the dust off her boots, and go back to the outskirts of Nashville, where she'd raise her sweet baby. She'd wanted a child for as long as she could remember, but the intensity had grown every year past the age of thirty. It had reached the point where she'd be on the verge of tears every time one of her friends or colleagues announced their pregnancy. She wanted to be happy for them, but when would it be her turn?

The "baby contract," which she'd worked out with her manager and lawyer, Kimberly Foster, left nothing open-ended. Everything was covered. Simply put, if the man agreed to her terms, he'd be the biological father of her child, and would hand over sole custody. If they wished to, of course, they could have visitation but she didn't expect that they would. But so far, the young men interested in being the father of her baby were so young they were not thinking much beyond making their "deposit."

Not that she blamed them because she'd been wild in her twenties, too, and most of her thirties. But Winona would be forty later this year and it was time to settle down. She'd longed to be a mother for years but none of her marriages had stuck. Nobody's fault. They'd just been the wrong men. Either abusive and controlling (her first husband), cheating (her second), or in love with someone else (Jackson, her third and last).

She heard a knock at her front door and rushed to open it. This had to be another prospect, arriving for his appointment. Her jaw gaped when she saw the man standing on the other side of the door. She had an interview scheduled for today but could have never hoped for someone like him. Holy cow, this man had been built in cowboy heaven. Judging by his height in comparison to her own average one, he had to be well over six feet tall. He was *exactly* what she'd had in mind. She'd peg him to be in his late thirties or early forties. Not a kid but a full-grown man. Tall, lean, but muscular, he wore a tipped Stetson slightly shadowing a penetrating gaze. Eyes the color of whiskey matched dark hair slightly graying at the edges, with some light beard scruff on a square jaw. Testosterone leapt off him in waves. He'd probably started shaving when he was *three*.

He made her think of long, lazy days in bed. Her womb woke up, ready to do the two-step.

Yes, girl! Yesss! This is more like it!

"Please come in, sweetheart. You're early. You get extra points for that," she said, trying not to drool.

"Actually, I'm a little late." He followed her into the living room. "And I'm never late."

She pointed him to the couch and sat in the chair in front of him, ready to begin the interview. "Tell me, why are you the perfect person for this job?"

He straddled the chair between two long legs. "I have a lot of experience."

"You do?"

Dear Lord, what were the odds of this kind of man dropping right in her lap like this?

"Of course. I'm a rancher, but I fill in here and there for these types of jobs."

What a progressive town! "And they *let* you do this? Does everybody know?"

"Does everybody know what?" He looked annoyed and hooked his thumb. "Look, I'm wastin' daylight here. Can I just get on with it?"

While she'd be willing to drop everything here and now for this man, that was the old Winona. The new and improved version wanted to have a baby and she couldn't just hook up with a handsome stranger. Besides, he had to sign the contract and have a visit to the doctor for a clean bill of health. So far, she'd had two interviews, and not one returned contract, which made her think these young men weren't taking her seriously.

"I love the enthusiasm!" She winked. "But I have a few more questions before I can offer you the position."

He cocked his head. "I thought I already had this job."

"Well, you pretty much *do*, but there's just few little things we have to go over first."

"Like what? I don't have much time."

Oh dear. Well, looks weren't everything. He wanted to get this over with. Not too promising.

She sniffed. "I had hoped this would at least take an afternoon."

"Well, it's goin' to take me more than one *afternoon*. I don't do shabby work and I always get the job done well."

"Oh boy, I'll just bet you do."

"What else did you have in mind?" He leaned back, splaying large hands on his thighs. "Because all Merle mentioned was the patio addition."

Merle. That name was familiar as Merle Stephens was her landlord.

Every randy thought, every hope she'd held for a virile hunk of a man her age ready and willing to knock her up, evaporated. With looks like his, he was probably married with children. Taken, like most of the good ones. Her hopes fizzled and dropped dead of exhaustion. At least she hadn't asked about his sperm motility. It was hard to come back from that one. She could act as if she'd been talking about the same thing.

"Oh no. That's it. The patio addition. Right this way, please." She led him through the kitchen to the connected patio.

Even though she'd hopefully be renting this home a short time, she'd wanted an enclosed area protected from the heat and elements where she could enjoy Hill Country and possibly write some songs. Mr. Stephens had agreed because he'd planned to sell this property after she left anyway and agreed it would be a selling point.

She supposed this drool-worthy cowboy would be here

every day until the work was complete. Torturing her with his big, hard body. Well, she didn't care. She had a mission to accomplish.

"What is your name? I assume it isn't Jeremy Pine."

"Riggs Henderson."

"I'm Winona James."

"I know."

He shook her hand, a strong firm shake and a gaze that met her eyes without a hint of male appreciation or interest. She, on the other hand, felt a sizzle whip through her like a category three hurricane. Story of her life.

There remained only a slight glimmer of curiosity in his eyes. *Who are you, again? You look vaguely familiar.*

His wife was probably a fan.

He stood outside the open patio, hands on hips. Then he nudged his chin in the direction of the house. "Okay, Miss Winona, you can go back to whatever you were doin' when I got here."

"I hope it's not askin' too much, but I have interviews scheduled almost every day, and while that's goin' on, I would appreciate a little quiet out here. Just so that I can hear myself think. I have some big decisions to make."

He quirked a brow. "Sure. I'll work *quietly.*"

A truck pulled up to the side of the house, kicking up gravel, and Winona turned toward the sound. "I think that's my appointment."

"Don't mind me. I'm good."

Winona went inside to meet Jeremy Pine and after a short greeting, led him into the living room and pointed to the couch. "Have a seat."

Jeremy Pine was blond but also tall and built, as were most of the cowboys in these parts. The young single men had been following her around like puppies since she'd arrived. She'd actually come to stop her ex-husband from

7

getting back together with the woman who stood him up at the altar. Also, she'd asked him for his sperm, since she'd already made the trip.

That hadn't gone well. Awkward.

"How old are you again, sweetie?" Winona asked, holding her pad and pen.

"I'm twenty-five, darlin'," Jeremy said.

Oh, sigh, he was so *young*. She couldn't remember the last time she'd dated someone her own age. Unfortunately, all the single forty-something men she knew were in relationships with twenty-something women.

He cleared his throat. "Well, I will be twenty-five. In about six months."

She gave him a small smile. Lying about your age to be older. Lord, how *sweet*.

He was certainly attractive enough physically, though there were no real sparks between them. She'd have to feel *something* for a few minutes at least, longer if she got lucky. See, Winona had decided early on, after Jackson had refused, that she'd go ahead and do this baby thing the old-fashioned way. There were two reasons for this. First, Winona hated needles, although the word "hate" wasn't strong enough. And secondly, Winona enjoyed sex, as long as it was on her own terms.

"Have you had your physical?"

"Yep, doctor said I'm as healthy and clean as I could be."

"You sure look good."

He grinned, but rather than a wicked smile it was sweet, and far too innocent for her liking. Despite all the filthy tabloid lies printed about her in the past, Winona didn't set out to make men out of boys. She far preferred men her age and only wished that one of them would give her the time of day. But here in Stone Ridge, most of them were already married. And anywhere else, well, she was far too *old* for them.

Winona went back to her questions. These were important, because she not only wanted good physical attributes in a father, she also preferred he have some intelligence and higher-level education. Her child would probably get musical talent from her, as well as the stubborn ability to survive just about anything. But for education, she'd need the father's help. Winona had barely graduated from high school back in Welch, Oklahoma, and though she had it on good authority that she wasn't stupid, she certainly wasn't educated. It was one of her deepest regrets.

"How well did you do in school?"

"All As and Bs."

"Wonderful. And—"

Bang, bang, bang.

She blinked, then tried again. "…how about—"

Bang, bang, bang, bang, bang!

Winona threw a glance to the window. "I told him to work quietly when I'm interviewing."

The hammering stopped and Winona smiled. "Okay. Where were we?"

"You were asking me about my education."

"Oh, that's right. Now, do you have a—"

Buzz, buzz, buzz.

"Degree—"

Buzz! Buzz! Buzz!

He had the saw going now! Looker or not, he was going to die!

"Oh, now that's it!" Winona stood. "I will *not* tolerate this."

"Ma'am?" Jeremy stood, voice laced with concern.

Winona stomped to the back of the room, hauled up the window and hung halfway out of it. "I asked you not to make noise while I'm busy in here."

He stopped sawing on a two by four long enough to give her a long, patient look. "You were serious about that?"

"Yes!"

He scratched his jaw. "But I'm runnin' behind schedule. Ma'am."

And he'd probably added the ma'am to make her feel older. By the tiny crinkles around his eyes, he was probably slightly older than she was anyway. Maybe she should start calling him "sir" and see how *he* liked it.

"I'm almost done in here."

He went palms up and stepped back from the saw. "If you don't care when this gets finished..."

"Thank you!"

She stomped back to Chris, or Jeremy. Pine, was it? She was so bad with names. And the buzzing appeared to be in her head now.

"So *sorry* about that." She took her seat again. "Your degree is in—"

Bang, bang, bang.

"Here's the contract, sugar." Giving up, she reached and handed over the four-page document. "Just read it over, and if you agree with everything in there, we'll talk some more."

"Okay, then." He stood, holding the hat to his chest. "I think we could make a beautiful baby, and I know I'd sure have a good time doing that. And you would, too, of course. I'd make sure of that. Thank you, ma'am."

The second "ma'am" pretty much spelled the end for Jeremy. She would *not* have sex with a man who'd referred to her as ma'am.

But her chest tightened because she had to pick someone soon. The ovulation kits she'd purchased indicated she should be at the height of ovulation for just a few more days, and yet so far, she'd failed to find the right father for her precious baby. It wasn't all that easy to do since she was shoving months, or years, of courtship and relationship into a few weeks. And if she didn't find someone in a few days she'd be stuck out here for another month.

Kimberly already thought Winona was nuts but given that she had once married in a Las Vegas drive-through, Kimberly was used to a high bar. Those had been her hard-drinking and partying days and they were over. She'd been in training to be someone's mother for a year. That meant no more drinking, smoking, and no more hookups. Not that she'd ever been nearly as active as the press liked to believe.

She'd been examined, and the doctor said that even if her age made her a bit high risk, there was no reason she couldn't have a healthy baby if she took good care of herself. But after forty, her chance of conception would drop to less than ten percent. She'd bought all the baby books and read them every chance she had. With so many differing opinions on everything from co-sleeping to potty training, she was grateful she'd make those decisions on her own. She just had to find the right man to be the father of her child.

After Jeremy left, she stomped over to the window again. Riggs tipped his hat to acknowledge her, a nail caught between his lips. The grin he slid her was wicked. Teasing.

"Hammer on and saw all you want, buddy, as loudly as you want. I'm done in here. And when you want to take a break, I've got some iced tea in the kitchen for you. I promise not to spit in it!"

And with that she shoved the window shut.

CHAPTER 2

"*I*f you think that's goin' to stop me, lady, then you obviously haven't lived on a ranch." Riggs chuckled to himself and went back to his grinding.

Winona sure had an interesting way of going from zero to sixty in five seconds. It was hard to believe this woman had been married three times. How she'd managed to find *three* men to put up with her, he'd never know. Sure, she was beautiful in that ridiculously glamorous "Hollywood" way that had no place in Hill Country. The moment he'd laid eyes on her he assumed that she shopped at www.CountryWesternFashion or something. A place where wealthy women shopped for clothes that made them look down to earth and approachable. Ha!

He didn't know too much about her as he stayed away from gossip, preferring to keep to himself, take care of his family ranch, and anything or anyone else that needed tending to in this town. A pride of ownership fell over him to be a man of Stone Ridge. The town had become home to him and his two brothers after their parents lost custody of them.

All three had been adopted shortly after going into the

foster system and had the good fortune to wind up in the home of Calvin and Marge Henderson. They'd been an older couple, already in their sixties when they took in three boys, and had been gone a few years now. All three brothers had inherited the cattle ranch since there were no biological children. Riggs took primary management for its running, with help from his younger brothers.

Though he worked part-time as a carpenter to supplement his income, he would first and foremost consider himself a cowboy. This patio addition job shouldn't take long, but he'd had a few days last week when he couldn't start work on the ranch-style home owned by Wanda and Merle Stephens. He'd gotten a late start. The princess had decided the patio, which would be fine in its current condition for any reasonable person, should be made into a "Florida room."

Basically, an enclosed patio to be protected from all the elements, for one to sit and do nothing. He hoped nobody in *Texas* had a Florida room. But Merle had indulged her, as he imagined most men did.

Riggs wiped his brow with the back of his hand. The Texas heat beat down on his back and he wanted to pull off his sweat-soaked shirt.

So, Jeremy Pine had shown up for an interview. Riggs had no idea what the interviews were about, nor did he care. But she'd made no effort to hide the fact that she'd checked him out head to toe, and he'd done his best to school his expression into one of disinterest. It was a damn lie, of course, as he appreciated a good-looking woman as much as the next guy.

She was no girl, this one, but seemed fully at home in her own body and skin. Confident enough to give him hell. Ever since she'd arrived in town a few weeks ago, it seemed every single guy had noticed her. They often followed her around town in groups. He didn't want her to get the stupid idea that he'd also be interested in being one of her groupies.

Still, he dropped the piece of cut wood and headed into the kitchen for that iced tea.

He found her in the air-conditioned kitchen strumming her guitar and singing softly. As far as he could tell, she wasn't an expert at playing the guitar, though her voice was much better. Surprisingly sweet melodic sounds coming out of someone so damn ornery. She'd gone from sweet to menacing when he'd ignored her request to work quietly. Sue him, but he'd never been trained to hammer and saw softly.

She now slid him a look that would stop a clock. Those tight jeans of hers no doubt had tassels on the rear pockets. She wore a shiny pink halter top with plenty of glitter and tassels. On her feet were boots with intricate designs that would never see the dirt of a real ranch, and her platinum blond hair was styled long and straight. She wore a shit ton of makeup including eyelashes so long they could not possibly be natural.

"What?"

Apparently, he'd been staring too long.

"Nothin', ma'am, came in for some of that sweet iced tea if you don't mind." He made this sound as if he was a twenty-year-old, the age of most of the men who worshipped at her altar.

At forty-two years of age, he *never* said, "if you don't mind."

She might have growled. "Stop calling me ma'am. I hate it."

"Just tryin' to be respectful."

He opened the refrigerator door and helped himself to the pitcher. She didn't seem the kind of woman to wait on a man and he wasn't the kind to wait for a woman.

She helpfully pointed to the cabinet with the glasses. "No, you're not being respectful, sir. You're tryin' to make me feel old."

"A little sensitive?"

The moment she'd figured out he was here for the patio work she'd treated him like a leper. She was a strange one but maybe carpentry didn't go well with her vision of a true cowboy.

"Have your iced tea and leave me alone," she said now. "I'm tryin' to write a song."

"Just one thing. Don't you think it's *Jeremy* making you feel old? He's about twenty-one, isn't he?"

She strummed at her guitar and wouldn't look at him. "He's almost twenty-five, for your information."

"Ah. A whole quarter of a century old." He smiled as he gulped the iced tea.

She looked up, eyes narrowed. "Why are you such a smartass?"

"Comes naturally, I guess."

"So what if he's young?" She stopped strumming. "No man my age is interested in me."

Because you're a first-class ballbuster?

"Forty-something single men that I meet are always with twenty-something women. That leaves me with few options." She looked up at him. "Besides, I'm not datin' these men. They're just comin' to see me and to...to say hi."

"Gotcha." He drained the glass and set it down. "Well, Jeremy says 'hi' to a lot of women. Just thought you should know."

"What do I care? He's just a kid."

It almost sounded as though she meant that, which puzzled him. He figured her for a famous woman who wanted a younger man to both keep up with her and serve as a status symbol. Not that *he* couldn't keep up with her,

15

because he was certain that he could. He didn't care to. Too much makeup and all that. He refused to be attracted to her on principle. The sooner she got out of town the better for the young men of Stone Ridge. As a pseudo big brother to everyone in town, he wanted to caution any man who would get too close to her. She was trouble, and due to his age, at least *he* saw her coming.

"I'm sure that will break his heart," Riggs said.

She snorted, then turned those incredibly blue eyes on him. He thought they would be even more beautiful were they not framed with fake lashes. He ignored the punch of attraction that hit hard and swift.

"You look to be around my age, so I'm sure you're either married, in which case you have nothing to say to me about this, or you're competing with Jeremy for all the girls."

"I'm not married anymore, and I prefer *women* not girls."

Look at that. He'd left the woman speechless.

Something told him he ought to record the day, the hour, and the minute.

Later, Riggs finished up for the day and decided he wouldn't bother saying goodbye to the princess. He'd head to the only watering hole in town, the Shady Grind, for a cold beer. Maybe a game of pool to unwind. Just as he'd packed up his truck, the princess came wandering out and nearly tripped on a rock in those ridiculous boots.

"Hey, I'm sorry I fought with you," she said, coming up to the tailgate.

"That's alright. I'm tough enough to take it."

"It's just… You don't know how hard it is for me."

"Maybe your jeans are too tight?"

Despite the fact that he disagreed with them being too tight, seeing as they showcased one of her best assets, he didn't mind indulging in the jab. He deeply resented the comment she'd made about forty-something single men going for younger women. She wasn't wrong in that most forty-year-old men were married and settled down, and he would be, too, were it not for the fact that after his first failed attempt, he hadn't wanted to risk that again.

Instead of glaring at the comment about her jeans, she hopped on the back of his tailgate. "If they were too tight, I couldn't do this, could I?"

"That was a joke." He smirked and set his toolbox on the truck bed.

"Funny. Look, I'm new in town and I don't have many friends. Jackson is the only one and Eve hates me so we can't really hang out."

"I doubt Eve hates you."

He felt compelled to defend his favorite veterinarian, who ran a tab for him and let him pay monthly on the bills he'd accumulated on the ranch. But he understood why Eve probably didn't want Jackson spending too much time around his ex-wife, even if they'd apparently been married for only a matter of months.

"You'd be wrong about that," Winona said, swinging her legs off the tailgate. "Ever since I—" She stopped herself and wouldn't look at him.

"Since...?"

"Well, since I got to town and tried to talk him out of getting back together with her."

"Hmm."

Riggs often tried this approach with people. He didn't comment after a bombshell statement like that one, to give the speaker some time to think it over. Come to their own realizations and conclusions. He really should have gone to college to become a counselor instead of law school to become a lawyer who didn't practice law. People seemed drawn to tell him their troubles.

Her palms went up. "Okay! I guess I wouldn't like that,

either. But you didn't see Jackson after what she'd done to him. I had to put him back together again. And he was a mess. He loved her and leaving him at the altar was cruel."

He didn't disagree so he nodded. "Our town is somewhat known for runaway brides."

"It is? Why?"

"Different reasons. But I guess here a woman has so many options. Too many of them change their mind at the last minute."

It hadn't happened to him. But he'd been married young, straight out of college, when Jenny got pregnant. It hadn't been the best beginning to a marriage even if he'd loved her. After losing her the way he had, he'd decided never to marry again. Having children would have been nice, yes, but at this point, he figured it wasn't going to happen. Neither was love. And he wasn't nearly as despondent about this as some thought he should be.

He enjoyed his freedom and ability to put in as much work into the ranch as required daily without being nagged about spending "quality time" together. Here and there over the years he'd had girlfriends and it was never worth the trouble. When he wanted a woman, he knew where to find one. No commitments and zero complications. He figured he was now too old and set in his ways for love and marriage. And as for kids, he served as pseudo big brother to half the men in town, and substitute dad for the younger ones.

"Hm. A town known for runaway brides." Winona stopped swinging her legs and drew them up to her chest. The move was so decidedly down to earth and girlish that it unnerved him.

He put his hand out to help her down and she accepted it a moment later. "I've gotta go, princess."

"Alright, well, princess is at least better than ma'am. You've probably got places to be." When she jumped down, he took a step back to give her room. "Is there a woman waitin' for you, Riggs?"

"No woman. Just a cold beer at the Shady Grind." He cleared his throat. "You expectin' anyone over tomorrow? For your interviews?"

"In the afternoon."

"Okay, well, I'll be sure to be done here early so you can have your quiet."

She did a double-take and then smiled. It made her look ten times sweeter. "Thank you so much, Riggs."

He tipped his hat, thinking this might be the end of their strange beginning, and headed off for that cold beer.

His phone buzzed and, glancing at the caller ID, he decided he had to take this, so he pulled over.

But Phil Henderson was the last person he wanted to deal with. "Yeah."

"The developer wants your answer."

"I already gave you my answer."

"Yeah, but you said you would think about it some more."

"I never said that, Phil. You have a way of hearing what you want to hear."

"You're still relatively young. Why would you want to saddle yourself with that cattle ranch when the developer is offering you several million for that land? Between you, Sean, and Colton, you could live the easy life."

"Not interested in easy, or haven't you heard I'm a rancher? This land has been part of the Henderson legacy for a hundred years, and we're not going to be the firsts to give up."

"You're not even a real Henderson. You shouldn't *have* that land."

For Phil, this was what it always came down to. He was Calvin's cousin, and a "true" Henderson. Despite the fact that he would have loved to dispute the land Riggs and his brothers had inherited, Phil didn't have a case. Riggs had proved it time and again, citing case law, and his adoptive father's iron-clad Living Trust. The land went to his sons, whom he considered Hendersons in every sense of the word.

"Tell the truth. Why do you care whether or not I sell? It's long been decided you don't have a stake in it. The developer has offered you a finder's fee if we sell, hasn't he?"

Riggs had recently suspected this. Right after his parents had died, Phil tried to stake a claim to the land. Many lawsuits later, Riggs thought he'd given up. And he had gone away for a few years, returning only a few months ago, coincidentally at the same time that a major developer had expressed interest in their land. Riggs didn't believe in such big coincidences.

His parents had owned the land through generations, never selling or splitting up lots, and that's the way Riggs would keep it. He regularly received inquiries from other ranches wanting to expand, and worse, offers from land developers. One of them had been quite persistent lately and thought they could fit quite a nice hotel on Henderson land. It would never happen under his watch.

"So what if they have? It's not much, but it's the only way I'm going to get any of what's rightfully owed to me. You can't hang on to that land forever."

"Guess you'll just have to stand by and watch me do it."

"You know what your problem is?"

But Riggs had heard it all before. Trailer park scum.

Loser.

And the worst of them all: thief.

"You think you're smarter than everyone else in the room. But your fancy schmancy law degree won't get you out of this mess. You're hanging on to that land by a thread and someday you're going to lose it. But you think you can save the ranch, so you hang on. Don't be the smartest idiot in the room. I don't know how much longer this offer will be around."

"Hell, I'm hoping they give up soon."

"It would be your bad luck if they did, seeing as it might be your only way out of the mess you're in."

"I'll manage, thanks." And with that, Riggs disconnected the call and got back on the road.

THE SHADY GRIND was crowded for a weeknight, but it had been nearly every night since Jackson Carver had bought it from Priscilla, the former owner. All the regulars were in attendance. His brother Sean would be here, too, if he hadn't sent him to a cattle auction in Dallas yesterday. Riggs hated to admit it, even to himself, but he didn't want to go straight home to a quiet and empty house tonight. Delores, his housekeeper, was like a second mother to him and she'd nag him about this or that. And when his brothers were around, those two never stopped talking or arguing.

Jolette Marie was one of a few women here tonight and a regular. There was Lenny in the corner, retired now, though he filled in as one-third of the volunteer Fire Department and did other odd jobs. Jackson Carver currently stood behind the bar, but if every other night Riggs had stopped in so far was any indication, he'd soon be pulled onstage for a song or two. Levi, a horse wrangler, was his back-up bartender.

"Hey, Riggs!" Jackson said from behind the bar. "Wanna beer?"

Riggs took over an empty stool. "I'll have one."

A couple of months ago, Jackson had come back from Nashville for his brother's wedding and wound up reuniting with Eve, his runaway bride. He'd taken over the bar and grill, appropriate, since he'd had his start singing here. Riggs hadn't minded the place when Priscilla ran it, but he had to admit that just having Jackson around had infused it with a new life and kind of younger vibe. He was working on replacing the old tired jukebox in the back with a first-rate sound system.

"Here, try this." Jackson set a bottle down. "It's an IPA. Something new."

Riggs wound up sitting next to Jeremy, and his friend Todd, so after a few minutes of small talk he couldn't stop himself from asking. "Hey, what were you interviewin' for today?"

Jeremy gaped at him. "She told you?"

"No, we didn't talk much."

"She's…um, she's lookin' for a personal assistant," Jeremy said, and his friend Todd elbowed him, grinning.

Riggs didn't see why she would need a personal assistant when all she'd done today was stay in the house trying to play her guitar and complain about how loud he was. Maybe she'd be sending someone to complain on her behalf. Though, he imagined there were probably lots of behind the scenes stuff that celebrities had to do. He had no idea. All he really knew was that Winona was renting the house for the summer and that she was Jackson's wife for about two minutes.

Riggs stuck around long enough for a game of pool and one song from Jackson before he called it a night. As he left, he noticed for the first time the flyer in the corner of the bar:

Winona James
Live
Proceeds of ticket sales will go to the new medical clinic

THEY'D USED AN OLDER photo of her, a glamour shot if ever there was one. Her hair looked windblown, and she appeared to be walking down a hill in the middle of a wide field as she looked steadily into the lens, those blue eyes intent and dramatic. She looked beautiful enough to be a model. A spike of longing thrummed through him that he was determined to ignore. He was a confirmed bachelor and had been for years. There was no room in his life for a woman, and certainly not one like this. She had high-maintenance written all over her. Not that she was staying, which in some ways might be kind of perfect. Maybe a fling would be in order, not that she'd be interested in taking scraps from any man.

He wasn't willing to give any woman a commitment, because his life was perfect. Quiet. Content. No need to switch things up now. Marriage and children were for other people. Not him.

But for the first time since he could remember, Riggs wondered what a certain woman was doing tonight.

CHAPTER 3

The next day, Riggs arrived early, just after his morning chores at the ranch. He thought the princess was probably still sleeping because she didn't come out to complain about the noise. He might have enjoyed that, seeing her hang out the window, her fresh face with no makeup, and maybe wearing a frilly nightgown or big T-shirt. Definitely would have enjoyed watching her swing a fist at him and yell because she'd been trying to get her beauty sleep. No such luck.

He pounded and sawed away all morning, bringing up the rest of the frame. It wasn't until noon when he opened up his lunch pail and decided to go inside for some of the iced tea she kept handy.

Lenny sat exactly where Jeremy had been yesterday, scratching his head.

"Hey, there, Lenny," Riggs called out. "You interviewin' for the personal assistant position?"

Lenny blinked and his neck swiveled back like a chicken's. "Is that what you kids are callin' it these days?"

"Huh?" Riggs helped himself to a glass of sweet tea, which

he guzzled. Then he walked toward the great room where Lenny sat on the couch. "Where is she?"

"I have no idea. She let me in, I sat down, and she didn't even ask me any questions. Then she excused herself and hasn't been back yet. I mean, I know I'm old, but I know what I'm doin', ya know. Doesn't experience count for somethin' anymore?" His palms went up, frustrated. "I have four grown healthy kids!"

Riggs was getting more puzzled by the minute. He didn't know what Lenny's kids had to do with anything. "I'm sure it has nothin' to do with your *age*."

"Go find her, will ya? I don't have all day!"

"Sure, buddy. Just sit tight."

This was ridiculous and quite frankly, maddening. Just yesterday she'd been discussing ageism and now she wasn't going to give Lenny, a healthy sixty-something, a chance to be her personal assistant. Typical. She was a full-blown celebrity hypocrite.

He walked down the hall and knocked on the only closed door, one of the bedrooms. "Winona. Open up."

"No. Go away."

He knocked again, a little harder this time, but used softer words. "C'mon, princess."

He heard movement inside and a moment later she opened the door a crack. "Could you just tell him to go and I'll call him later?"

"Why?"

"I'm not feelin' well all of a sudden."

He squinted. "You look fine to me."

"Well, I'm not!"

"Look, let's not argue. What's this really about? Don't you think Lenny could work as your personal assistant? At least give him a chance. I can personally vouch for him."

Her eyes went wide and she squeaked. "Personal assistant?"

"Jeremy told me you've been interviewin' for one."

She briefly closed her eyes. "Um, yes. That's exactly right. But I can't face any more interviews and it's your fault."

"*My* fault?"

"You were out there at six in the morning hammerin' away and I couldn't sleep. I was up early and now I need a nap."

"It's noon." He scratched his jaw. "I planned to get done early in time for your interview. And why didn't you yell at me if I was too loud?"

"Because," she said, her gaze briefly flitting to the ceiling as if praying for patience, "I wasn't dressed."

"You weren't dressed."

"I sleep naked, cowboy." She sent him a sly smile.

He swallowed hard. "Okay, that makes sense. I'll go tell Lenny that you'll call him later."

"Thank you." The door to her bedroom closed softly.

Pushing away thoughts of a naked Winona, Riggs joined Lenny.

"She's not feeling well, and she doesn't look good. I think she's going to take a nap and try to sleep it off. Probably drank too much last night," he added for spite. He would prefer not to have the image of her naked that she'd put there. He was afraid it would follow him around all day now. "You know how it is with these celebrity types."

"Yeah, I know, brother." Lenny stood up and ambled toward the front door. "I know."

Riggs followed him. "She'll call you."

"Either way. I'm startin' to lose interest. Not as young as I used to be, and not sure I can keep up with her uh, demands, if you know what I mean." He winked. "But tell her I'll look at the contract anyway."

"Contract?"

It would be just like her to make someone sign a contract for this! Ridiculous. The image of her soft naked body was leaving him now, thank the Lord.

"Lenny, don't you sign any damn contract before I look at it first."

He hadn't specialized in contract law just for the family ranch, but he protected his friends, too.

Lenny nodded and clapped his shoulder. "Thanks, son. What about you? Don't you want to interview for the personal assistant job? Or are you too busy?"

"You couldn't pay me *enough* to be her personal assistant."

Lenny's eyes went wide. "This a *paid* position?"

"You were goin' to work for *free?*"

He shrugged. "Wouldn't exactly call it work, heh, heh, but yeah. Sure."

"Just because she's easy on the eyes and a celebrity, don't let her take advantage of you. Nobody works for free."

With that, he shut the door and went back to work where he could take his frustrations out on a piece of wood.

WINONA FELT AWFUL. Last week when Lenny called her to interview for the position, she'd had no idea he'd be in his late sixties. He'd sounded a lot younger over the phone. Sitting with him for even five minutes had been excruciating. She'd discussed fathering a child with a man the age of her stepfather, and he'd been one mean son-of-a-bitch. Too many bad memories.

Last night, she'd nearly chickened out on the whole idea.

She blamed Riggs. The feel of his rough and callused hand as he'd offered it to her had pulled a strong memory. Some men were kind and gentle with their women. Jackson, for one. He'd been so good to her. But she'd only really been

27

in love once, with her second husband, and her longest marriage. Riggs reminded her of Colby, her second husband and manager. They were about the same age. Like Colby, Riggs was tall and generously built, with wavy dark brown hair and whiskey-colored eyes. She'd hoped one day that she and Colby would have children, but he kept putting her off because of her contractual obligations to the record label.

Each month, she'd ask him if they could finally have a baby. After five years, he'd never warmed to the idea. Meanwhile, her eggs were getting older and he didn't seem to care. Colby didn't smack her around like her first husband had, but he did have a coldness and bitterness toward her that she didn't understand.

"All you talk about is having a baby! Winona, you have fans who are waitin' for that next album. How can I get you pregnant when you have a fifty-four-city tour coming up? Think about your fans for a change instead of your own selfish needs."

Her own selfish needs.

Winona was proud of how far she'd come, and in the earlier years, Nashville liked to refer to her often as the woman who "had it all." If one called "all" enough money to never have to worry again, then she'd agree. But she'd never felt like she had it all. It was a calculated lie that made her and Colby look good. The power couple. No one saw the nights she went to bed alone because he'd stay up late reviewing a contract, or fielding offers for product endorsements. He cared more about appearances than he did about her.

Then came the day when she'd been informed by her accountant that both Colby and her publicist had been slowly embezzling from her in a dummy wardrobe account. She'd been in her dressing room about to go on an award show and present when she'd been informed. Colby hadn't even tried to deny it.

Winona threw him out and proceeded to rip up everything in sight. She took a pair of scissors to her evening gown, ripped out her hair extensions, threw everything she could pick up against the wall and watched it all shatter into pieces. Her reputation took a heavy hit and she'd fired Colby and sued him for divorce. She'd been forced to hire a "fixer" to salvage her career, but nothing had been the same after that.

After her divorce, she'd started drinking heavily. Having fun and trying to forget she'd been good enough to marry but not good enough to have Colby's child. She'd tried to forget Colby had used her as an ATM machine. A few months later, her former publicist was pregnant, and she and Colby married after the divorce was final. What really burned Winona was how Colby had used his position as her manager to get himself another much higher profile client. He still talked about her, too, in interviews and raunchy exposés on her life. She wished she'd never met Colby Jennings, because he'd ruined her. She'd wasted too many years recovering from him and now, here she was, nearly forty without a child. Without a family.

Too bad Riggs would never agree to father her child. Clearly, no man in town was going to tell him about her special situation, either, probably because being older and wiser, they knew he'd try to talk them out of it. Besides, she told herself, Riggs didn't have enough of an education to counterbalance her lack. Here he was, doing two manual labor jobs for a living. A rancher and a carpenter.

When the hammering resumed Winona felt safe enough to emerge from the bedroom. In the kitchen, she picked up her cell phone and dialed Kimberly. Her new manager happened to also be her best friend in the world. After five years together, Winona trusted her completely. Kimberly and her husband had been married ten years and had three children. It was Kimberly who had first given Winona the idea of artificial insemination. But Kimberly didn't approve of the route Winona had decided to take instead.

She tried to talk her out of the idea daily, which was why Winona found herself calling her now. "Hey, Kim. Want to talk me out of this today?"

"Sure thing, honey."

Winona heard a screaming toddler in the background, saying "Wipe meeeee!"

"Oh, the joys of motherhood," Kim said. "Hon, I've told you repeatedly, you're too wonderful of a woman to have to resort to this method. You're a catch. And don't start with the needle thing. At your age, you're high risk anyway, and so you'll probably have amniocentesis."

No, she would not, and had already decided, but wouldn't tell Kim. Winona was having this baby and would love her no matter what. She simply wanted to give her baby the best start possible. But biology would do the rest and she couldn't control the fact that she had old eggs or that sometimes it was the luck of the draw with Mother Nature.

She was ready to love a child, perfect or imperfect, with her whole heart.

"Is it wrong to want to know the father of my child? To see his face?"

"No, that's not wrong," Kim said. "And really? Don't let anyone tell you that your child is potty trained until they can wipe themselves. Okay?"

"Filed away for future reference." Winona chuckled.

A toilet flushed in the background. It was a good thing she and Kim were such close friends.

"If you have doubts about this, why are you calling me?"

"Because this is my process. I call, and while I argue with you as to why I should do this, I also convince myself."

"Ah, I see. Well, carry on."

"Something happened." Winona cleared her throat. "An older man came by today to apply to be my baby daddy."

"Oh. Oh dear."

"I only told a couple of men, but word seems to be getting out." She walked the length of the kitchen, then took a seat at the table.

"Have you...uh... Have you..."

"Have I gotten it on with anyone yet? No. I still haven't chosen him."

"Well, hurry on up. If you're committed to this insanity, then go for it."

Through the window, the spectacular Texas sun splashed rays of midday sunlight. Winona took a deep breath.

"It can't just be *anyone*."

"Yes, I'm aware. First, he has to sign the contract. Second, he has to produce the goods. A positive home pregnancy test. Then, you'll finally come home to Nashville and reboot your career."

Winona left the kitchen and paced the living room. "But I have to feel *something* for him. A connection. I want to see his face. I want to know him and that we've created a life together. If I have a son, he might look like him."

"You're romanticizing this again, and I thought we weren't going to do that." She said this in a sing-song voice she often used with her toddler.

"Oh, right. Well, sue me if I'm not a *man* who can get it on with just anybody!"

"And *that's* why you need a sperm bank. I rest my case, your honor."

"I don't need a sperm bank. There's a...a man."

"What man?"

Winona opened a blind and peeked through the slat. Said man was hard at work. He seemed to enjoy arguing with her. Or she loved arguing with him. Hey, it gave her something to do. Yes, she realized he had to make noise when hammering and sawing. But she loved the outraged look in his eyes when she asked him to keep it down. It hovered between annoyance and disbelief.

Riggs stopped sawing on a piece of wood and removed his T-shirt with one arm. Oh. My.

"Hello? Are you still there?"

"Um, yes." She sighed. "Oh, I'm here. I'm...here."

She couldn't take her eyes off the man. He moved with such ease in his body. That body was hard and muscular with a light smattering of dark hair between his pecs that lowered to his abs and disappeared into his...gulp...Wranglers.

"There's a man, you were saying?"

"He works for me. I mean, he works for the landlord, and he's here nearly every day. I'm sure he's about my age. The only problem is he's probably not well educated. He's a carpenter and he's working on the house I'm renting. I guess he's also a rancher."

"Is he nice?"

Nice. On the first day, she'd thought him to be a total jerk. But then he'd looked into her eyes and offered his hand. She'd felt a tingle, a dang *tingle*, and she was way past feeling that sort of thing for any man. He had such a good face and warm smile. Eyes that shimmered with humor and a crooked smile that was this side of wicked.

"Yes, he's nice. And he would never do it."

"He's single, right?"

"Of course!"

"Are you sure he wouldn't do this? I mean, if he's perfect, other than the education, I don't think you can afford to be picky at this point. Intelligence isn't always tied to education.

You ought to know. You're the savviest woman I've ever known."

"But I bet he wouldn't sign the contract or get the physical. He'd make fun of me for doing this. He kept hammering away when I was in the middle of an interview. When I yelled for him to stop, he just smiled. He loves to irritate me. Sometimes he calls me princess." That wasn't quite as irritating.

"Really. Is he flirting with you?"

"No, I don't think so. That's just his nature. Ornery."

"Hm. Sounds vaguely familiar. Okay, well. I have to say that I'm worried about you cooped up in that country house every day just writing songs. Are you getting out enough? Take a walk. Plant a tree or a shrub."

"Don't worry. I'm actually performing in Jackson's bar Saturday night. It's a fundraiser. They do a lot of that around here."

She wished she looked forward to singing. But Eve would be there, and she still wasn't thrilled with Winona. She didn't see why Eve would be the slightest bit jealous. Yeah, she made the mistake of asking Jackson for his sperm, but Jackson loved Eve unconditionally, no matter *what* she'd done to him in the past.

It was exactly the kind of unconditional love from a man that Winona had never had.

CHAPTER 4

When Saturday night arrived, Winona felt sick to her stomach. She hadn't had a good case of stage fright in ten years. Performing was what she did, and who she was, from the time she'd hitchhiked to a talent show in Nashville and changed her life. Granted, it was all an act. Everyone thought she was an extrovert, but apparently, she should have gone into acting instead. She was an introvert who did an extremely good job of faking.

But tonight, she was in a terrible mood.

Her prime ovulation window had shut, and she hadn't found a baby daddy. Instead, the picture of her cherubic-like baby faded a little more each day. For the past two nights she'd woken up crying, wondering when, why, and how she'd chosen to give up a family for...*this*. That hadn't been her plan. She wouldn't have traded the chance to have a baby for all the fame in the world, but it had still worked out that way. Now, it might be too late. Contrary to popular belief, she would *never* have it all.

If she hadn't lost her mother at such a young age, maybe Winona wouldn't be as determined to have a child. But for years now, she'd longed for a connection to family. A biological connection because her daughter would be Mary Jo's granddaughter. Dead or alive, her mother would live on not just through Winona but through her children. And their children. Just a little piece of Mary Jo might live forever, or at least for generations.

As she'd been trained to do for almost two decades, Winona brushed off her pain, pushed back her tears, and dressed for the show. She grabbed her guitar case and loaded it into her truck, then set off for the Shady Grind. This was a reminder of the good old days when she'd drive herself to gigs in her car, stopping on the side of the road to sleep. She'd had no one, and nothing but her own stubborn determination.

When she saw the line of parked cars from Second Street all the way up to Main where the bar was located, she should have been filled with pride. Instead, it would be a wonder if she could walk inside. She didn't want to let these good folks down with a mediocre performance, but she just wasn't at her best tonight. Hadn't been in years.

Jackson had told her to park in the back and set aside a designated spot. She carefully pulled in and parked, then began her before-performance ritual.

"Show, show, show, show," she chanted. "Kick ass! Take names!"

She punched the air. Had she forgotten to wear pink? She couldn't do the show without pink! Just before she hyperventilated, Winona remembered her pink panties. She'd never forget to wear pink before a show, her mom's favorite color. It wasn't just a color to Mary Jo, it was also the way she thought of Winona. There were tender memories associated with pink.

Inside, she heard the sounds of Jackson singing, "The Only One for Me," wafting out of the venue. His number one hit song. Written about Eve, of course. Winona didn't blame him. Heartbreak was the number one generator of the best love songs. Unrequited love came in a close second. Some would say there was no real difference, but having experienced both, Winona would disagree.

She took a deep breath. Her routine wasn't working as well as it usually did.

"Show, show, show." She rested her forehead on the steering wheel, feeling defeated already. "No, no, no."

She was thinking of her mother again. How much she missed the way she'd stroke Winona's hair every night and tell her she was the best girl in the whole wide world. When she'd died, it felt like someone had ripped the sun from Winona's orbit. And after that, she'd been alone. For years. It could be argued that she was still alone.

The knock on her driver's side window made her jump.

She turned to see Riggs on the other side of the window, gray Stetson tipped. *He* sure cleaned up nice. Tonight, he wore a starched white button up, sleeves rolled up to his sinewy elbows.

She swallowed and pushed the button to slide the window down.

"Eve asked me to come out and check to see if you were here yet. You okay? Jackson said you're never late, but you're supposed to go on in just a few minutes."

"I'm fine! So ready for this."

She swung the door open. Her short white sequined dress molded to her figure and made it difficult to get out, and her high-heeled red boots with pink and white inlays were ones she wore when she didn't have to walk far. She had her hair down tonight, with hair extensions to give her extra length and body. As she'd glanced at herself in the mirror before she left, she believed this was the best she could do.

And Riggs was holding his hand out once again. "Can I help you with anything?"

"You can take my guitar case, please, sugar." She pointed.

He carried her guitar case behind her, and she walked, no strutted, to the rear entrance. Her show persona would kick in any moment now. Because this was a smaller venue, as expected, she went through the kitchen. Every eye turned on her, but she was ready.

Five, four, three, two, one.

Smile like your life depends on it!

"Hey, y'all! So nice to meet you!"

"Miss Winona! I'm a huge fan." One of the cooks said. "I can't believe you're really here."

"I can't believe it, either, honey. This dress is so tight I can barely walk!"

Everyone laughed and she'd put them at ease though they didn't stop staring. She understood. She used to stare, too, when she met someone famous. Once, she'd nearly gone full-blown catatonic when she met her hero, Dolly Parton. Dolly had taught her that a consummate pro has time for everyone.

Probably because Jackson was still on stage, Eve met her at the door to the bar entrance. She didn't look mad, thank you, Jesus.

"We're almost ready for you," Eve said.

Winona turned and Riggs stood right behind her, having already pulled her guitar out. He handed it over and she pulled the colorful pink strap over her head and settled it in place. She would not call herself a musician, far from it, but she'd learned how to play guitar. Or at least fake it.

"Thank you," she said to Riggs, then turned to Eve. "I'm ready when you are, honey."

Eve nodded and went out the door.

"For you, Mama," Winona said under her breath.

A few seconds later, Jackson announced her, and Winona walked out to a screaming crowd.

"Hey, Texas! Thank y'all for having me!"

And then she launched into a rousing rendition of "Next Mornin'," her first hit song, one about hard drinking and partying.

RIGGS WATCHED Winona move on stage, nothing short of mesmerized. He wasn't a huge fan of country music. Yeah, he knew he *should* be. Born and bred in Texas, he still preferred hard rock. Sue him. But the woman onstage could sing the dictionary and she'd have everyone eating out of her hand. He didn't care whether or not she could play the guitar, because she made it look so damn good, and her sweet voice made up for everything. Not just a sweet voice, but a presence to be reckoned with. It wasn't just her beauty or how she dressed (which in his mind, anyway, was better than he'd seen so far) but the way she carried herself. Like she owned the room.

Every song of hers implied she was a hard-drinking woman who enjoyed a good party, but he'd never seen her drinking anything other than sweet tea. She never left the house other than to yell at him. This was so far from the woman he'd seen that it might as well be her twin up there kicking ass. Yeah, he'd definitely seen a hint of that side of her, but he'd seen the part no one wants to see. The mean, bitchy side without all the good stuff: the sexy, take-no-prisoners attitude. The way she spun and twirled around on that stage had him thinking...thoughts. Thoughts he hadn't had about a woman in a long while.

When he'd come up to her window, he'd clearly startled her. He'd looked into eyes so defenseless and exposed that for a moment he'd felt sucker punched. And then in the next moment, she'd transformed.

She sang five songs on her own, then joined Jackson in a duet. A love song. Good thing she wasn't Riggs's girlfriend because he'd be jealous. His head told him there was nothing going on between those two because Jackson was a goner for Eve, but they both faked it well. He supposed that's why they called it performing.

As they ended the night, both of them took a bow. Jackson held out his hand to help Winona off the stage, but they didn't walk far until he was in Eve's arms, and in a full-on lip-lock. Riggs briefly caught a flash of something unnamed in Winona's eyes as she tried to find her way around them. But even as the crowd parted for her, she was engaged in conversation time and time again. He'd watched her for several minutes, and when she caught his gaze, he looked away.

"Wow, she is something, right?" Levi, the part-time bartender, slid Riggs a beer.

"Right." Riggs took a pull of his beer. This was his first of the night, and he wouldn't be finishing it.

"I thought about applying to be her personal assistant, but I've got too much going on right now." He winked.

"You?" Levi worked on a horse ranch, nearly a horse whisperer, to hear Eve tell it. Riggs didn't understand why Levi would want or need to work for Winona. Maybe times were tough all around. "That hard up, huh?"

"No, hell, not at all. I'm spread too thin as it is."

"That's what I thought."

"But good Lord, I'm tempted." With that, Levi took care of another customer on the other end of the bar.

Riggs watched as Winona made her way to the bar, though there were some men she couldn't seem to shake. They were following her like they were dogs and she was made out of bacon. He would tell them to back off, but he didn't know that she actually wanted that.

"Call me," Jeremy said to her, a lovesick look on his face.

"Sure will, sugar." Winona extricated herself from the last man, pulled her guitar strap off, and came to sit on the stool beside Riggs. "I'm going to go. Tell Jackson and Eve I said good night, yeah?"

"Want a beer first?"

"Nah, I don't drink anymore."

"Huh. Your songs say something different."

"They sure do. When I wrote them, I *did* drink too much."

"On a health kick?"

"Something like that."

Her brilliant blue eyes were still in full glitter mode. It was almost like someone had wound her up and made her spin like a top. Pretty soon, he guessed, her battery would run out.

"Good night, then." Holding the neck of her guitar, she hopped off the stool. "See you tomorrow."

"Wait. I'll help you out."

She was stopped no less than ten times by his count. Lots of compliments on everything from her dress, to her songs, to her guitar. She was incredibly gracious of each and every person. Were it him, he'd be annoyed. Finally, he did assert himself because she might enjoy this adulation, but he did not, and he'd run out of patience.

"Make a hole," he ordered.

"Thank y'all," Winona said, as they were finally able to make their way through the kitchen.

"I made you a plate to go," one of the cooks said, beaming. "It's a Shady Burger with sweet potato fries, our specialty."

"Oh, thank you!" She behaved as if he'd just given her a diamond ring. "I'll eat this when I get home."

"If you ever get home," Riggs muttered.

Grabbing her guitar case, he swung the door open for her. The air deflated out of her when she climbed into the truck. He shoved the guitar case in the back and then came to the driver's side. She rolled down the window, turned on the truck, and dialed the A/C full blast.

"I'm gettin' too old for this."

He snorted. "Too *old?*"

No one would have guessed with the way she moved tonight that she was a day over thirty, but he'd become annoyed again by the way she kept mentioning her advancing age. She had a complex.

"Never mind." She shook her head and gave him one last smile. "See ya tomorrow."

He tapped the hood. "Good night, princess."

CHAPTER 5

*R*iggs went back inside the bar where he played another game of pool, this time with his brother, Sean, who'd come in at some point. Notably absent tonight were Lincoln and Sadie, but not only were they newlyweds, a rumor was floated through town that Sadie was already pregnant. Either way, he didn't expect they left their cabin too often except for food. Maybe a little fresh air.

"Hey, Riggs." Jolette Marie appeared at his elbow when he set the pool cue down to let someone else have a chance.

"What's up?"

Sometime after the last man she'd dumped at the altar, Jolette Marie often came to him for advice about some dude or another.

"Tell me again why I'm worth more than a casual hookup?" She finger-waved and smiled in the direction of Walker Wright a two-timing jackass if there ever was one.

He really did not have time for this.

"Look, you're only as worthy as you think you are. Don't let anyone else decide that for you. Like tonight. We all saw a woman that made her own destiny take the stage. No one tells her what to do. *Believe* me."

"Yeah, but *she's* beautiful. And a star. She can probably have any man she wants. Like, maybe even Sam Hunt, if she wanted to."

That might be true, so why did Riggs feel it was not even close to the truth?

"You're beautiful, too. And you better believe Winona thinks more of herself than to be anyone's casual hookup."

"But what if there's this amazing chemistry going on, like this animal magnetism?" She snapped her fingers.

"Oh, well, you didn't say *that*." When her eyes brightened, he shook his head and chuckled. "No. If there's that, then it will last longer than one night. Or it should."

"Okay," she said with a sigh.

He patted her back, his little pseudo sister. Beautiful and brimming with confidence but underneath it all a lot of false bravado.

Riggs said his goodbyes and headed out. For some reason, he turned his truck left on Main instead of right, the way to his ranch. Left was the turn to go to Winona's house. He'd never been out there at night and he told himself that he wanted just to check on her. To see whether or not she'd made it home okay after that amazing performance. It didn't seem right for someone with that level of celebrity to go home alone.

Shouldn't she have "people" here to watch over her while she was hiding out in Stone Ridge? Where were all her people? He wouldn't be surprised if she needed a bodyguard in Nashville, but he comforted himself with the fact that this was his hometown. Women here, in the minority as they were, were revered and protected. In fact, he should have followed her home and not gone back inside to play pool with his brother. Or one of the many men of Stone Ridge should have. Riggs would have thought that Jackson would have considered all this.

He continued to drive and talk himself out of going by her house to check up on her because he had too much work to do. He had ten pregnant first-calf heifers on the ranch, all artificially inseminated. He should turn his focus back to his family business, because he had enough going on. But he couldn't explain the pull that he had to Winona, except that there seemed to be a connection between them. He didn't believe he'd been imagining it. But he'd just had a talk with Jolette Marie about casual hookups. Winona was leaving soon to return to Nashville and Riggs wasn't interested in anything more than a casual hookup. At the moment, he was exactly the kind of man he'd just warned Jolette Marie about.

Sure, because it takes one to know one.

But Riggs would never take advantage of Winona. There was something oddly vulnerable about her, and he only wished he could figure out why. Jolette Marie was right. Winona could have any man she wanted.

The light was still on inside her home when he pulled up, excitement and attraction pulsating through him.

"You have one last chance to leave," he muttered to himself. "Leave, idiot. *Leave.* No good will come of this."

But he didn't listen to his own great and unsolicited advice. Instead, he found himself at her front door, and she opened before he even knocked.

"Oh, hey, Riggs." She glanced up and down the street, then waved him in. "Please come in."

She'd divested herself of the tight dress that hugged her curves, but she wore another white and nearly see-through sundress. Very plain, with no tassels, no glitter. Barefoot, her hair was loose and tousled. And if he wasn't mistaken, she wasn't wearing a bra. Gulp.

"A bunch of trucks followed me home and I just wanted to make sure they're all gone," Winona said.

"Who?"

"Some men, and when I got home, they just waved and left." She shrugged.

He chuckled with relief. "Yeah, they wanted to make sure you got home okay."

"Well, now, that's service. Anywhere else that would be considered stalking. But all they were doing was providing me an escort, huh?"

"That's the kind of thing we do around here. You may have heard there aren't many women in our town. So, they tend to be quite noticeable."

"In a way, that's why I'm here."

"I thought it was to visit Jackson."

"Yeah, that too." She wandered into the kitchen and he followed. "Hey, I think we raised some money tonight for the medical clinic."

"We did. A full house and Jackson had a cover charge. It's really a welcome help because they're operating in an older building right now."

"I'm happy to help. I've done a whole lot of fundraising in my career and this is a worthy cause."

He stopped at the kitchen table. "So, what happened tonight?"

"What do you mean?"

"You looked like you were upset sitting in your truck, but then you turned into this different person the minute you climbed out."

"Oh, that. I guess you now know me better than most people in town other than Jackson. You've just witnessed the transformation of Winnie Lee Hoyt to Winona James."

"Winnie Lee Hoyt?"

She went to the refrigerator and reached for the pitcher

45

of sweet tea. "That's my given name. The name my mama gave me."

"It doesn't seem right that you should have to be someone you're not."

"That's why I said I'm gettin' too old for this." She went on tiptoes to the cupboard and grabbed two glass tumblers.

"You're not too old. Stop sayin' that."

"Whether you want to believe me or not, I am too old in *my* business. I started when I was only sixteen, and now I'm thirty-nine. And there are always new young artists comin' out every month with a hot, chart-climbing single. It's about the time for me to fade into the background and let someone else have a turn." She set the tumblers on the table.

"That's horseshit. You're never goin' to fade into the background."

"What do you know about it?" Now she went hand on hip like he'd just pissed her off.

He smiled a little but told himself not to go too far with this. They were alone. The sun had set which always made him a little horny. And she was a flesh and blood gorgeous woman with a great set of tits if that dress was any indication. He was practically salivating to get his mouth on them.

Ignoring her last statement, he walked to the room that led to the addition he'd been building. Outside the night was quiet and calm for August. But inside him, a storm brewed. He really should get out of here because he was far too attracted to this woman. There were too many things about her he found engaging, like her feisty spirit. Her inability to back down. She reminded him of a scrapper. A survivor.

And it took one to know one.

He sensed her behind him before she spoke. "You do good work, just like you said. It's going to be a great addition. Too bad I won't be here to enjoy it."

When he turned to face her, she held out a glass of iced tea, which he accepted. "Why not?"

"I'm leavin' sooner than I'd planned."

Riggs had never seen her sounding this defeated. And tired. He pushed back the need to fix this for her, whatever it was. None of his business, that's what.

For a few minutes, they stood side by side looking into the dark night, the rushing sound of the nearby river in the background. "Never hired a personal assistant, did ya?"

"It's too late." She sighed. "No, I gave up on that idea. I don't need one anymore."

"I guess you must have scared off the younger men. Had I more time, I'd have applied for the job. You couldn't scare me off, and you know it."

She snorted. "You don't know the half of it, cowboy."

"Going back to Nashville?" He took a gulp of the sweet tea and let the cold seep inside of this fire growing inside.

She was leaving. No harm done for one night.

"My manager thinks that it's time to reboot my career. Give it another shot."

"Is that what you want?"

"I don't know. I'm sort of sick of my life." She shrugged. "All I'm good for these days is to trot out at award shows and hand over awards to the up-and-comers. I'm the old guard."

He turned to her, the wildfire of attraction settling into irritation, a safer place to be.

"Know what? I'm getting sick of hearing women complain about how old they are when they're still young. I hear them say they have a new wrinkle, or Lord forbid, a gray hair." He touched the spittle of gray he had on his side-burns, which hadn't killed him yet. "The beginning of the end. Maybe it's time for you to step aside but let that be your decision. You don't look like someone who's going to give up. As I just told someone else tonight, you determine your own self-worth. Not some arbitrary number."

"Spoken just like a man!" Lips pressed together, she turned and stalked back into the kitchen.

He followed her, not willing to back down, eager to get into this argument. It was a good distraction from the other, more intense feelings he had. This magnetic attraction to her was something rather inconvenient for him. Even if she was leaving.

She took the pitcher of iced tea from the refrigerator and slammed it on the table. "Do you want some more tea?"

She pretty much yelled this and, oh yeah, she was nice and pissy.

He loved this. "Sure. I'll have some more tea, old lady."

She stuck her tongue out.

"Do you know why you men have this opinion? Because gettin' older only makes y'all more attractive. You get a little gray and you look *seasoned* and experienced. And that's sexy. A woman goes a little gray and people tell her to dye her hair or she'll look like someone's granny. There are support groups online for women who want to go gray and just live with it. That's how bad it is! *Support groups!* I mean, just look at the products. There are eye strips for that puffy look under your eyes, wrinkle creams, creams for stretch marks, Botox, you name it. And they're always geared to women. You want to know why? Huh? Do you?"

"Sure." He smiled, enjoying himself *far* too much.

"Because men are too smart for this! Men are, 'take it or leave it baby.' Y'all rule the world, so why not?"

"Go on," he said, encouraging her. He should go to hell for this but damn she didn't look defeated any longer. Her fighting spirit was back. "We rule the world, and..."

"And it's not right!"

She went on for about ten minutes, in between a swallow

or two of tea, raging on how Nashville needed more women record label executives, and Hollywood more female directors, and producers. Also, how it wasn't fair to judge women for getting older when it was just a natural cycle of life. On and on she went, getting more and more riled up.

Her righteous anger was the sexiest damn thing he'd ever seen. Finally, he couldn't take it anymore. This wildfire would not abate. He went right to where she stood near the refrigerator.

Crowding her, he lowered his head. "You're gettin' a little red. You might want to take a breath."

She went wide-eyed. "Riggs."

"Damn, baby, I love the way you fight." He traced the curve of her lower pouty lip, slightly bigger than the top.

"The way I *fight*?"

"You're beautiful. Strong. No one could ever take advantage of you because you know what you want. You go after it. And damn it, I've wanted to kiss you since the day you threatened to spit in my sweet tea."

She snorted. "You might have a problem."

"Oh, I have a lot of problems."

She opened her mouth, about to argue more, he assumed, but he covered it with a kiss. He nearly lost his mind with lust as her mouth opened for him and she deepened the kiss. She tasted like sweet tea and mint. A small concern rippled through him that he was taking advantage of this fiery moment, and he nearly stepped back. He could walk away right now while he still had the strength to do it. But then she untucked his shirt, and her hands drifted up and down his pecs. She was fast, he'd give her that. But he could keep up with her, however far they went tonight.

Only as far as she wanted. They were both experienced enough to know exactly what they were doing. Playing with fire. Two strangers. Her body, under his hands as he explored, was soft, supple, and perfect. Her thigh was silky but taut as his hand glided up and under her dress to her behind. Her light flowery scent inspired lust and desire in him. He hadn't been with a woman in so long, certainly not one that excited him like this. That challenged him.

He was vaguely aware of where they were headed, and fast, as they continued to grope and reach for each other, but he'd stopped thinking rationally. When she tugged at his belt, it was too late to stop this train. If she wanted to stop, she'd have to quit climbing him like a tree.

"I want you," she whispered.

He should slow them down from this crazy, no-holds-barred passion. But then she slipped off her panties, not even bothering with her dress, then lowered his pants and underwear for him.

Holy country music, he wanted this woman more than he wanted his next breath.

"Condom," he said.

"I… I don't have one."

"I do," he said and reached for his wallet, taking care of business.

He lifted her into his arms. "Wrap your legs around me."

"Oh yes."

When she did, he thrust inside of her, finding her wet, and warm, and perfect.

And he took her against the kitchen wall.

WINONA WAS HAVING up-against-the-wall screaming-hot sex with the most exciting man she'd ever met. Riggs felt dangerous and strong. The feel of his hard biceps under her exploring hands had plunged her headfirst into a tizzy of lust. In the back of her mind there was the nagging thought that she should have explained why she'd come here. Told him about the interviews. But she didn't see the point when her chance to conceive had ended.

She was leaving and would never see Riggs Henderson again. He tweaked her nipple through the thin cotton of the dress, and she stopped thinking and started feeling. Everything. She plunged her fingers into his thick dark hair, which she found surprisingly soft. Their bodies were molded against each other from lips to hips and when he began to move inside of her, the powerful thrusts only drove her further into a frenzy. She clutched at his shoulders, pulling him deeper into her. Closer.

She woke up to every sensation flowing through her body. The tingles of heat he left when he nibbled at her neck, his hands on her behind, holding her, driving into her. She heard the sounds they were making, the moans and groans, the creak of the wall as it took their weight. He smelled like leather and lust. This was madness of the purest and best kind. For however long this took, she would forget everything else in her life that wasn't working. Because this moment, this, was working. Oh, how it was working.

Her body tightened and trembled as she climaxed, arching her back. A few moments later Riggs joined her, his body hard as granite under her touch. He continued to hold her against the wall, seemingly effortlessly.

"Princess, you drive me crazy."

"It's mutual, cowboy." Her legs quivered from being wrapped around him, but she wouldn't be the first to let go.

Let that be him.

He pulled out and lowered her, carefully, into the circle of his arms. From this vantage point, he towered over her and she felt a tiny spark of intimidation at his size.

In his eyes, she saw utter remorse and regret, and it kicked her in the heart.

Then she realized what had happened.

"Damn it. The condom... It broke."

"What? It did?"

"Shit. It's been in my wallet too long and that's probably why." He ran a hand through his hair looking absolutely disgusted with himself.

She bit her lower lip. The truth was, she didn't have a good chance of getting pregnant. Her ovulation window had closed. It would take a small miracle. But on the long odds she'd get pregnant, she wasn't cold and calculating enough to leave Stone Ridge and never let Riggs know. Though that would certainly be easier on everyone.

"I want you to know I haven't been with anyone for a long while. And I'm always careful." He rubbed his jaw, looking sheepish.

"I've recently had to have a battery of tests and I'm perfectly healthy. You don't have to worry about me."

"What about, you know, pregnancy? You're probably on birth control, right?"

"No. I'm not in a relationship so I didn't see the need." She nearly choked on the lie. She'd stopped birth control a year ago when she'd decided to have a baby on her own. "Besides, I'm nearly forty, so the chances are pretty slim."

"Good. I know you wouldn't want that complication at this stage of your life."

"Right."

But she'd lusted after this man from the moment he'd shown up at her door. She'd seen his face, and they had an odd connection and chemistry she would guess neither one of them fully understood. No one would have had to talk her into getting naked with him to have a child. Obviously, she would have done it without the promise of a baby of her own. Because this moment just hadn't been planned at all.

Guilt sliced through her. She still had a long way to go to

have faith in herself that she didn't need a man in her life to feel worthy.

She tousled his hair. "Don't feel bad about this, okay? We just...are both probably lonely and needed someone tonight."

"You're amazing." He gazed at her warmly from under hooded lids and tucked a stray hair behind her ear. "I didn't mean to take advantage of you. You know that, right?"

"You didn't. This has happened to me before. Men following me home after a show. They believe the illusion."

For years, she'd had people protecting her from men like Riggs. Men who were attracted to the woman performing. Kimberly had taken lead the last few years and had she been here tonight she'd have run interference and never allowed Riggs inside the house.

And Winona would have missed out on being with this rugged, handsome cowboy, even if just once.

He quirked a brow. "That's not what I did, you have to believe me."

She pushed against his chest. "Not *you*. You saw the difference between me and the Winona onstage immediately. Because you've seen the real me and you're not thrilled with her."

"That's not true, either."

"Liar." She sparred back but added a smile.

He accepted the dig with one of his wicked grins and his callused hands slid down her arms. "You could wear a few less tassels, and a pair of boots that would tolerate Texas dirt."

"Okay. I'll go shopping then."

"You do that."

They cleaned up and dressed quickly but Riggs wasn't done with her yet. When she walked him to the door, he turned to her again. "Are we okay, princess?"

"We're okay." She tipped on her toes to give him a light kiss on the lips.

"When is your period due?"

"Not for another week or so. I'm not always regular."

"You'll tell me if anything happens."

"Happens?"

He lowered his gaze to her stomach. "A baby."

"Oh, sure. Right. You'll be the first to know."

She couldn't leave now, so she'd wait it out another week or more. Even though she couldn't be *this* lucky, hope remained a flickering light in a very dark room.

Anything was possible. Just not likely.

"I'm sorry again. And whatever happens, I'm here for you."

At the simple but significant words, her heart gave a powerful tug. And then he was gone.

inona decided to stay in town on the long odds that she'd accidentally become pregnant. Irony at its finest. The early home pregnancy tests all claimed they were accurate within one day of conception, but Winona still waited over three weeks. She *had* to be sure.

Riggs would ask her every day whether she was okay, which was code for had she gotten her period yet, and she told him not to worry. That she wasn't technically late and sometimes irregular. This was true. Still, she avoided him when he'd come to work every day. She'd stay in her bedroom, and sometimes drive to town and back again.

But at the end of the third week, with no period, Winona lined up all six tests that she'd purchased online and took the first one. Waiting for the result was the longest few minutes of her life.

The stick was pink. Her stomach tensed. Her heart ready to burst with joy, she took another one because she'd read that sometimes these tests were wrong.

The second test was positive, too. What were the odds of that?

"Oh my Lord."

She gripped the edge of the bathroom sink and didn't know whether she could allow herself to feel happiness. This had never happened to her. In the past, she'd had a few close calls with Colby, but *never* a positive pregnancy test.

But if one test could be wrong, maybe two could also be wrong, and after all, she'd bought six. Might as well use them. So, she took one right after the other, and all were positive. There was no way that all six tests could be wrong.

She was going to have a baby.

Riggs's baby.

For a moment, she couldn't breathe. She'd given up on the idea of a baby and had protected sex without thinking this outcome could be possible. And holy cow when he found out what she'd been up to…he just might kill her.

She'd need to tell him everything and explain what she'd hoped to do here, because how else would she get him to sign the contract and let her raise their child in Nashville?

She couldn't just leave Stone Ridge without telling him. And she did want her child to know her father. Once she told him, he'd mistakenly assume that she'd used him that night when she'd done nothing of the sort. She'd been as caught up in the moment as he had, equally brain-dead, or she wouldn't have had sex with someone she'd just met. That was totally unlike her and veered wildly off the plan.

Okay, so maybe she'd been known to veer off plan in the past, but never like this.

She didn't look forward to this dicey conversation, but she would think that Riggs probably felt too old to be a father. He wasn't married anymore, but she'd never even asked him if he already had children. They might be teenagers by now, if he did. If so, he was surely not wanting another child at this late date. He might just let this go without a fight and sign her contract. He didn't seem like the type of man to let something this significant go, but he could surprise her. Maybe.

After noting the date and time of this significant, life-changing event, and considering who her baby daddy would be, Winona burst into tears. She'd gotten what she wanted, but not in the way she'd hoped. It would have been better to have a father already be on board with this situation.

"My baby." She tenderly placed a hand on her flat stomach. "I've waited so long for you."

If she could be lucky enough to carry this baby to term, she'd be a good mother. Her baby would be first in her life, ahead of career and friends. Ahead of *everything*. This child would be her family. Because they'd go it alone, they'd be closer than most. Just like Winona and her mother.

Outside the bathroom, she heard Riggs's loud footsteps in the kitchen and the sounds of ice tinkling in a glass. He'd been extra kind to her, going out of his way not to be too loud outside at the hours she'd asked for him to be quiet. When he'd see her in the kitchen, or outside, he'd smile and tip his hat and ask if she was doing okay. No more fighting, which she kind of missed quite honestly. When he fought with her, he was at least engaged with her.

She washed her hands, dried her tears, and went into the kitchen where Riggs stood drinking iced tea.

"Hey." He took in her appearance and did a double take. She was dressed in cut-off shorts, a tank top, and hadn't bothered with makeup today. "You okay?"

"Yep."

"You don't look okay. Have... Have you been *crying?*"

Happy tears. But he wouldn't understand. "Maybe."

She sat on a chair at the table. "We need to talk."

The apprehension and abject fear were written so clearly on his tight jawline. She'd assured him that this couldn't happen.

"I'm shocked, but yes, I'm pregnant. I'm sorry, Riggs. I really am."

For you.

He fell, more so than sat, onto the opposite chair. It was as if she'd told him he had four months to live.

"You're sure?"

She reached for his hand and squeezed it. "There are six tests all lined up in the bathroom, if you'd care to check. I can't believe it myself."

"Damn it, this is all my fault." He stroked a hand down his face.

He looked miserable which made her feel so much better about all this. She would soon take this enormous burden off his shoulders and he'd be forever grateful to her. So eternally appreciative that he might even wind up liking her in the end.

"No, it isn't your fault. I can't let you say that. You brought the condom. I'm the one who's sorry."

Lord, they were being so *nice* to each other.

"Don't be, princess. I wanted you, and I showed up that night. But I hadn't planned on failed birth control. I'm the one who used an old condom. I'm an idiot."

"No." She sucked in a breath as her stomach fell to her toes. "Please believe me. I didn't think this could happen to me at my age. And I-I didn't mean to involve you or tie you to me in any way."

"Of course. What woman in her right mind wants to be pregnant at nearly forty? This is going to be rough." He squeezed her shoulder. "Don't worry, I told you I'd be here for you, no matter what happens. We'll get married."

She choked on her tea. *"What?"*

"You'll come to live on my ranch with me and I'll take care of you. And the baby. It's my responsibility."

"Wait. Wait a minute. *No.* I... I can't *marry* you. I've been married three times, or haven't you heard?"

"It's not a big secret. Jackson was your third husband."

"Right, and I can't afford another mistake."

"This wouldn't be a *mistake*, since I'm the father of your baby."

She held up her palms. "No, thank you. You don't want to marry me."

"Of course I do. I wouldn't ask if I didn't want to do this."

"Well, you didn't *ask*. Though that's a kind offer, I don't want to get married."

"Then what *do* you want?"

There really would be no other more perfect moment to answer that question, and so she rose.

"Wait here. I'll be right back."

She found the contract on the nightstand in her bedroom. In the doorframe, she paused, and sent up a little silent prayer that he'd see the reasoning behind all this and go along with her well-laid plans. Clearly, he didn't really want this baby, not the way she did.

He accepted the contract when she handed it over to him. "What's this?"

"Just read it and you'll see."

As he read, his eyes went narrower with every second that passed, his jaw tighter. He looked up from his reading. "You can't be serious."

"Look, I didn't plan for it to be *you*. That's what all those interviews were about. All of the men were to read and sign the contract before they could be the father of my baby."

Oh dear, this didn't seem like the right thing to say because now his eyes went so dark, his mouth so tight, he appeared ready to go nuclear.

"You *slept* with all those men? Jeremy? *Lenny?*"

"No! Absolutely not! I wasn't lying when I said I haven't been with anyone in a very long time. Before you."

"Forgive me if I have a hard time believing that! And this contract isn't worth the paper it's written on. You can't take a father's rights away with the sweep of a pen."

"Well, it was written by my manager, and she's an attorney."

"So am I, and I can tell you that any good attorney could tear this contract apart with his hands tied behind his back."

Her world began to implode around her as her hands shook, and she realized the grave enormity of her mistake.

Riggs was an *attorney*?

She touched her stomach, as though she could somehow protect her unborn child. Could things *possibly* get any worse than this?

"You're not taking my baby away from me," he growled from between gritted teeth.

Apparently, things could get a whole lot worse.

RIGGS WAS NEVER ANGRIER at anyone in his life than he was at himself. For God's sake, he'd used an old condom in his wallet that crazy night. Probably expired, but had he cared at the time? No. He took a chance. But he was way past the age to go out of his mind with lust and desire over a woman. Way past the age when he felt invincible and untouchable. Oh, he realized he could be vulnerable. He'd already had something precious ripped away from him. Now this.

But if he was angry with himself first, Winona James came in a *very* close second. After telling him how older men took up with younger women, she was ready to have young Jeremy Pine's baby and Lord knew who else she'd "interviewed." She definitely hadn't considered *him* for a donation, though he would have laughed in her face. No, she didn't want someone her own age. She required someone she could push around.

The contract that she'd flashed in front of him was the last straw. To him, that meant she'd wanted this outcome, and at the moment it was difficult to believe that she hadn't used him. Like she'd tried to use a prospective sperm donor. Just when she'd become likeable and desirable, she'd proved him right. Entitled celebrity, as he'd first assumed. Not a sweet woman who had a lonely and vulnerable side.

"Did you read the part about Skype calls on all important holidays?" She gnawed on a fingernail.

Possibly the most ridiculous part of this contract. "I don't do *Skype*."

"FaceTime?" she squeaked.

"If you weren't a woman, I'd knock you out. This contract is insulting to anyone with a brain. None of this is okay. Nor will it ever be." With that he stood, held the "contract" between his hands, and ripped it neatly in two from top to bottom.

With every word she said, she lowered further in his estimation. His poor baby. He'd have this *woman* as a mother. Riggs would need to step in and do everything within his reach and power to counteract the terrible influence she'd have on him. For now, he refused to entertain the possibility that he could have a daughter. The idea was too painful.

And no wonder the guys never told him about this ridiculous situation. Personal assistant his ass. He'd have ripped them all a new one for even considering signing this contract. And *Lenny*! Like he didn't have enough problems. As if Winona hadn't already done enough, Riggs would look like an idiot for falling for her scheme when word got out. Maybe now the only way to save face was to pretend he'd fallen in love with her and accidentally knocked her up.

"I have wanted this baby for so long and this is my last

chance!" Winona yelled now, enraged when he ripped the contract. "You don't want a child. You made that clear."

"Maybe I don't, but I won't turn away from my flesh and blood. This is my responsibility."

"It doesn't have to be!"

"That's where you're wrong, because you don't understand old-fashioned homegrown values. You don't understand me. I was raised better than to be a man who would walk away from his child. That's *not* happening."

She covered her face with her hands. "I can't believe this."

"You better believe it, princess. Finally, someone is standin' up to you. You can't just go through life mowing everyone else down. People, even the *little* people, have rights and choices. Not just you."

"That's not fair. I'm tryin' to make this *easier* for you."

"You want to make it easier for me? Let's get married."

Although fatherhood carried with it certain rights, marriage would cement those for him. There would be no question as to his rights to a shared custody arrangement even with a powerful and entitled celebrity. If it came to that. But if she wanted to travel and tour instead of raising their baby, then he'd step in and do it himself. It would mean his life would change. Everything would change.

But on the other hand, he also never thought he'd have this chance again. A child.

Unlike Winona, he hadn't gone out of his way to make it happen. Planned and schemed. That didn't mean he would turn away from his baby and have him somewhere in the world, possibly being raised by another man someday.

"We're not gettin' married! You don't even *like* me."

"There were several minutes there when I liked you just fine." He threw a significant look at her kitchen wall.

"Okay, say we get married. Then what? What's your plan, cowboy?"

"Unlike you, I haven't had all kinds of free time to come up with a plan. I haven't schemed my way to a baby. But this is what I'm going to suggest. We can draw up a new contract, one I'll agree to. Our marriage can be for convenience only, but I'd want you to stick around until the baby is born. I need to make sure you're not off traipsin' around bars."

"Well, how interestin', since you didn't mind me traipsin' around bars a few weeks ago." This time she turned to glance at the wall.

"I don't mean *Jackson's* place. That's practically a family place. I meant *Nashville.*"

"What you're sayin' is that I can traipse around a bar, sing and perform, and do my *job*, as long as you pre-approve?" She crossed her arms.

"I didn't say that. You're puttin' words in my mouth. We could get married, then after the child is born, we do that unconscious coupling all you celebrities are doin' these days." He made air quotes. "And we agree to a shared custody arrangement that's fair to *both* of us."

"I think you mean conscious *un*coupling."

"Whatever. A divorce, the way us normal folks say."

"You want another divorce? That *can't* be what you want. It's not a homegrown value."

He scoffed. "I've never *been* divorced. I'm a widower."

And at that moment, as Winona's jaw gaped wide, he stood. "I'll be in touch soon."

Riggs stomped out of her house, packed up his tools, then drove savagely back to the ranch. Several minutes of glorious sex had just given him a lifetime commitment to a woman he could barely stand. Just the idea that he'd consider signing that contract infuriated him. She obviously had been used to dealing with much younger men, and whether that was her choice or not, she'd forgotten what it was like to deal with a grown man. An educated man, not the hicks she assumed she'd find in Stone Ridge. He would not be talked into any kind of shady arrangement. Having already lost one child, he would never purposefully lose another.

What he needed to do now was to cool down and put his mind on other matters for at least a few minutes. He had to wrap his head around this life-changing news. Sit with it, stew in it, and finally learn to accept it. No doubt Winona thought he'd think it over and come to a different answer.

Here, sweet, famous lady, take my baby and give it a good home. I'll be in touch every birthday.

She thought he'd give her his baby so that she could raise him on her own without any interference. *Skype* calls! The woman was certifiably insane, and he'd involved himself with her.

He pounded his steering wheel. "You are a full-grown man and a total jackass!"

The very nature of what had happened made it impossible for his mind not to wander to Jenny, his late wife. His college girlfriend. He hadn't thought of her in years.

He'd married her, because it was the right thing to do, and she'd wanted his help. And whether or not he'd been ready for marriage, he'd loved her. Jenny had been his best friend. They might have eventually married anyway, though he'd always had misgivings about Jenny's maturity level. Those misgivings had come back to haunt him when she'd lost her life and that of her unborn child.

She'd been drinking, driving home from a party, and as if the guilt he'd felt at not having been around to drive her home that night wasn't enough, he'd faced other facts. He'd known Jenny to be a party girl, and a hard drinker. She'd promised to stop drinking when she became pregnant, and he'd trusted her, when on some level he realized he shouldn't.

She'd carried on with her drinking, and in one night he'd

lost his wife, his best friend, and their baby. He might have been able to prevent it had he been more mature himself, more given to protecting his wife and child instead of obsessed with getting his law degree.

Not this time. This time he was taking full control of the situation, whether the princess liked it or not.

Because she'd picked the wrong man if she wanted one who would simply walk away.

CHAPTER 7

*R*iggs parked his truck near the barn and headed to the main house. He'd had a heifer in need of some attention, and a call in to Eve, who had promised to drop by.

And sooner rather than later, he'd have to deal with Phil Henderson, because the man would not give up. Not with developers' money on the table.

Winona was the last thing he needed right now, piled on top of everything else.

He stopped in at the main house to change. Maybe he needed a ride on Spur to get rid of this hostility and frustration. He found Delores in the kitchen sitting at the table with Lillian Carver, one of her good friends and the family matriarch at the Double C Ranch.

Now he'd have to tamp down the temper that Delores was far more used to seeing than someone who didn't live with him. Delores Wallace had been with him and his brothers for ten years now, cooking and cleaning and helping keep the house running. She had a cabin on the property and because she'd never had children of her own, she considered the Henderson men her sons.

"Ladies." He tipped his hat. "Good to see you, Mrs. Carver. How are Lincoln and Sadie doing?"

"She has amazing news." Delores nudged Mrs. Carver. "You tell him, Lillian."

"Sadie is pregnant!"

The rumors were true. Another baby. Riggs and Lincoln, fathers about the same time. Riggs wondered if Lincoln was also quaking in his boots. "Great news."

"Thank you! I pray we get a girl." She held her hands together in a prayer hold.

"What are you doin' home?" Delores said. "Got done early?"

That was one way of putting it. "I just wanted to check in on the heifer having some trouble. Has Eve come by yet?"

"You should ask Sean. He came blusterin' through here a few minutes ago without a minute to stop and say 'hey.' Don't know where he's got off to now."

"You need a chart to keep track of them men of yours, Delores," Lillian chuckled.

"Don't I know it."

Riggs helped himself to an ice-cold water from the fridge and eyed the apple pie inside. He was famished after the trauma of finding out he'd be a daddy. Delores would be happy about the news, seeing as she and Lillian conspired to fix up the "Henderson men" on a weekly basis. But Riggs would have to break the news to Delores gently. If she got a hint that he'd knocked Winona up one crazy night, she'd have his hide. He'd have to get her to believe he loved Winona. There was no other way he could pull this off.

"Riggs has been workin' on an addition over at Merle and Wanda's rental. Guess who's rentin' it? None other than Winona James, the country and western singer."

"Oh Lord, Riggs, stay away from that woman!" Lillian went palms up.

Now she tells me.

"She's nothin' but trouble with a capital T," Lillian said. "You know that my Jackson was married to her?"

Everybody in town did. "Yes, ma'am."

"Well, I guess I can say so now, because it didn't happen. But don't you know she had the gall darn nerve to ask my Jackson for his sperm!"

Riggs nearly spit out his water. *"What?"*

Jackson! She'd asked her ex-husband to make a deposit. Did the woman have no shame?

"You heard me. Well, when Eve heard this…you can imagine. That girl does have herself a temper, after all. Not that Jackson would have *considered* the idea."

Riggs scrunched his water bottle with one hand. Winona was going down faster and faster. He now looked forward to marrying her and making her utterly miserable for nine months. Miserable, but healthy. Oh, he'd make sure of it, toeing that line like an expert acrobat. Maybe he'd make her eat kale. For the baby, of course.

"Good Lord," Delores said. "What is this mess?"

"Don't ask me. She's like all of these entitled celebrities who think they can have whatever they want, lickety split." Lillian snapped her fingers.

"She's not so bad," Riggs said between his clenched teeth.

How else was he going to explain marrying her in a few days?

Lillian regarded him as though he'd grown a second head. "Really?"

"Maybe she's changed, Lillian," Delores said. "A place like Stone Ridge could do that to a woman."

And this was why he loved Delores. She'd see the good in a field mouse.

"Yeah, she…she…" Riggs wracked his brain for something selfless she'd done. Something kind. Other than the sweet iced tea she served him and occasionally threatened to spit in, he had nothing. "She performed at the Shady Grind for Jackson. They raised money for the new clinic. I'm sure she didn't charge him, and he had a full house."

There.

"Oh, good. I hear Judson hired a midwife, and Linc will be taking Sadie there from now on," Lillian said.

"See? She has her good side." Delores clapped her hands once.

He'd seen her only *good* side, and it got him into this mess. "Well, if you'll excuse me, ladies. I've got work to do."

"You don't understand." Winona sniffed into the phone. "He's actually an *attorney*."

She'd gone through half a box of tissues since Riggs had left her house a couple of hours ago. The tears wouldn't stop coming. How she'd managed to hook up with probably the only cowboy attorney in town, she'd never know.

"I explained that your contract wasn't terribly binding. I did the best I could with it but there are too many gray areas, ethical, and moral problems surrounding this kind of a thing. Especially considering your financial status. You *should* have gone with a bank."

All she'd wanted was a baby. Her own precious child to love and raise. This is what she got for being honest and above board. And for wanting to see the face of her child's father. For wanting to know him. She now knew far more than she ever wanted to about her baby's father. He was a jerk!

"That contract would have been fine for most of these men."

"That's what you get for not checking the condom's expiration date, I guess."

Winona covered her face. "Please don't pour salt in the wound."

"Well, honey, let's take a look at his contract suggestions and see what he's thinking before we fly off the rails. Maybe he'll be reasonable. And for God's sake, do *not* get married again without a prenup! There is only one Jackson Carver, I assure you."

Despite the fact that Winona wanted to believe there was another man somewhere with as much character and integrity as Jackson, she had to admit it was a longshot. He'd had the chance to take her for half of everything she had when they'd divorced, but he'd simply walked away from the marriage with only what he'd brought into it.

"I don't want to marry him. You have to get me out of this."

"What do you have against getting married just for a short time? You're getting what you wanted, but with a few conditions. He'll be the father of your child. And, I hate to bring it up, but I'm sure it hasn't escaped you that Nashville is a fairly conservative community. Divorce is one thing, though still not popular, but a child out of wedlock? Well, I believe that's still frowned on."

"Because I swore the *next* time I got married, it would be for life."

One night shortly after she'd received her quickie divorce from Jackson, Winona had sat down on her bed holding the Dissolution of Marriage papers. It was official. She was a three-time loser. She didn't cry or rip up the papers. Instead she stared at the words and understood in that moment that she had to change her life.

Then and there, she'd made a vow to the memory of Mary Jo Hoyt.

Mama, the next time I marry I will know the man. I will love him with all my heart. And I won't give up on him, or us.

"You had the best of intentions..." Kimberly let that remark draw out.

"Just give him your legalese. He'll see reason. A marriage isn't necessary, but if we do get married, I should *not* have to live with him until the baby is born!"

"Agreed. And I will do everything in my power to make that happen for you."

But a week later, no progress had been made. Over the phone and a dozen or more emails, Riggs stuck to his guns. He wouldn't budge or give an inch. Kimberly said he had one of the finest legal minds she'd ever met when it came to contract law, which wasn't good news for them. But in the good news department, Riggs had signed a prenup with zero hesitation. Their other contract was useless, and they'd thrown it out and started over.

The only contract Riggs would agree to had some ridiculous demands in it that were questionable, but seeing as he currently held all the cards, he'd inserted them willy-nilly. In exchange for a quiet and uncontested divorce, Riggs insisted she marry him and live with him until their baby was born. At that time, and only at that time, they would entertain a joint custody arrangement. Also, he agreed not to sue her for full custody if she would do the same.

How generous of him!

Contract negotiations became so heated that Kimberly flew out to personally meet with Riggs. Settled at the kitchen table over dual laptops and papers, the man with a Stetson and a law degree argued over addendums and clauses. Winona sat quietly and stared out the window toward the hill that faced the nearly completed Florida room and tried to picture her beautiful sweet baby. As she gazed out into the early September morning, she imagined autumn rolling in soon. The blazing Texas heat would abate. Leaves would begin to fall and change colors. Her baby would be born in the month of May, around Mother's Day.

Maybe she'd have Mama's beautiful golden curls and bright blue eyes. Winona could name her daughter after her mother, a way to honor the woman who'd been the only person to ever love her unconditionally. Mary Jo might be a plain name, or simply a classic. Surely, when she held her tiny miracle in her arms, all these negotiations would have been well worth it. She reminded herself that had she gone about the normal way of having a child, she might be arguing over naming a child with her boyfriend, fiancé, or husband anyway. But it wouldn't have involved a legally binding agreement over custody. Instead, she was letting a virtual stranger determine her and her unborn child's future.

And that was all on her.

"We're very close to an agreement and I don't know why you're being so unreasonable," Kimberly said from the next room. "We absolutely won't budge on this last point. Winona has been more than generous, but she can't stay here until the baby is born. Nashville is her home."

"Sorry, that's a deal breaker."

"What about…" and Kimberly's no-nonsense voice droned on and on.

All Winona wanted was a nap. Every day she grew more exhausted and worried something could be wrong with her baby. She'd do everything in her power to give her a good start. Eat well, take her vitamins, take walks for the fresh air. Anything.

Just please let me have this. I'll do anything.

She didn't know if it had been hours or a few minutes, because she was suddenly jarred awake by Kimberly.

"We've reached a deal."

Riggs stood just behind her, gray Stetson tipped, an

unreadable gaze in his hooded lids. "Is everything alright? You were sleeping again. You've been doing that a lot."

"I'm exhausted lately." She blinked at the two attorneys who'd been trying to work out the next year of her life.

"Perfectly normal," Kimberly bit out.

Unfortunately, Winona heard the deep sound of resentment in Kim's voice. And that look in Riggs's gaze became obvious now. It was triumph. He'd won.

Beat her at her own game.

She stood and crossed her arms.

"I have something to say. I'm not marrying you, Riggs! Absolutely not. Anything else, okay, but I won't do that. You can have your visitation, your joint custody, whatever. I give up. But I won't, on principle, marry you. I absolutely *refuse* and neither one of you can make me!"

THE SMALL PRIVATE wedding was held a week later at Trinity Church, because Stone Ridge didn't have a courthouse. They also didn't have a police department and barely had a school. She took some pleasure in the fact that after her baby was born, she could argue that with only one small K-4 school in town, and no preschools, it was unreasonable to expect her to raise her child in Stone Ridge.

In attendance was Pastor June, the officiant, and Kimberly, as a witness. She'd stayed in Kerrville, the next closest town over, so she could attend the wedding. The guests were Riggs's younger brother Sean, and their housekeeper, a middle-aged woman named Delores. His other younger brother Colton was in the Army and stationed somewhere overseas. Delores seemed the only happy one, wiping away genuine tears. Winona was already all cried out as she'd sobbed for hours the night before.

The utter humiliation of marriage to a man who didn't

love her was beyond cruel. She'd done a desperate and crazy thing to have a child, sure, but she honestly had never meant to involve him. Privately, Kimberly had explained that Riggs took full responsibility for his actions. However, he blamed her for the contract, for the interviews, and for daring to think she'd get away with this. He believed her to be selfish, dimwitted, and didn't trust her with *his* flesh and blood.

Kimberly assured her that this marriage was a stopgap measure meant to appease Riggs. At the end of the year, if it even came to that, Kimberly would work to have the marriage annulled. It would be as if it never happened. The only requirement was that she not sleep with him because that might make it difficult, if not impossible to annul the marriage. Winona assured Kimberly, on pain of death, that she would *never* sleep with this man! Again.

"I'm holding you to it," Kimberly said.

Despite the specter of despair clouding this day, her fourth wedding was the finest one she'd ever had. The first had been to her high school sweetheart and had involved a courthouse in Oklahoma. The second one, to Colby, was another courthouse somewhere on her fifty-four-city tour, because Colby claimed *he* couldn't wait to be married to her. And the third one to Jackson...when they'd both been drunk, hurting, and lonely in Las Vegas.

Trinity Church was a white clapboard building with a steeple and a belfry. A stained-glass photo of Jesus was its only real decoration. The pews were old, wooden, and looked uncomfortable. Riggs came dressed in a dark suit, green tie, and black cowboy boots, clean-shaven, and wearing his ever-present Stetson. He seemed to be taking this ceremony somberly, but she'd expect nothing less from a man this traditional.

The gold band Riggs gave her was traditional, too, but surprisingly beautiful and it touched her that he hadn't purchased a cheap ring. Winona wore the same tight, short, white dress she'd worn the night she performed at the Shady Grind. The same night she'd conceived her baby. She wanted Riggs to know that, to her, this was nothing but another performance. Just as it obviously was for him.

She'd heard him talking to his brother and Delores before the ceremony.

"Well, when cupid strikes, I guess no one can predict. I had no idea I'd fall so hard and fast for Winona."

"I'm so happy for you," Delores had blubbered.

And she was still sniffing as they finished their vows.

"I now pronounce you man and wife," Pastor June said. "You may kiss the bride."

Their kiss was so fast and chaste that Winona thought for sure they'd blown their cover. They'd have to spend a lot of time apart on his ranch, or sooner or later they'd all figure out their marriage of convenience. For reasons she couldn't understand, Riggs was insistent that no one in his family believe that he'd married her because she was pregnant. This seemed a fine point to him and not one she could just write away to traditional pressures. Riggs wasn't fooling her. He was a grown man, and no one told this bullheaded man what to do.

"I need at least one photo for the press release," Kimberly said and whipped out her phone.

Riggs draped an arm around her waist and Winona smiled the way she did every time she took the stage. *Show time!* They'd all agreed that the press release would say Winona and Riggs met through Jackson Carver, and that they'd dated quietly for months before their private wedding. No pregnancy announcement yet, but spoiler alert: Winona would get pregnant pretty damn fast.

As they filed out of the church, Delores gave Winona a sideways hug and walked with her. "I'm so happy to have you

at the house. Finally, another lady. Where are you two goin'
for your honeymoon?"

"There's no time for a honeymoon," Riggs said gruffly
from behind them. "I've got too much goin' on. And I have to
finish the addition to the Stephens's property."

The one *she'd* never get to enjoy.

"Hell, man, don't act like you're the only cowboy in this
family," Sean said. "I can take up the slack."

"I'm not goin' anywhere for a while."

"Oh, well, you'll go on a honeymoon after everything on
the ranch is settled," Delores said, beautifully ignorant.

They all parted ways in the parking lot. Riggs waited for
Winona by his truck, giving her a look that said he was in no
mood to argue. But she went straight to Kimberly, her only
contact to her former and rapidly disintegrating world. A
world that, if not always satisfying, at least made sense to
her. In her world Winona knew what was expected of her.
Here, she didn't know what Riggs wanted from her, or what
he expected she'd do for nine months, stuck on a cattle
ranch.

Kimberly folded Winona into her arms. "Try to make the
best of this, honey. We'll keep in touch every day. The year
will go by quickly."

"No, it won't." Winona's voice broke.

"Hey, is this the same lady that clawed her way to the top
of the music business? You're tougher than this." Kimberly
pulled back to study her. "He doesn't *know* you. I don't like
this, either, but maybe it will work in your favor. Once he
gets to know the real you, he won't be able to help liking you.
After that, co-parenting with him will be a lot easier."

But Winona didn't think Riggs would ever forgive her.
They had nothing in common other than the baby they'd
someday share. He'd proven that he liked having sex with
her, but even that would be something he'd now regret. She'd

never regret it, no matter how she'd conceived. Maybe pregnancy hormones were already making her too emotional, because normally when a man treated her like this, she'd want to key his truck.

She eyed his truck now, and the man who stood resolutely by it. He reminded her of a warrior about to take home his spoils. "This will all be worth it when I hold my baby."

"That's right." Kimberly rubbed Winona's back. "Just keep your eyes on the prize."

"Winona," Riggs called out in irritation, and then when he saw that Delores and his brother were within earshot, "Baby, we really gotta go. C'mon, now. I already miss you."

With one last squeeze to Kimberly, Winona walked to the truck that would take her to the ranch where she'd be imprisoned for the next eight months.

Riggs held the door open, but then hauled her into his arms, lifting her by the waist, above his shoulders. The smile he gave her was slightly wicked, but mostly frozen, his normally shimmering eyes vacant.

"I can't wait to get you home."

Riggs hoisted her in the passenger seat and shut the door.

"You should have been an actor," she said as he buckled up and started out of the parking lot.

"There's a little bit of an actor in every attorney," Riggs said fiercely.

"I don't see why we have to pretend to be so in love."

"Why else would I marry you this fast? I don't want anyone to think that I'm the idiot who signed up to be your personal assistant."

"No, we did this the old-fashioned way. A faulty condom."

"By the way, I think we were married quickly enough that we can get away with a wedding night pregnancy. Just give it a couple of weeks and I'll announce it to the family."

"The proud papa," she spit out.

"That's right," he said and turned on to the main road. "And Sean took your rental back to Kerrville earlier today. No use in wasting your money."

She bit her tongue at the way her new husband was already making decisions for her. *That* wasn't in the fine print. "How will I get around town?"

"If you need to go anywhere, either Delores or I can take you. Doctor's appointments, I'm there."

"Basically, I'm literally a prisoner."

"You're *not* a prisoner. I said I'd take you wherever you want to go, not that there's many places."

"Am I allowed to see my friends, Master and Commander?"

He threw her a contemptuous look. "*What* friends?"

She pretended that didn't hurt. It was true that she didn't have many friends here, and now she couldn't even count Riggs among them.

"Jackson," she said, wondering if she could claim anyone else. She traced the hem of her skirt. "I think Annabeth, the veterinarian, likes me, too."

And many of the men, she felt tempted to add, but they'd stay away from her out of respect for Riggs. Even if it had been fun to flirt, Winona had to start thinking like a mother, if not a wife. That carefree part of her life was over for good and she wouldn't actually miss it contrary to what anyone else might think. The attention had been harder to handle than she'd ever cared to admit.

"You can see your friends. I'm not a monster."

"Thank you, Sir. Oh, and do I call you 'Sir' in front of the family? Will *that* also be expected of me?"

"You better not," he said in a husky tone. "This has to be *believable*."

"Thank you for Delores, by the way. She might be the only way I stay sane."

"Don't get too close to her. I don't want her to be devastated when we divorce."

"Right." She bit her lower lip, trying to push back the tears. "I'll be mean to her then."

"Don't do that, either. She's a kind woman and deserves your respect."

"Face it, nothing I do is going to make you happy."

He had nothing to add to that truth nugget.

Her luggage had been moved to the ranch earlier, but Winona still hadn't seen the place where she'd spend nearly a year growing her baby. Her hope was that it didn't stink too badly but she'd visited a dude ranch before, and the smell had been pungent. Her only real experience with a real farm was the little vegetable garden that her mother had grown every spring. It was only a six-by-five-foot piece of dirt by their trailer home, but in that small space Mary Jo had grown the most delicious cherry tomatoes, basil, mint, and cucumbers. Winona had both photos and memories of picking bright red cherry tomatoes with her chubby fingers, biting into them, the juice dripping down the front of her dress.

The neighbors used to say that Mary Jo could make silk out of a sow's ear. Even now, another memory washed over Winona, hurting in new places. She wondered if at some point she'd tell Riggs about her mother, especially when it came time to name their little girl. Shockingly, naming hadn't been in the contract, leading her to believe Riggs didn't care much about first names. But it had been clearly and notably spelled out that her daughter would carry the Henderson family's last name.

Another deal breaker for the cowboy.

CHAPTER 8

*R*iggs pulled down the long dirt lane that led to the ranch, trying to see it from Winona's eyes. In her eyes, she'd probably be living in a hovel for a year. He wondered if she realized, or if it would even matter to her, that Henderson Grange was one of the largest parcels of land in Stone Ridge.

"You live *here?*" Winona said now as they approached.

Every muscle in him tensed and he'd been about to give her a smartass remark about her entitled celebrity status, when she continued, "It's so big."

"The Hendersons were one of the oldest and original ranching families in Stone Ridge."

"Do you always talk about your family in the third person like that?"

"Cal and Marge were our foster parents that turned into real parents."

That made her speechless again, so he continued.

"We don't use all of the land for ranching, but we have about five hundred acres in total." He pointed. "That stream divides our property on the western slope."

"I can see I'm going to be taking long walks on this beautiful property."

"Don't get lost out there. And stay away from the livestock. They're not friendly."

"I know you believe I'm dumb as a post, but I promise you I know how to walk and everything. I even graduated from high school."

While that wasn't quite true, he chose not to call her on it. Late nights, he'd been researching the mother of his baby. Since she was famous, it was all public information and biographies were all over the Internet. She'd dropped out of her Oklahoma high school but obtained her GED later. The mother of his future son had led an interesting life.

Her mother had died when Winona was only ten, and she'd lived in a trailer park with her stepfather until age sixteen, when she'd self-admittedly lied about her age and married her first husband. She'd left that husband in the dust when she *hitchhiked* (again, bad choices) to a talent contest in Nashville, which she'd won.

Since then she'd won several Country Music Association awards over the years and had two number one hit songs. Both had been years ago. Since he'd been occasionally forced to listen to country music, through no fault of his own, he'd heard the songs. Both upbeat tunes, not a single ballad in the mix. She'd claimed many of her songs to be semi-autobiographical, including one about keying her cheating boyfriend's truck. He'd be paying close attention to *his* truck from this point forward.

He pulled said truck up the circular driveway of the ranch-style home instead of the barn up the hill where he usually parked. Not for the first time, he wished the house was larger, if for no other reason than she could stay on one side and he on the other. But he also wouldn't mind impressing her a little. Because he hadn't been able to impress her with their rings. They were two simple gold bands, to remind her this was a practical arrangement. Nothing fancy or romantic. He'd bet her shoes were worth more than the gold band he'd purchased.

She had more wealth and financial stability to offer their son, but he wasn't a slouch in that department. Money just wasn't everything. He intended to prove to her that he'd do a good job raising their child on his end because he wasn't foolish enough to believe that both she and her attorney would keep their half of the deal not to sue him for full custody after their divorce. He'd agreed to that, and forced them to do the same, but contracts were violated often, and it just meant more time and money spent in court.

She'd have a hell of a fight on her hands if she decided to sue for sole custody, but that wouldn't make it any less of an irritation to him. He'd left his law career for a reason. Though he loved the law there were too many loopholes, and the day he realized he'd make his living exploiting those, he quit.

"Listen," he said. "For now, we have to share a bedroom."

He caught the panic clearly etched in her bright eyes and hated that she disliked him this much. But he'd essentially brought this on himself, hadn't he?

"Calm down. I won't actually sleep with you, but this has to look good. Until I figure out how I can realistically give you the spare bedroom. We're supposed to be madly in love newlyweds."

"You snore."

"No, I don't."

"How would *you* know? You're asleep. And I'm just givin' you a reason why you might give me my own bedroom."

That actually made a lot of sense. "Just might work."

"See? I'm good for somethin'."

She was good for a lot of things, not the least of which

was driving him crazy. Something about this woman teased his lesser self. That bottom-dweller mentality he thought he'd left behind. Obviously, he hadn't done so. He just used legalese now instead of his fists.

"But for tonight, we're goin' to have to pretend. After I know that everyone's asleep, I'll go sleep in the spare room."

With that, he came around to help her down from the passenger side of the truck. He offered his hand even if no one was looking because he wanted her to know that despite all the fighting, he thought they could possibly get along. It was only eight months or so. He was a reasonable person, and since she'd agreed to his demands, he'd been placated for now. There had to be *some* redeeming qualities to Winona Jones, because she'd come a long way from the trailer park.

Somewhat reluctantly, he respected her for all her accomplishments and only wished he hadn't had to research his wife. Two people who were about to have a child together should know each other a hell of a lot better than they did. Hopefully, she'd take the time to get to know him, too, the father of her child. He was miles out of his comfort zone, getting married again at forty-two, and would attempt to be a decent husband. It would all be worth it when he met his son. And as long as Winona didn't pick some ridiculously trendy name like Eleven, or name him after a fruit, he'd go along with whatever she chose.

Riggs led her to the front door, hand low on her back. Inside, Delores had a cake and a full meal ready. He'd told her not to make a big fuss because he and Winona had both been married before and were old enough not to need any fanfare. But Delores lived for fanfare. He didn't have the heart to stop her from baking all night. He'd seen the elaborate cake this morning, and it was entirely pink, because she'd read that was Winona's favorite color.

Before he opened the door, he thought maybe he should

apologize. All along, after discovering her pregnancy, he'd taken control without caring what she thought or wanted. He regretted being a grump, but she'd hit him where it hurt. The thought she'd take away his child, the thought she didn't think him *worthy* to raise their child...that stung. And as always when stung, he retaliated. Sooner or later, he'd have to stop that, but it went against his nature to let others walk all over him. Even a beautiful and wealthy woman who could do a lot better than him.

"Look," he said at the front door. "I should apologize before we walk inside. There hasn't been a wedding in our family in two decades, and Delores is excited. She may have decided, on her own, that we should have a party. I want you to know I tried to talk her out of it."

"Why would you do that?"

"I've already pushed you hard enough. Wouldn't really blame you if you didn't want anything to do with any of us."

She tipped her chin. "I'm always up for a party."

That gave him pause, because she had a well-documented history of drinking. This was a sensitive issue for him given Jenny. But he couldn't imagine that Winona, who obviously desperately wanted a child, would do anything to risk their baby's health. Still, he'd neglected signs once before. Jenny had also wanted the baby. He mentally shook his head and put the idea out of his mind.

Holding open the door for her, he waited for her to walk inside. He observed as she paused in the granite floor foyer and took it all in. She also seemed to be waiting for some kind of permission and glanced back at him, an uncertainty wavering in her eyes that completely threw him.

"Welcome!" Delores appeared, threw her arms open, and Winona easily went into them. "Sean put your luggage in the bedroom, and I want you to just relax. Kick off your heels. I know how you appreciate your privacy, but we're havin' a little family party, and I made y'all a cake."

She led Winona into the separate dining room with a large farmhouse table. The pink two-tier cake sat in the middle of a spread of country cooking. A ham, chicken fried steak, Delores's famous fried chicken, mashed potatoes and gravy, grits, buttered rolls, corn, green beans, and several pies in addition to the cake.

"Oh my, this is so nice of y'all," Winona said. "I'm so happy to be here."

He noted it was the same thing she'd said the night of her performance. Say what you wanted to about Winona James, she could sure put on a show. But then again, so could he.

"It will take us two months to eat all this food," Riggs said, reaching for Winona's hand.

She nearly jumped in surprise and gave him a wary look. This had to look real, damn it. Had she already forgotten?

"Not with all you cowboys," Delores said, waving them to the table. "I bet the food doesn't even last much past tomorrow."

"Alright, are we eatin' yet?" Sean walked in, rubbing his hands together.

"Not until we cut the cake," Delores said, waving him away. "It's a weddin' cake."

Riggs led Winona to the wedding cake, and she squealed in surprise. He honestly didn't know whether that was real or fake delight.

"It's all pink," she gushed. "Oh, thank you, Delores!"

He wanted to whisper that she didn't have to lay it on so thick, but he'd just noticed the inscription on the cake:

Riggs and Winona Henderson
True Love

THERE WERE red and white hearts on both sides. Guilt pulsed through him at the lie he'd perpetrated and for a moment he wondered if he should take Delores into his confidence. She'd understand that these things happened, two people hooking up out of loneliness and need. Definitely not true love. More like hot sex. But Delores had been like a second mother to him, and he'd rather not confess to that incredible lapse of judgement on his part. The other problem was that Delores didn't know how to keep a secret.

"Hurry up and gimme a piece of that cake then," said Sean, hopping on Riggs's last nerve.

"Sean!" Delores said. "Behave."

"Well, did you make it so we could stare at it all day, or are we actually goin' to eat some?"

"The bride and groom have to cut the cake and have the first piece." Delores handed the cake cutter to Winona.

"This is almost too pretty to disturb." She took the cake cutter and poised it.

"Please, disturb it," Sean added and then an "oof" sound after Delores elbowed him in the gut.

Riggs remembered this part, and obviously so did Winona. When he laid his hand on hers as she cut the first slice, she glanced up at him with the hint of a smile. They cut a slice and did the obligatory feeding it to each other. When she took a bite out of his hands, she licked some frosting off his finger, and his dick twitched with a memory of that tongue. He swallowed hard, wishing he could dislike her more. Wishing that she weren't so damn beautiful. It would be difficult enough living with someone who would count the days until she could leave his family, and he sure had no plans to repeat the performance that got him here in the first place.

Besides, he liked her far better when she was yelling at him.

They eventually sat down to eat the banquet Delores had prepared and Winona entertained them all with memories of the Grand Ole Opry.

"Did you ever meet the one and only Johnny Cash?" Delores asked wistfully.

"Just once."

Then she told them about meeting Dolly Parton, her hero, and how kind and generous she'd been. She'd taught her that a professional had time to be nice to everyone and should take the time to acknowledge each fan. Riggs had witnessed that skill in action the night he'd knocked her up.

"Did you ever have a chance to meet any rock stars?" Sean shared Riggs's own taste in music.

She paused, her fork poised before her mouth. Dear Lord, that mouth. It was full and sensual, the lower lip slightly fuller than the top.

"I met Mick Jagger once," she said. "He made a pass at me."

"Of course he did," said Sean. "I will go to my grave admiring that man."

"He's very sweet and very British. I could hardly understand a word he said but he claimed that *I* was the one with the accent."

"What was it like being married to Jackson?" This question earned Sean a glare from Delores.

"Big mistake. He's such a sweetheart and he obviously never got over Eve. We were just good friends who should have never been married in the first place. I regret it." She slid Riggs a look. "I think marriage should be forever."

"In a perfect world," Riggs grumbled quietly.

"I can see the love between you two, just firin' off and

sparkling like cannon balls on the Fourth of July," Delores said. "I'd bet my life savings on you two lasting forever."

"Well," Winona said. "I believe it, too. I love him, of course."

"What do you love most about him?" Delores pressed.

Riggs really wished she wouldn't. Winona knew little about him other than he was strong enough to hold her up against a wall, could wield a hammer, had his law degree, and didn't shoot blanks.

"I love that he's so *honest*," she said, scoring a direct hit. "And, of course, traditional. You don't meet many men like him in show business. He insisted we get hitched...in a church."

"Riggs was brought up the right way," Delores said. "He's a good man."

"Guess Winona is about to find out how good," Sean added. "Heh, heh, heh."

Delores sent him her withering, you're-never-too-old for my switch look. "And what do you love about Winona?"

All eyes were on Riggs. Sean had a sly grin on face, showing Riggs he had a real good feeling exactly what he loved most about Winona.

He reached under the table for her hand. "I love how she *listens* to me. And how she takes such good care of her man."

She squeezed his hand, but with an I-wish-I-could-hurt-you death grip. He gave her a satisfied grin, having scored his own hit.

Delores stood. "And now let's adjourn to the living room, because it's time for your first dance as a married couple."

CHAPTER 9

"*D*ance?" Winona squeaked.

This party masquerading as a wedding reception had already outmatched any of her previous weddings. She realized that didn't say much about her previous ones. But she didn't want this marriage of convenience to outshine her next and last wedding day, whenever *that* might happen. She could tell that Riggs was horrified by all the romantic touches, and at the words "true love" on the wedding cake, he'd turned pale.

His true love was obviously his late wife. But Winona thought it all so beautiful, from the two-tier pink wedding cake, to the homemade meal with so many of her favorite foods, to the love and attention to small details from Delores. Winona only wished it *were* real because it hurt that all this warmth and comfort was based on a lie. In that moment, she hated Riggs.

The home itself was nicer than she imagined it would be. There was a wrap-around porch and a rocking chair similar to the one her mother used to sit on when she shelled peas. Despite Winona's resentment, she had to admit this was a warm family home. Even with the shotgun propped behind the front door. She was familiar with shotguns, having shot copperheads by age eleven. She filed this away for ammunition should the case arise:

Father keeps a loaded shotgun behind the front door.

Delores led the way to the living room where she had an old-fashioned turntable set up in a corner of the open, rustic room. Decidedly western, there were leather couches without a single pillow in sight, recliners, and one huge plasma TV above the stone brick fireplace. A woman's touch was literally nowhere.

Delores lowered the needle to the vinyl and out came the words from George Strait's number one hit, "I Cross my Heart." Winona's heart tugged in a powerful ache. For years, it had been one of the most requested songs at wedding receptions. When she'd first started performing, she'd played weddings, and sang the love song many times. George sang about a man who swore his woman would never in the world find a love as true as his. The sweetness of the memory of better times, when she'd been younger and full of hope, sliced through her.

In the middle of the room, Riggs held out his hand to her, and she saw in his dark gaze a quiet kind of acceptance. He looked strong, and tall, like an oak tree in the middle of a storm. Like nothing could bend or break him. Not the strongest wind or the hardest hit.

She hated him more than she thought she could hate anyone.

He tugged her into his arms, and she went into them without looking at him, flashing her "show" smile, though it felt limp as a noodle. She came attuned to every single sound, from George's soothing vibrato, to Riggs's soft breaths, to the sound of the needle against classic vinyl. And she was painfully aware of the muscles in Riggs's forearms as they bunched under her touch, and the hot searing brand of his hand low on her waist. Scorching anger pulsed through her because she wanted him to ache like she did. She wanted him to *hurt*. He'd forced her into a charade when she wanted this to be real.

She wanted a man to love *her*, not her body or her money, or the fact that she might be able to introduce them to Carrie Underwood. She wanted that unconditional love that she'd never had from anyone but her own mother. Finally, the song ended, and Winona could not take another moment of this slow torture.

She yawned. "I'm so tired."

Riggs was all over that. "She didn't get enough sleep last night. So much to do. Let's let her rest now."

"Oh, of course, sweetheart." Delores once again squeezed her tight. "You go on and get ready for bed."

"I'll be right behind you, baby," Riggs said.

Lord, he was good.

"Well, that's *my* cue," Sean said, and swiping one last piece of fried chicken, he went out the door.

"Be back before dawn tomorrow, we've got work to do," Riggs called out after him.

"This has been such a wonderful party." Winona meant every word. It had been far *too* wonderful. So wonderful she was sick with grief.

"I'll bring y'all breakfast in bed tomorrow morning," Delores said.

"No, don't," Riggs said a bit too forcefully. "*I'll* bring her breakfast in bed."

Delores blushed three shades of red. "Well, I wasn't going to barge in. I would knock and leave it outside your door like room service."

Winona glared at him because from now on, no one would be a bigger champion of Delores than she would.

Apparently realizing his mistake, Riggs softened. "Of course, I knew that. I'm sorry, I just don't want you goin' out of your way."

"You've done so much already." Winona reached for Delores's hands. "And I will never forget it."

"It was my pleasure, sugar. Let me show you to your room," Delores said.

Winona followed Delores down a long hall and to a separate wing of the spread-out, H-shaped ranch-style floor plan. They went down a long hall to the last door on the right. It opened to a large, neat, bedroom suite with a large bed and an ornate mahogany headboard. Her suitcases were lined up next to the closet.

For Winona, it wasn't unfamiliar to spend the night away from home. At the beginning of her career, she'd driven herself to shows, sometimes sleeping in her car. Later, she'd stayed in the homes of her fans. This would be more of the same. Staying in someone else's home. Only it would be for several months and not a few nights. In the home and bedroom of the man she hated.

"You have your own bathroom in here so no need to run into any of us. All the privacy you need."

"This is perfect," Winona lied.

The drapes were dark, the bed covers were dark, the photos on the wall were black, brown, and white. Monochrome. This was a man's room, not a stitch of color in sight, let alone any pink.

"Well, it definitely needs a woman's touch, I'd say. But that's what you're here for."

"I'll start with pillows. A splash of pink." She brightened.

He was determined to make her miserable, so she'd return the favor. By the time she was done, he wouldn't recognize this room.

"Who lives in this house?' she asked Delores, who was fluffing the bed pillows like a hotel maid.

"Just Riggs and his two brothers. Colton is on another tour of duty with the Army. He hasn't been home in a few years, but I've got high hopes he'll be back soon. This was the family house, and after their parents died, all the boys came back home to take over the ranch. Riggs had been away for a few years going to law school. Now all three of them run the ranch."

"Don't you live here, too?"

"I have a cabin on their land, not far from here. It's perfect because I have my privacy, but I walk to work every day. Riggs was kind enough to give me the house, and after my husband died, it was just enough room for me. We never had any children." She took a deep breath. "The Henderson boys are like my own. Marge was my best friend. It's going to be so wonderful to have female company around here."

When Riggs appeared in the open doorway, Delores excused herself, shutting the door. He walked to the closet and wrenched off his tie.

"I'll never forgive you for this," Winona said.

He glared at her. "I told you this wasn't my idea."

"That's not good enough! We wouldn't even be in this position if you weren't so damn traditional. We didn't have to get married!"

"Lower your voice," he growled. "Delores is still here. You're forgetting this isn't about us. It's about my son, who deserves to be born to married parents. Too bad you think that's not important."

"Your *son*?" She laughed, on the verge of hysteria. "She's a girl, and she's going to be hell on wheels!"

His eyes narrowed. "How do you know?"

"Just a feeling."

"So, you could be wrong. And you're not the best judge,

so I'm going to hang on to the hope of a son if you don't mind."

"Well, buddy, I have mother's intuition, so good luck with that!" She seemed to be shouting.

"I said quiet down!" He crossed the room in two long strides and made the enormous mistake of putting his big hand over her mouth.

She pushed back and bit down hard.

He drew back his hand. "Damn it, Winona! What the hell's wrong with you?"

"What's wrong with me is you put your *hand* over my mouth. And I bite back, mister. That's something a husband should know about his wife." She plopped down on the bed.

He flapped the injured hand in the air. "Should I go get my rabies shot?"

"I would." She crossed her arms and smiled.

"Lord, I *hope* we don't have a girl."

"Get out of here so I can change." Ironic, but she was having his baby, and he'd never even seen her naked.

"Change in the bathroom if you're that shy." He untucked his shirt and started unbuttoning it.

She didn't want him doing that. Didn't want to see his bare chest, which she saw hints of now as the buttons slowly came off. Going by the feel of him the night she'd conceived, her arms under his shirt to touch him, he was all hard planes and taut muscles.

"What are you *doing*?"

"Changing, because I'm *not* shy." He tore off his shirt and threw it to the floor.

"Jerk!" She stood and grabbed the handle of her carry-on, rolling it into the bathroom and slamming the door behind her.

Removing her cosmetic bags, she set up shop. Riggs Henderson wouldn't know what hit him. Try several thousand dollars of Ulta products, for starters. He wanted to marry her? Well, she'd show *him*! Because she came with product. She lined up all her cosmetics, shoving all his toiletries to the side. Before long, she'd taken over the formerly sparse granite countertop with hair extensions, curlers, hair straightener, hair spray, blow dryer. Several makeup bags, her toothbrush, teeth whitener strips, dental floss, and toothpaste. Just for fun she laid out her bikini wax kit since she wouldn't have other feminine products around for a while.

She peeled off the skintight dress and relieved herself of all the spandex that kept her fleshy, curvy, figure under tight control. She vowed that Riggs would never see her fully naked. She'd had her bare legs wrapped around him, and his hand had stroked her behind, but he would never *see* any of it. If he insisted on being one of those fathers that saw his baby born, she supposed he'd see *that* much of her. But that would be *it*. No more!

She changed into the long T-shirt she had in the bag. A size extra-large, it came to her knees, plenty of coverage. When she emerged from the bathroom, she'd removed every inch of makeup from her eyes. Let him see what his wife *really* looked like. It wasn't as if she cared what *he* thought, and she would sleep in comfort tonight, just as soon as he left the bedroom.

Riggs wore gray sweatpants and a Dallas Cowboys T-shirt. He sat on the leather chair at the side of his bed, scowl firmly in place, looking perturbed.

He took her in, did a doubletake, and went brows up. "What did you do with Winona?"

She ignored that comment and crawled into bed. "When are you leaving?"

"As soon as I hear Delores go out the door." He glanced at his wristwatch. "Should be soon."

"All it takes is once to get pregnant, as we both know, so we'll tell her I got pregnant tonight."

He nodded. "After that, we can say that I snore."

And with that small but powerful agreement between them, Winona rolled over and gave him her back. She had no idea when he left, because she fell asleep within minutes, dreaming of her sweet baby.

CHAPTER 10

*R*iggs should have helped Delores with the massive clean-up, but he was supposed to be in this bedroom with Winona having great wedding-night sex. Fat chance. Damn Winona had made their argument so loud that he half wondered if after all this effort, she'd blown their cover. How should he explain a honeymoon night argument to Delores? A night of rough sex? Yeah, sure, that would go over well with the woman he thought of as his second conscience.

He wanted to tell his family the truth, especially Sean, but a forty-two-year-old man shouldn't have had an accidental pregnancy with a one-night stand. He was normally a lot smarter and set the example. Not just to his brothers, but to nearly every one of the younger men of Stone Ridge. To demonstrate how he'd failed to protect himself, and his partner, was downright humiliating. He was far better than that.

And Riggs had now done his research. Once he'd heard about the personal assistant position, a little digging led to discovering that no one had actually slept with Winona.

Jeremy and a couple of other men said they'd never heard back. No one had.

He glanced over at Winona, because she hadn't moved in several minutes. She'd come out of that bathroom looking like a different woman. Far more beautiful, in his opinion. One of the few women he'd met who looked better *without* makeup, she was a natural beauty with flawless porcelain skin, deep green eyes, and that sensual mouth.

Once he heard Delores leave, Riggs rose from the chair and stretched his legs. Winona rolled over in her sleep, facing him. Her mouth slightly parted, a stray hair fell over one eye, partially covering it. Funny. In her sleep, she looked perfectly harmless. Almost…vulnerable. But anyone stupid enough to think *that* should beware, backup, and leave the way they came. This woman was a scrapper down deep and could tangle with someone twice her size.

He'd almost laughed when she bit him, because it had been so unexpected. But she excelled at surprising him. His next immediate reaction, which he'd restrained, had been to fight back. Without a doubt, she'd met her match. He had half a mind to take her over his knee and spank her. Not the sexy kind, either. But no doubt she would have screamed so loud that someone in the next county would have heard her.

Quietly, he left the bedroom, closing the door behind him. Mutt, his half beagle, half border collie and the best herding dog he'd ever known, met him in the hallway. He sat on Riggs's boot, as was his custom.

"Believe me, you don't want to go in there. She's mean as the devil."

Mutt slept at the foot of his bed every night even if Riggs had been raised to believe dogs lived outside. But thanks to Delores's soft heart, and Mutt's advanced age, he regularly made the rounds usually winding up with Riggs.

"C'mon, let's go. I have an early mornin'."

Riggs headed to Colton's empty bedroom further down the hall, Mutt tagging along. When Riggs walked inside, Mutt seemed confused. He hesitated in the doorway until Riggs waved him inside.

"I'm sleepin' in here tonight."

And every other night for the next several months. He went to bed, pushing away all thoughts of his sexy and impossible wife.

THE NEXT MORNING, Riggs woke before the sunrise, and scrubbed a hand down his face. Last night, he'd made another firm decision. He wouldn't make any other foolish choices like the first one he'd made with Winona. No sex between them, even if consummating the marriage would make it more official. This wasn't a real marriage, just a temporary fix, and having a sex life would mislead her. It would make him feel truly married, and he didn't want that. He wanted to walk away from this unwanted commitment the first moment he could.

Winona was too angry with him anyway for ruining her perfect scheme. She'd expected to be on her way back to Nashville to be a single mother. But even though he'd be willing to get over his anger long enough to have make-up sex, he wasn't thrilled with her, either.

She'd made him out to be a monster for simply exerting his rights as a father. Everything else, like the marriage, made sense. Hopefully in the light of a few weeks, she'd forgive him and see the sense in it. He wasn't holding out hope for another night like the one that got him into this hot mess, but he wouldn't rule it out, either. It would have to be up to her. His attraction to her was maddening on so many levels. The magnetic pull his body had to hers was something he'd never experienced before. Never on this level.

He showered, dressed, and met Delores in the kitchen where he found her taking out the skillet. She usually made a big and hearty breakfast for them, then drove it out to the field. The coffee thankfully already made, Riggs helped himself to a cup. Mutt had followed him out of the bedroom, where he plopped down under the kitchen table. Though she denied it, Delores regularly fed him scraps, and Mutt knew where to find them.

"Stop feeding him bacon. He's gettin' fat."

"Well, good mornin' to you, too, Mr. Married Man." She set the large pan on the stove range and went to pull out the slab of bacon from the Wooten's farm. "I know you're putting off the honeymoon, but you could have at least slept in today."

"I've got a heifer calving soon and Eve coming by to check."

"Winona is so sweet. I just love her to pieces."

"Yep, that's why I fell in love with her. Sweet." He nearly choked on the lie.

"Be good to her, Riggs. Don't ignore her if you want to keep her."

If Delores had heard anything last night, she wasn't talking. "I don't plan to."

"I know you. You'll get all caught up in the ranch and forget you've got a beautiful wife in there waitin' for you to get home every day."

"Yeah, not likely I'll forget." He drained his coffee. "She won't let me."

"She's a firecracker, I can tell." Delores smiled at him. "Exactly what you need."

"If you say so." He wasn't at all sure about that.

He'd always thought if he ever settled down again, he'd find someone sweet. Nurturing and caring. Someone like Sadie

Stephens, for instance, who for God's sake, was a *schoolteacher*. Definitely never anticipated anyone like Winona, a damn hellcat. Then again, he carefully reminded himself he *wasn't* settling down. He would simply have a child with this woman who was currently his wife, and since they would share a child, he would tolerate her one way or another for the rest of his natural life.

Fun times.

Riggs had just finished morning chores when Sean showed up on his horse.

"Mornin'." He tipped his hat. "No idea what *you're* doin' here this early. Aren't you supposed to be enjoying married life?"

"What makes you think I'm not?"

"Seems weird. All this is pretty sudden you gotta admit."

"That's how it happens sometimes."

"Not to you."

Riggs ignored that. "Your turn to muck the horse stalls. I'll spread feed today. One of us also needs to mend the fence on the north pasture. And we need to look into our castration schedule."

"What are you up to today?"

"I'll be checking on the heifers all day. We've got two in labor. One of them's gone on now for hours and might need some assistance."

"Call me if you need me to help pull 'em out." Sean hopped off his horse and took its lead. "Did you really just meet Winona at the job? Never see her at the Shady Grind or anything?"

"Just like I said. Met her on the job and saw her the night she performed at Jackson's. It was a good show."

They walked together toward the calving pens. "'Cause brother, I just heard somethin' and I wouldn't feel right not bringin' this to your attention."

Riggs should have known this was coming. He braced himself for what he suspected. "What's up?"

"Well, it's just that a few of the guys, they were sayin' that Winona had been on the hunt for baby daddy. That she was havin' herself some interviews and tryin' to find herself a...*sperm* donor."

His poor brother looked horrified to give Riggs this information. And it took courage to hand over this kind of bad news to a new husband. If only he didn't already know.

"She gave up on that stupid idea after we met."

"But you heard about this?"

"Sure, I heard. Don't worry. We talked about it before I asked her to marry me."

"Yeah, and about that." Sean cleared his throat. "That was...really fast. For you, especially. You don't fall in love easy, like some other people do. I'm just worried."

"Well, don't be." To give additional assurance, he clapped his brother on the shoulder. "I know what I'm doin'. I'm as sure about this as I've ever been of anything in my life."

That seemed to reassure Sean, and it should, because it was the honest truth. Whether or not he loved Winona wasn't the issue. Marrying her was the right thing to do and he'd never regret it.

Riggs got busy in the calving pens and checked in on the first heifer, the one who'd been suffering for hours. Births on the ranch were commonplace and usually nature took its course. But occasionally the ones who'd never given birth before needed assistance, when they'd been going on for hours without any progress. Riggs had pulled a calf or two out of a weary first-time mother, and as he examined this one, he gathered all the equipment he'd need.

Rubbing the heifer's belly, he wished this could be easier on everyone. It did not escape him that Winona would be going through this in several more months, but he imagined she'd want to be pumped up with drugs. He wasn't stupid enough to think he'd have a say in *that* matter. It was her body, so her choice. Wonder if she'd even let him in the delivery room. He could hope, but that, too, would be her choice. She might not want or need his support.

"But you," he said to the cow. "Might need to give you a little help, girl."

"Hey." A loud and harsh voice came from just outside the pens.

Riggs straightened. Right. Phil Henderson again. He was going to need to secure this ranch better, if only to keep away the likes of Phil. He trusted everyone else in this town, but Phil wasn't from the area. He occasionally lived in Kerrville, about forty minutes away, and dropped by once every few years to remind everyone he was a Henderson. Guess Riggs was due a visit.

He pulled off his gloves and joined Phil on the other side of the fence. "What is it?"

"Guess congratulations are in order." Phil tipped back on his heels. "You got married."

"That's right."

"Well, well. If only Marge and Cal could see you now. The happy husband."

"*Why* are you here?" Riggs threw his gloves to the ground.

"Thought you might like to hear the developer has upped their offer on the land. I don't think they'll go any higher. You better take this."

"Not interested."

"That's a mistake." Phil scoffed. "No wonder you won't sell. Your wife, Winona James. She's a wealthy woman, isn't she?"

"I don't know, don't care. I love her, *that's* why we got married."

"Sure. Yeah. Uh-huh. Buddy, I've seen her so I can't blame

ya. Though, mighty convenient for you how love came right along. Perfect timing. But you're a good-looking guy, Calvin always said so. Not surprised. And why sell now when you've got yourself a millionaire for a wife?"

Riggs resisted hauling off and slugging the old man because just the insinuation insulted him to the core. He opened the gate latch and came around to the other side of the fence. "You need to get on out of here before I kick you out myself. I'm busy runnin' a ranch and I don't have time for this."

"Will sure be a lot easier to make do now with your *wife* bankrolling the operation."

Riggs advanced on the man, just to startle him, and only stopped moving when Phil gratifyingly retreated, his eyes wide. His palms were up in an "I give up" gesture.

Riggs spoke through his tight jaw. "Don't talk about my wife, old man."

"You won't win, Riggs." He gestured to the land around them. "Can't. You're not a true Henderson so you don't know what you're doing. When your wife figures that out, she'll probably want to sell off, or turn this into a dude ranch. And hell, maybe that would be the way to go."

"Here, let me help you to your vehicle," Riggs said. "I wouldn't want you to get lost on the way out."

A few minutes later, Riggs watched as the old man drove his truck down the lane, kicking up dust. He'd have to put a lock on that gate soon because now that Phil *thought* Riggs had money, he might get even more desperate.

CHAPTER 11

*W*hen Winona woke the next morning, for a moment she didn't recognize her surroundings. Having lived half of her life on the road, it wasn't the first time this had happened. She'd wake up on a tour bus, or in a hotel room, alone and disoriented. It took her a few seconds to remember and get her bearings.

She was in her new husband's dark bedroom. Her hand dropped to her womb as it did now every morning. *Still there.*

One day, she'd find a way to forgive Riggs. After all, thanks to his apparently healthy swimmers, it only took once to get her pregnant. But she'd have to share her child now. She'd always thought this baby would be hers and hers alone because the men she'd married never wanted this responsibility.

She reached for her phone on the nightstand. No text messages from Kimberly. Winona was already so homesick she thought about texting her but instead checked email. Even that was as slow as a dial-up connection. And it probably *was* a dial-up connection! She waited several minutes for the emails to load. She had one bar. One! For the next few months, she'd be living in the country with even less Wi-Fi than she'd had at the rental. Finally, after about thirty or so minutes, and plenty of fist shaking on her part, the emails loaded.

Nothing too exciting, just the usual fan mail, most times answered by Kimberly's assistant. Maybe Winona would start doing it now since she had plenty of free time on her hands.

Holding her breath, Winona googled her name, and waited several interminable minutes. Finally, a photo of her and Riggs appeared, with the press release covered by all major media:

Singer Winona James marries Texas cattle rancher in private wedding ceremony

It's marriage again for thirty-nine-year-old CMA Award–winning vocalist, Winona James. She was recently wed to Texas cattle rancher, Riggs Henderson, in a secret ceremony with no press in attendance. She and her husband met through Winona's third husband, Jackson Carver. It is the second marriage for the forty-two-year-old Riggs, a widower. It's the fourth marriage for Ms. James. The couple will be honeymooning at an undisclosed location on the island of Kauai.

THE LAST LINE was a fabrication Kimberly gave the press to throw them off. She'd hoped that within two weeks this story would be old news and Winona wouldn't have to deal with any snoopy press coming to Stone Ridge. Almost a certainty, since she wasn't exactly topping charts these days. All anyone seemed to be interested in anymore was counting her husbands. Another marriage! She would be the laughing-stock of Nashville.

In the weeks since the night she'd performed to raise money for the local clinic her life had completely changed. Her baby was a six-week-old fetus and the books said she'd already have a heartbeat. Maybe it was time to see the doctor, but since she'd waited this long, she could wait a little longer. As long as everything was progressing smoothly, and she was healthy, she didn't see a need to rush anywhere and have them confirm what she already knew to be true.

She found her robe and fished it out of her suitcase, knowing it would be just her and Delores this morning. Later, she'd put on her face. Do her hair. Get dressed. At the moment, she required sustenance as she was famished. She'd given up her caffeine fix the moment the stick turned pink and had been in a foul mood every morning since. Headaches were commonplace but now her stomach growled and pitched as she shoved her feet into slippers and peeked out the door. Down the hall, the coast was clear, and in the distance, she could hear Delores rattling around in the kitchen, humming "Beautiful Morning" to herself.

"Good morning," Delores greeted when Winona strolled into the kitchen. "You missed breakfast, but I'll whip you something up right quick. What do you want? Pancakes? Waffles? Fruit?"

"Yes." It all sounded wonderful.

"Oh good, you're hungry. Well, that's good. I worried you might be one of those celebrities who's vegan, or you know, doesn't eat much."

"Normally, I might be watching my weight, but I've been famished since I—" Winona stopped herself, realizing she'd been about to announce her pregnancy. "Since I got to Stone Ridge and tasted all that amazing Tex-Mex cookin'."

"Well, you won't starve round here. Plenty of home cookin' in the Henderson household. I wouldn't have it any other way. My boys like to eat."

"Where are they?"

"They're usually out in the fields from before dawn till late in the day. 'Course I'm sure you'll see Riggs pop into the house more often than he normally would." She winked. "He won't forget ya."

Not likely, since she was the biggest pain in his neck. A completely unplanned event in his life. No wonder he hated her. She'd turned his life inside out. But now he'd returned the favor two-fold.

While she had Delores to herself, Winona could ask a few more personal questions she might not feel comfortable asking her new husband.

"Did Riggs date much, um, before me?"

"Not really," she said. "If he's dated anyone, guess I don't know about it. Never brought a woman home. You may have heard there's a shortage of ladies in our small town. Everyone married up young around here. And Riggs is the kind to give the shirt off his back, so he hasn't exactly been in the runnin' for a while. He hasn't had the time. I'm so glad you came along and changed all that. He's been lonely. Not that he'll admit it."

"What happened to his first wife?"

"He didn't tell you?"

Winona shook her head. "No. This has all been so...fast. A lot happened. I guess we're still gettin' to know each other."

"Well, sugar, you should ask him. That's too sad of a story for the day after your wedding."

"Let me help you." Winona hoped that the comfort of working side-by-side would encourage conversation.

"I never turn down help."

Delores offered her the mixing bowl. She poured flour, milk, and eggs into it. The last time Winona ate homemade pancakes was probably when her mother had made them. She stirred for a few minutes, enjoying the sounds of the metallic spoon scraping against the plastic of the bowl. With the hum and familiarity of being in the kitchen, time slowed to a stop.

"I know that Riggs's first wife died. He told me that much," Winona said after a few minutes.

Perhaps preoccupied with buttering the waffle iron, Delores lowered her head. "An accident. So sad."

Winona had thought it might be an early illness like the abhorrent C-word that took too many women far too young.

"Car accident?"

"Yes, and unfortunately, she was pregnant with their child."

Winona stopped stirring and stared blindly out the kitchen window. Outside, a bluebird perched on the branch of an oak tree. Everything inside of her stilled. His actions made a lot more sense now. He didn't want to lose another child.

Poor Riggs.

Delores kept talking. "Riggs blamed himself but that's just who he is. He has this idea he's everyone's protector. But I blame Jenny. She got behind the wheel of a car when she'd had too much to drink. Nothing good ever comes out of that."

Drinking, when she was *pregnant.* Winona told herself only an alcoholic would do that. Someone like her stepfather, Leroy. No wonder Riggs was so paranoid and untrusting of Winona. He had a false belief based on his unfortunate past.

"Did you know her well?"

"No, she never lived in Stone Ridge. They were college

sweethearts, I guess. Jenny was a real party girl. They weren't well suited to each other, frankly. How she wound up with Riggs I'll never know."

True love, Winona imagined. Such as when two radically different people couldn't stay away from each other. Like two magnets. Riggs had that kind of love and passion at one time in his life and she envied him because she never had. The inscription on her wedding cake belonged to someone else. The pain twisted in her gut and she briefly lowered her hand to her womb. Thankfully, now, she'd never be alone again.

The thought cheered her enough that Winona feasted on the waffles piled with sliced peaches and delicious preserves. She had pancakes drenched in syrup and ate like she hadn't in a long year.

I'm eating for two. I'll work like a fiend after I give birth and lose all the extra weight.

Though, she'd read it was harder to lose pregnancy weight after thirty-five. She'd hire a trainer to torture her if it came to that.

"Maybe I'll take a walk and work some of this off," Winona said.

"Now that's an idea, but we're having a typical Texas fall. It might actually rain later. God only knows. If you want to know what the weather's like, step outside."

"I do know that about Texas," Winona said, taking her plate to the sink.

Her stomach suddenly churned and pitched, protesting all the food she'd rewarded it with. Incredibly, she still felt empty, which didn't make any sense.

"Oh boy. I don't feel good," Winona said, just before everything she'd swallowed started to come back up.

. . .

Riggs made sure to be home for supper, seeing as he was a "newlywed." But he didn't want to deal with Winona after the day he'd just had. Her hostility toward him was expected, but still not welcome. Right about now he could use that sweet wife he should have ordered from a mail-order bride service or something. No idea why his life's purpose seemed to be being drawn to women who were salty instead of sweet. Dangerous instead of boring. He walked inside, throwing his Stetson on the hat ring in the foyer. He needed a shower before he could be presentable for dinner.

Delores was at the stove, cooking something that smelled delicious.

"Is that fried chicken?"

"Oh, Riggs. I'm afraid I've got some bad news. Your new bride has the flu. She threw up this morning, and again sometime after lunch. I've been feeding her saltines. Now she's refusing to eat anything and just laid up in bed miserable. Poor thing. I'm sorry, honey. I guess it's for the best that you two put off that honeymoon after all."

He stomped toward the bedroom and let himself in without knocking. It would seem odd to knock anyway, but at the moment, concern and worry curled in his stomach and he honestly didn't care if he interrupted her in the middle of undressing. But she wasn't on the bed, or in the bedroom. He heard the retching from the other side of the closed bathroom door.

"Winona?" He twisted the doorknob, but it was locked.

The toilet flushed. "Go away."

"Unlock this door."

"No! I'm sick, and I think we both know why. You can't tell Delores."

Then he heard more retching.

"Is this normal, or do you need the doctor?" Just the

thought he'd lose this baby, too, filled him with unwelcome fear. No answer, and he became agitated, yanking on the doorknob. "Unlock this door or I swear I'll do it myself."

He could see why she might be embarrassed to let him inside, but he couldn't help but want to take care of her. It wasn't in his nature to walk away when someone needed help. A moment later, he heard movement and when he turned the knob, it was unlocked. He found Winona kneeling in front of the porcelain bowl, her hair tousled every which way to Sunday.

"You bastard," she said.

"Why? Because I want to make sure you're okay?"

"I don't want *anyone* to see me like this, least of all you."

"That's ridiculous." He wet a wash rag and bent to place it over her forehead. "We're going to have to drop any shyness between us sooner rather than later."

She moaned, cradling her head. "This is horrible."

"What is it? Why are you like this?"

"Morning sickness, idiot. Or all-day sickness."

"Should I get a doctor?"

"My mother went through this. She used to tell me about how miserable I'd made her."

That little morsel certainly didn't endear him to Winona's mother. "Okay, so this is normal. We'll just hang in there."

She turned to him, those piercing eyes flashing anger. *"We?"*

He grimaced, feeling idiotic. "You know what I mean."

Her reply was to throw up again, and he grew worried by her flushed and sweaty face. He knelt behind her, wiping her mouth when she was done. To his surprise, she leaned into him, and he realized she was far too miserable to care who had her back. He brushed her matted hair from her face and let her sit there for a few minutes, just quiet and calm in his arms.

When she hadn't thrown up in several minutes, he rose and took her with him. "Let's put you back to bed."

She didn't complain but buried her face in his chest. "I'm so sorry."

"There's nothin' to be sorry about." He gently placed her on the bed, where she curled up into a fetal position.

"I meant I'm sorry about your wife and baby."

The loss was two decades old now and the pain no longer piercing. It used to bring him to his knees with grief but now he simply felt like it had almost happened to another person.

"That was a long time ago."

"It doesn't matter. I'm still sorry it happened to you."

He cleared his throat, changing the subject. "You sure you're alright? I keep thinking we should go to the doctor."

"There you go with the 'we' again."

He sighed. "What I mean is that I'll *take* you to the doctor. Should I make the appointment?"

"No! I'll make my own appointments, thank you."

"Whatever you say."

"Gee, thanks. I get to make a decision."

He wouldn't go there with her now. She was too vulnerable and weak, and he didn't kick puppies. But she'd made all the decisions in his estimation. She'd wanted this baby, enough to be interviewing sperm donors. Yeah, he was also to blame.

But to believe she hadn't planned this was difficult sometimes.

"You're welcome," he said to the smartass. "But don't you think it's time you see a doctor? I read that most women go right after they find out they're pregnant. We have a new clinic in town, run by a general practitioner. Dr. Judson Grant is his name."

"Okay, I'll think about it." She waved her hand. "You can

go now. I'll be okay. Go have some of that delicious dinner I smell."

"Do you want some? I'll bring dinner to you."

She opened one eye. "No, thanks. I couldn't eat another bite."

He left quietly, shutting the door behind him.

inona fell asleep, even though she'd already slept for a solid ten hours. She didn't seem to have energy to do much else. The pregnancy books she'd devoured before she ever became pregnant all said that the first few weeks were exhausting, and that hadn't included all the women like her, blessed with morning sickness. She'd felt awful to run for the bathroom after Delores's wonderful breakfast. There hadn't been anything wrong with the food, except that maybe she'd eaten too much of it.

When she woke, beams of moonlight filtered through the blinds. She turned and startled to find Riggs slumped on the chair beside the bed, a plate of half eaten fried chicken, corn, and biscuits in his lap. She'd guess he was tired for different reasons. Hunger swelled in her at the sight and smell of the fried chicken and she reached over and carefully took the plate from him. He didn't budge. Good to know her new husband was a heavy sleeper. They shared that quality although hers had been a byproduct of years sleeping in cars and rolling buses.

Shameless, she took a bite of the cold chicken as she

watched him sleep, noticing that he looked far less imposing than he normally did. It was his height, and his build, that reminded her a little of a mountain man. Someone you'd never want to tangle with or disagree with often. He was, however, incredibly handsome, and for the first time since the day she'd first laid eyes on him, she took her time and appreciated his smoldering dark good looks. She drank him in, the mocha wavy hair, the square and powerful jawline dusted with beard scruff. The gray Henley he wore that strained against his biceps.

Her heart tugged. If only this was different. In another reality, they might have fallen in love. She supposed she hated his sense of honor because it reminded her of what they didn't have. Even if in the past it had been far too easy to fall in love, she couldn't fall for Riggs. She couldn't love the father of her baby even suspecting that he'd fallen asleep watching over her.

Even suspecting that he cared about her well-being beyond being the housing for his baby. He would decimate her heart if she even dared to love him. She'd seen that side of him. The side that took control, that bulldozed over people who stood in the way of whatever he believed belonged to him.

And she didn't belong in this small town. She'd shaken off small-town living ages ago and didn't care to return. They were in a partnership together and that was all. They had a contract. He still resented her, whether he'd admit it or not, and she understood why.

He didn't know that she hadn't been with a man before him in years. That her last "fling" was her actual marriage to Jackson. She'd promised herself to do better. But Riggs had a way of bringing out the stupid in her, because he'd kissed her, and she forgot everything except how much she'd wanted him from the moment they met.

After she finished his plate of leftovers, still hungry, she climbed out of bed and headed to the kitchen. Groping in the dark, she found the light switch, opened the large refrigerator, and inside found neatly labeled Tupperware bowls. Bless Delores, she was a saint. So organized. Winona pulled out the fried chicken, another container labeled cherry pie, and mashed potatoes. This was home cooking the way her mother used to make.

"Well, I'm goin' to get fat anyway, might as well enjoy it," Winona muttered as she piled the Tupperware on the kitchen table. "Thank you, Delores. You cook just like my mama did."

"Hey."

She jumped at the sound of that deep, sleep-soaked voice.

"Glad to see you feel better." Riggs stood in the frame of the kitchen doorway, large and imposing, and framed by the ambient glow of the moonlight shimmering through an open blind.

"Um, thanks. I figured, hey, why not? And the baby needs food. Right?"

"Right."

Dear Lord, he had the most adorable bed hair. It fell over his forehead and eye on one side, giving him an almost boyish look.

"Let me help you with that." He reached above her for the plates.

The old-fashioned clock on the wall said it was ten. "I know you get up ridiculously early. You should go back to sleep."

"I will in a minute," he said and set a plate down for her and found some silverware.

Winona picked out a cold chicken drumstick and a hunk of pie to start. "You need to know that I'll take good care of this baby. She's going to be healthy and have the best start in life."

"*He*," he said, but this time a hint of amusement creased the corners of his eyes. "And I can see that. You want this baby."

"More than anything. This isn't just a passing fancy for me, or some new toy I want. I've wanted to be a mother for years, but it never worked out for me."

He nodded. "I just want to be involved. That's all. I'm not tryin' to crowd you, even though it might seem that way."

She thought about his lost baby. "I know. And it's okay. You're going to make a great father, even if you didn't plan on this."

"I'm going to try and be a great husband, too, for as long as we're married."

As long as we're married. There went that unwelcome tug again as she wondered how he defined a *great* husband. She could see for him it meant taking care of her, but did it also mean he'd be faithful to her for all these months? Should she even ask?

"We're going to be parents, so I'd like it if we could get along." He leaned against the counter, crossing his arms.

Maybe if you'd stop trying to control everything. She decided not to say this out loud and ruin this momentary truce. "I'd like that, too, Riggs, but we both know I don't belong here."

"I don't know about that. You can belong anywhere you'd like."

He then sat across the table and helped himself to a bite of her chicken like he'd been sharing with her for years. "Don't give me that look. Think I didn't notice my empty plate?"

She smirked. "Help yourself. And it should be easy to be a good husband to me, since I don't even know what one looks like."

Her first husband had been a kid, Jackson simply a good friend, and Colby? He'd been a decent manager, an adequate lover, and that was about it. Not even a good friend, as it turned out.

"I'm not sure I do, either, but I had a great example in Calvin Henderson."

"That's more than most can say. I had a great example, too."

"Your mother?" He gazed at her from under hooded eyes.

"Yes, *she* was my everything."

"Tell me about her." He took a bite of pie and then offered her the fork. "The stuff I won't get if I were to do a Google search on you."

"Well, her name was Mary Jo and she sang to me all day. Nursery rhymes, and Patsy Cline, some Disney songs. Anything. I think she loved to sing more than she liked to talk. She baked the most amazing apple pies. And she could grow anything in her garden. All we had was a little patch of dirt, but she grew juicy tomatoes, cucumbers, and squash. I was an only child, so the center of her world. She died when I was ten, and because I'd never known my biological dad, I had to stay with my stepfather. He hated me and the fact that I looked so much like my mother."

Riggs's eyes were soft and warm. Kind. "How did she die?"

"Suddenly. They said it was a rare aneurysm of some sort. She was only thirty-two, younger than I am now. I know this doesn't make any sense, but I used to wish it had been cancer, or anything else. Something to give me a little time to get used to the idea of her being gone."

Her throat tight, she didn't want to talk about her mama anymore. She shoved a bite of pie in her mouth, so that maybe he'd stop asking questions.

"No one gets that more than I do." Riggs reached to

squeeze her hand, then rose. "Good night. I won't ask you to remember anything this sad again. I swear."

"Wait." She stopped him before he left the room. "Tell me something. How does a lawyer wind up being a cowboy?"

He ran a hand through thick, dark hair and gave her a small smile. "It's more the other way around. How does a cowboy wind up a lawyer?"

"Okay. How?"

"First, he grows up in a trailer park with parents who care more about getting high than putting food on the table. When they lose their parental rights, he winds up a foster kid with Cal and Marge Henderson, and later their adopted son. Honestly, I would have been happy as a rancher my whole life. But my parents wanted me to go to college. I knew if I did, I'd do something that would help the ranch. So, I went to law school. I saw how Cal had trouble with some of the contracts he had to work with, and I specialized in contract law."

"Just my luck," she muttered.

"Cal Henderson was a great rancher, father, and husband. Just not much of a businessman."

"What do you think *makes* a good husband?"

He studied her. "Same things that make a good wife. Honesty, loyalty, faithfulness."

"You and I… We're going to be faithful to each other?"

He quirked a brow and cocked his head. "Yes. We *are*."

"Well, I know *I'll* be. I just wondered…about you."

"Don't wonder anymore."

"And by the way, you forgot something about a good husband. You forgot *love*."

"There are different kinds of love," he said, a hint of sadness in his dark eyes.

And with that he turned and left her in the kitchen.

. . .

A WEEK LATER, Winona was still throwing up. Riggs would hear her in the morning and late at night after he'd retired to the spare bedroom. She seemed miserable, and worse, weak. Finally, Riggs couldn't take it another blessed minute. By his calculations, she was now seven weeks pregnant.

How would his baby get the proper nutrition if Winona couldn't hold her food down? Granted, he'd read that morning sickness was common. But it could also lead to complications if it got out of control, and in his opinion throwing up several times a day was out of control.

He made the appointment at the new clinic in town and informed Delores that he was concerned his new bride's flu might get her too dehydrated. Delores gave him a long look filled with questions, but he ignored that.

Riggs took a break after lunch and found Winona in the bathroom retching again. He rapped on the door and let himself inside.

"Go away."

"You're going to the doctor. I made the appointment."

"I *told* you this is normal. I'm not worried, why should you be?" She turned to him, holding a washcloth to her lips.

He glanced at his wristwatch. "We have to leave in thirty minutes."

"Thanks for the heads up! I can't go in thirty minutes. I'm not ready."

"You look fine."

She stood, washed her mouth out with water, and nudged the door closed leaving him on the other side. This was fine. She wanted her privacy and he could wait. But he didn't do such a great job of waiting, pacing the bedroom floor. He had to tell Delores the truth about the baby and soon. She was nobody's fool and would resent being lied to. So, he'd take her into his confidence. Maybe later tonight after they got through this exam. He'd lie about everything else: he fell in love with Winona, love at first sight, and they were a good fit. All that rot.

Riggs didn't need the doctor often, but he'd still visited the clinic on opening day. He'd put his support behind the latest project funded by the biddies of the SORROW (Society of Reasonable, Respectable, Orderly Women). It was still a work in progress, with more funds needed for cutting-edge equipment and a full staff. But now there would be no more hightailing into Kerrville with a broken nose or a sprained ankle. It was either that or patch it up at home, which Riggs and his brothers did most of the time.

Winona emerged, blinking to find him there. "I told you, I'm not ready."

"This is a come as you are situation. You look perfect." He took her arm and led her gently out the door and down the hallway. "We'll be back in a bit, Delores."

"Feel better, Winona." Delores waved and opened the front door for them.

"Riggs!" she complained as he led her to his truck. "Stop it."

Damn, her arm felt weak. She couldn't even manage a good shove.

Worry seeped through him as he let her go. "Did I hurt you?"

"No, but I think you're worried for no reason. I'm fine."

He opened the truck door and helped her inside. "Don't tell me not to worry. Even Delores is worried."

"That's because she doesn't know about the baby."

"Well, she's about to figure it out if we don't do something about this and soon."

"Well, excuse me for breathing." She buckled in. "We have another week if you want to keep this pretense up. Or we could just tell everyone the truth. It's not like we're the only two people on earth this has ever happened to."

But he might be the only forty-two-year-old man in town who'd used an expired condom like a jackass. Damn humiliating.

They didn't say another word to each other for several minutes, and he just let the music play on the country western channel. It grated on his ears and nerves, but he knew that she preferred it.

"Are you okay?" he tried.

"Well, since you asked. I lied, because I *am* worried."

"Were you avoiding making the appointment?"

"Maybe I was, I don't know." She wrapped her arms around her waist. "I'm afraid...somehow...they're going to take this away from me. It's not going to be real."

"Ridiculous. That's not going to happen."

"You don't *know* that. Maybe this morning sickness isn't normal like I want to believe."

"It's normal. I'm just worried and want you and the baby checked out."

"Maybe I should see a specialist. I don't think a GP is what I need."

"Dr. Grant has a midwife. Trixie something or other. She came out from Dallas, just like Dr. Grant did."

"A midwife."

"Is that okay?"

"I always wanted to go with a midwife, do the whole home birth thing, give birth in a kiddie pool." She looked out the window, then back to him. "Plant the afterbirth at the bottom of a tree."

"You have *got* to be kidding me."

She laughed, or more like cackled, and the feeling that shot through him was almost unrecognizable. Relief.

"I wish I could have taken a photo of your face." She held up her fingers, as if framing his face. "Click."

"You're hilarious. I didn't figure you for the crunchy

granola type. Figured you'd want some luxurious private suite at a high-end hospital.

"Is that right? Well, you know what? Maybe I am crunchy granola! If the midwife says it's okay for an old coot like me to have a home birth, it's happening, baby." She snapped her fingers. "And I don't care what you have to say."

"Say old coot again and see what happens. If you're an old coot, does that make me a geezer?"

Winona crossed her arms. "Sensitive much?"

But it was all he could do to hold back a smile. He loved sparring with Winona. And the truth was that they'd been fine the past few days when they didn't talk. Maybe they'd been getting along *because* they didn't talk.

He pulled over in front of the clinic, an old formerly abandoned building kitty corner to the veterinary clinic. Since there were more cattle and horses in Stone Ridge than people, Eve and Annabeth's business was doing better than Dr. Grant's at the moment.

Holding open the passenger door for Winona, he offered his hand, but she didn't take it. Still, he went ahead, opening doors, closing them, ready to carry her inside if needed. But she waltzed right inside like a queen or a princess dressed in her Wranglers and sweats, her hair pulled back in a ponytail. He doubted anyone would recognize her.

"Hi there, how can I help you?" A fresh-faced young woman greeted them.

"I have an appointment," Winona said before he could. "My husband made it, without *asking* me, which is why I look like I've been dragged through a muddy field. My apologies."

"I think you look great!"

The comment came off with false enthusiasm and no apparent recognition, so Winona turned to him with a smirk.

"She's sick a lot. Every day, several times a day," he said.

"My *husband* doesn't seem to understand morning sickness." She slid him a withering look.

"This is more like all day sickness."

"Well, it's nice to meet you both. I'm Trixie Lee." She offered her hand. "I'm the midwife here and also kind of the receptionist until we get the practice up and rolling. Dr. Grant is with a patient right now. We take turns at reception."

"Well, it sure sounds like y'all are busy today. I'll come back." Winona turned but met his large body in her way.

Riggs smiled and crossed his arms.

"No, please, Mrs. Henderson, I have plenty of time for you," Trixie said. "Right this way to one of our patient rooms."

"Should I—" Riggs said.

"Wait here," Winona ordered, sending him a clear message that whatever warmth he'd imagined between them had simply been an illusion.

CHAPTER 13

There was another little fact that hadn't made it into Winona's bio and probably wouldn't be found with a simple internet search. She hated doctors *more* than she hated needles. When she'd been ten, a doctor in the waiting room told her and Leroy that they'd done all they could. But unfortunately, Mary Jo had suffered too much brain damage from the aneurysm. Winona could still smell the antiseptic smell of the hospital the moment before she'd thrown up all over the tile floor and Leroy's work boots. In a way, this clinic was worse, because she could smell the freshly dried paint on the walls mixing with the sterile smell.

Her stomach roiled and pitched, and she prayed she wouldn't get sick all over this young woman.

At the same time, she deeply resented her sweet face because she had the power to tell Winona that she'd made all of this up. She wanted this baby too much. Those six tests had all been wrong. The sickness? Possibly just her body behaving psychosomatically. The way her mind thought it should. Her mother had morning sickness. Winona would have expected the same.

"I'm pregnant," Winona said this firmly, daring the young woman to tell her she was wrong. "Seven weeks."

"Congratulations. Is this your first?"

"Yes." Winona tipped her chin. "And I'm thirty-nine."

"How bad is the morning sickness?"

"He was right. It's all day sickness."

"Well, we can do something about that. But the good news is that it can't hurt your baby and it should be over soon. Most morning sickness doesn't last past the first trimester. I'll take a full history first and then we'll do the exam."

The questions were exhaustive and thorough, and Winona was impressed. She promised to send along all her previous medical records. If Trixie had any clue that she was the singer Winona *James*, she gave no indication. Refreshing.

"I don't have any information on my biological father's health history," Winona said. "I never met him. Is that a problem?"

"Usually a woman takes after their mother's side of the family in this situation."

Then, Winona was forced to tell Trixie about Mary Jo's health. Health, which up until the day she died, had seemed perfect.

"I know it's scary to think that could happen to you, but in all likelihood, it was a random event." Sympathy flashed in Trixie's eyes. "We'll monitor your blood pressure carefully. Honestly, I know some like to refer to thirty-nine as geriatric age for pregnancy, but I disagree. As long as your health is good, you could have a perfectly normal full-term pregnancy."

"I-I don't need to go to a specialist?"

"It's up to you, but I feel perfectly confident working with you. If I thought there was any risk, I'd refer you to a specialist." She paused a beat. "Were you thinking of delivering at home? Because we have a birthing room here. And Dr. Grant is on standby for emergencies."

"Um, maybe at home? I'm not sure yet."

Winona was weighed, and surprisingly, despite the sickness, she'd still gained three pounds. Trixie said this was good news and her blood pressure was also normal.

Then came the exam portion and the moment when Winona pictured her happy place as Trixie fumbled in there. For a moment, she stopped, then continued.

"Huh."

"What?" Winona sat up on her elbows. "Is something wrong?"

Please don't tell me there's no baby. Please don't. This is real.

"Oh, not at all! Please don't worry. It's just...you seem a bit larger than I'd expect for seven weeks."

"That's not possible! I know the exact date I conceived."

Thank goodness Riggs wasn't in here. He'd take that and run with it. Accuse her of trying to pass off the baby as his. But *why* would she do that when he'd been such a pain in the ass? Any other man would have handed over full custody and possibly sent her a thank-you note, too.

"I'd love to try out our new ultrasound machine if you don't mind. Then I could just rule out twins."

"*Twins?*" Winona squeaked out.

"Sometimes that's why a woman can feel larger than the time of conception. Of course, there could be other reasons."

Not happy reasons, Winona guessed. "I... Why would I have twins?"

"No fertility drugs, I take it?"

"Absolutely not. I was trying to do this the natural way. I *hate* needles."

"Possibly some history, perhaps on your father's side? Any history on Riggs's side?"

"I... I don't know." Winona gnawed at her lower lip.

If Trixie thought it weird that she didn't know this major fact about her husband, she didn't say anything. Damn Riggs for bringing her here today. Twins! How would she do *twins*?

Okay, don't panic. Maybe Trixie was wrong.

"Let's get the daddy in here and ask him," Trixie said. "Besides, it's always fun for them to see the fetus. Makes this all the more real."

"Oh, it's *real* to him." Winona sighed.

Trixie left the room and a moment later Riggs walked in. He looked murderous, his jaw tight, his eyes blazing.

"She said you're farther along than you should be. Got something you want to tell me?"

Anger spiked through her that he would doubt her for a second. "Yes! Did she also tell you it could be twins?"

"She said she's doing an ultrasound."

"To rule out twins." Winona cleared her throat. "Are there any twins on your side of the family?"

"No. Are you telling me it's either you're pregnant by someone else, or we're having twins? I don't like those choices!"

"They're not choices, Riggs! And these are your babies. I'll do a DNA test if you want. I'll swear on a stack of Bibles. There hasn't *been* anyone else, though I almost wish there had been! Anyone *else* wouldn't be such a royal pain."

Neither one of them said a word for several beats. Then Riggs rose from the chair and began to pace the room. "Twins? *Twins*, Winona!"

"Don't you yell at me! Don't you think I'm freaking out? Take it easy. You know, maybe she's wrong." She threw a look at the door Trixie had gone out of. "She looks awfully young. And inexperienced. Right?"

"Right." He held up his palms. "Look, we're both letting emotions cloud our thoughts. We don't know what's happening *yet*, so let's just wait to hear."

Trixie wheeled a monitor into the room. "Well, hello there, Daddy. Isn't this exciting? I can't wait to see if we're having multiples!"

"Wait. What the hell do you mean by *multiples?*" Riggs came closer to the cot, pointing his finger in accusation. "You said twins."

"Oh, that's what I meant. Ha! *Please* don't panic. Hope you already started saving for college! If not, I'd start today." She rubbed some made-in-the-arctic goop on Winona's stomach that made her jump.

Her wand moved up and down as if looking for something. For several long seconds she said nothing at all. Winona squeezed her eyes shut just as she used to do as a child before bed every night, praying that when she woke up her mother would still be there.

Please let everything be okay.

"Here we go," she said, pointing to the monitor screen.

Winona turned and saw a form that reminded her of the little guppies she'd seen in Kim's ultrasound photos. Like a lima bean. *Two* lima beans. She swallowed. Sound waves echoed, a whirring sound.

"How lovely," Trixie said. "Beautiful. Do you see this right here? Two heartbeats!"

Winona heard the sound of Riggs collapsing into the chair. "This is not happening. We didn't plan for twins."

"Well, nobody really does," Trixie said with a snort.

Of course, they hadn't planned for twins. They hadn't *planned* on any of this. Not technically. *She* had, on her own. But all Winona wanted was one precious baby and now she was getting two.

Tears rolled down her cheeks before she could stop them. "Are my babies healthy?"

"Looking good! I'm going to take all these measurements and data down. But this *totally* explains why I thought you were farther along. From my perspective, everything looks good, but we can't tell anything about genetics from an ultrasound. I can estimate the date of conception fairly accurately. Are you interested?"

"Yes," Riggs said.

The woman preceded to give a date of conception within a two-day window of the night that she and Riggs had been together. Then she went ahead and took an "educated" guess.

It was the actual day. Winona took the opportunity to slide Riggs a satisfied smirk.

"How did this happen? Am I having twins because I'm older?"

"Women over thirty are far more likely to have twins spontaneously, because they're more likely to release two eggs per cycle. The risk goes down further into your thirties but it's still there. Therefore, it's not all that amazing, At least not from my perspective. I'll monitor for signs of high blood pressure, gestational diabetes, the kind of issues which would move you quickly into a higher-risk status. But please don't worry, I see this all the time and I've even delivered sets of twins, all natural. Advanced maternal age isn't linked to risk factors. Don't let anyone tell you that it can't be done." She shook a finger.

"I... I haven't decided on a birth plan." She'd joked with Riggs about this but delivering naturally did have some appeal. She'd read it could be healthier for the babies.

"If you come back in a few weeks, I can try and hazard a guess as to sex." Trixie wiped the goop off Winona's stomach.

"Is that somethin' you want to do? Find out the sex?" Riggs asked.

"Maybe. It might be nice."

Riggs shrugged. "Amniocentesis is more accurate."

She stared at the man. He was constantly amazing her.

He put up his palms. "What? I've been reading. It says that a woman over thirty-five usually has one."

"That is true," Trixie said. "It's a fairly common procedure but not at all necessary."

"I don't want to have that done." She'd long ago made up her mind that she wouldn't do that invasive procedure.

First, the huge needle. Second, she couldn't stand the thought of it going that close to her baby.

"Why not?" Riggs asked.

"There's a risk of miscarriage."

"It's a very small risk, and we wouldn't do this until you're solidly into your second trimester," Trixie said. "But entirely up to y'all."

He cleared his throat. "If there's any risk at all, it's not worth taking."

For once they agreed.

"I know sometimes they can tell if there's something wrong, like Down's Syndrome, but I'm having these babies. No matter what."

OUTSIDE, the September day was warm. Winona kept silent. Her emotions were all over the place. She swung from shock to joy to hurt and...anger. And as usual, she settled in where she felt most comfortable. The place where she'd lived most of her life, fighting and protecting, sometimes with her fists. And sometimes with a fireplace poker if it happened to be handy.

They reached the truck and Riggs held the passenger door open for her. Winona walked past him.

"Hey. Where are you goin'?" Riggs called out.

She didn't answer him but kept walking further into the parking lot of vehicles because she didn't really *see* anything right now. If not for Riggs, she could be in Nashville, preparing the nursery in her mansion with two of everything. Anger pulsed through her. Even if for just a few minutes, he'd *doubted* her.

Doubted that these were his children. How dare he.

He caught up to her. "Didn't you see the truck? We're right over there."

"I know where we're parked." She stopped and glanced around at all the vehicles.

It gave her something to do and a way to avoid looking at him. The worst thing about being married to him was all the feelings he'd brought up in her just by...being so nice sometimes! So incredibly *accommodating* even while he'd taken away her freedom. This man confused her. Baffled her. It would be easier if he fit into the molds of men that she'd become used to.

Across the street at the Shady Grind, a few patrons walked out and glanced at her curiously. So strange to have people appraise her like they should know her but couldn't *quite* place her. She was Winona James, but today she *wasn't*. Most days she felt Winona-less. It was uncomfortable, like being naked in a crowd of people. She needed her armor to feel like herself.

She slid Riggs a glare. "I don't appreciate what you did in there. You *know* that these are your babies. How could you have ever doubted me for a second?"

"The midwife gave me that doubt. She said the pregnancy looked like it was even further along than you said." He cleared his throat. "And you have to admit, anyone else would have doubted you. We barely knew each other, and you got pregnant the first time. Both of my brothers would have demanded a DNA test."

"Riggs, do you honestly think I'd *lie* to you when you refused to sign my contract? When you *insisted* we get married? Maybe I should have lied and told you that it *wasn't* your baby!" *Babies*, she corrected in her own mind. "I could have left town and never told you a thing. Maybe I'd be better off right now."

He shoved a hand through his hair, today being one of the few times he wasn't wearing his ever-present hat. "You're right. It's just that…right in that moment, I don't know, I…"

"Wished you'd never met me?"

He blinked. "No."

"Admit it. Your life would be easier if you'd never met me." *She was about to cry. Stupid hormones!*

"I'm not going to admit to something that's just not true." He reached for her hand and tugged her to him. "Okay, maybe it would be easier. But…not better."

Fizzling out of hostility at his warm touch, Winona gave up and allowed Riggs to walk her back to the truck, where he helped her inside, then buckled her seat belt before she could.

Her hand lowered to her stomach in wonder and amazement.

She didn't even want to consider what this meant to Riggs. Would he suggest that they each take a child? But no, surely, he would never want that. Having brothers, he knew better than most how important it was to keep siblings together. She didn't know what it was like to have a sibling, but she certainly didn't want to deprive her children of that experience.

Her children.

Riggs started the truck and turned to her. "Well, damn, Winona, when you do something, you do it big."

RIGGS DROVE HOME IN A FOG. Again, he and Winona didn't talk. They didn't fight. He figured they were both trying to get their brains settled around their new reality.

For one terrible moment, he thought he would lose this baby, too. He'd worried that the baby might belong to another man. He'd have to step aside. Because this time, there was no helpless and needy twenty-year-old former lover who wanted his help. Now, he had a full-blown woman who didn't need him. Who barely tolerated him. Who didn't feel that she belonged here.

She'd have laughed if he said he'd still help her raise the baby whether or not it was his. If he offered to be the child's father. At that point, she would dissolve the marriage and hightail it back to Nashville. He'd have no rights, no recourse, and simply wind up alone again just when he'd started to get used to having someone in his life.

Just when he'd started to get used to her.

She was right. It made no sense for her to lie about the baby being his when it would have been easier not to tell him at all. She didn't need him, so she might have left town, and he'd have never known one way or the other. But the thing he'd hated most about the doubt was the thought that she'd been with another man. This was crazy talk and he recognized it. Neither one of them were blank slates. He hadn't been a jealous man at any point in his life and it would be a stupid time to start now.

The moment she'd said that she wanted these babies no matter what, Riggs realized that he didn't know Winona at all. While in foster care, he'd been in a home for a few months with a boy who had Down's Syndrome. The sweetest kid he'd ever met. He loved baseball and Twinkies and was a friend to everyone. His big grin settled on people a little like the sun. His parents hadn't wanted him, but they hadn't known what they missed.

Like Winona, he wanted these children no matter what. He wondered if she'd understand why he'd freaked out back at the doctor's office if he told her more about Jenny.

She'd been one of his best friends in college, someone who hung out with the same crowd. One misguided night, they'd slept together after a party. That led to a relationship of sorts, one he fell into as a clueless twenty-one-year-old who loved regular sex. Jenny was great, and fun, but he'd never quite fallen in love with her. She had other men in her life, and he was fine with that. He had other girlfriends, too. It was college. Being pre-law, he told himself that he had no time to fall for someone and make plans for a future together.

When he hadn't fallen in love with Jenny, Riggs began to think he couldn't love anyone. He had a gene missing. Or maybe he'd been ruined by his parents' toxic relationship.

But in his first year of law school, Jenny had come to him with a problem. She was pregnant with another man's child.

"Listen, I know you don't love me."

"Of course I love you. You're my best friend."

She chucked his shoulder. "Aw thanks, big guy. But you know what I mean. Still, I think we could make this work. We get along so well and we never fight. I want this baby, Riggs, and I'm keeping it. I'm ready to be a mother and I don't think anyone in the world would make a better father than you. You know what it's like to have lousy parents and you won't make the same mistakes they did. And you have a ranch. A legacy. If anything happens to me, I want you to raise my baby. Let's get married. I love you enough for the both of us."

Their marriage had lasted six weeks.

He and Jenny had lived in student housing and she wasn't particularly happy that he spent most of his time studying. Still, they never argued. Even though she had a degree in education, Jenny took a job as a waitress.

Looking back, he had no idea why they'd married. No idea how he thought he could support a child *and* finish law school. But he was excited to be a father. Calvin had been supportive as usual and told him they could come and live at the ranch until they figured things out.

Riggs thought everything would work itself out because he had supportive parents and resources. More than most people had.

"Let's go to Eddie's party," Jenny had said one night.

But Riggs was bogged down in reading case law. "Too busy. You go ahead."

"Okay, but you're missing out."

He didn't ask, simply assumed Jenny wouldn't be drinking. She was pregnant, after all, and wanted this baby.

But he should have asked more questions, because after that night, he never saw Jenny again.

CHAPTER 14

For the next week, Winona woke rejuvenated and rested. She'd take a shower first thing in the morning, then eat an amazing breakfast cooked by Delores. Sometimes she threw up before breakfast, and sometimes after. The rest of the day, she managed to hold down her food and drank plenty of water. Some days she'd help Delores with kitchen cleanup, but mostly she'd rest on and off all day. She'd started to take short walks around the property to get a sense of the area.

Riggs was kind, often bringing her breakfast in bed, staying out of her way. Never provoking an argument.

But one morning, just as she thought everything was going well, her world blew up.

Delores was waiting for her in the kitchen when she came back from her morning throw up, and with one look at her, Winona realized the show was over. She'd been so excited about a trip Delores said they would be taking into town later today. Now this.

She went hand on hip. "How far along are you?"

Stunned, Winona tried to think of something, anything,

but she couldn't account for throwing up in the morning and being fine the rest of the day. She couldn't think of a reason for throwing up with no other symptoms. They should have thought this through better.

Maybe if she'd spent the day in her bedroom instead of taking walks and falling asleep reading books on the comfortable living room couch. Pure instinct had her placing her hand on her stomach. It had become routine. She quickly lowered it to her side when she realized what she'd done.

"I'm old, not stupid." Delores crossed her arms. "Are you going to deny it?"

"No. I'm about eight weeks. We were going to tell you. I'm sorry."

"Oh, honey. Do you think I'm upset with *you*? It's Riggs I'm angry with."

Winona had no idea why, when he'd done everything in his power to do right by her. It seemed that expectations for Riggs were set a little *too* high. He was a mere man, after all. And birth control had a failure rate.

Delores didn't have to know that Winona had been interviewing sperm donors.

Please, please, let her never find out. "Don't be mad at Riggs. I'm way more to blame than he is."

"I highly doubt *that*." Delores pursed her lips.

But Winona would stop short of telling Delores the whole story. She wanted to protect Riggs from being known as the town chump who got caught in her net. Plus, Delores already felt like a second mother that Winona hated to disappoint. She had a feeling no woman in this town would appreciate her idea to find a sperm donor, not a husband, or a real partner.

"Riggs is an honorable man and he doesn't want anyone to think less of me because of the accidental pregnancy. He's the one who insisted on gettin' married. I'm obviously not nearly as traditional as he is."

"That does sound like my Riggs. I know this is a ridiculous question, honey, and I'm sorry to ask. But...well, you didn't ask Riggs for his sperm after Jackson turned you down, did you?" She grimaced as though the very thought horrified her.

Winona was grateful she could tell the truth.

"No, definitely not. I wouldn't do that. And, asking Jackson? By now, everyone has heard that." She wished Jackson had kept his mouth shut, but that was hindsight. "Well, I was desperate. I realize now how crazy the whole idea was. I just wanted a baby so badly that I lost my head there for a little bit."

How about that? Another truth.

"No one understands that more than I do. My husband and I couldn't have children. We tried everything. Everything but all the fancy things that cost so much money. I just couldn't see doing that to us. He worked so hard. In the end, I had to accept it. At least we had each other, and we were crazy in love right up until he died."

Winona choked back a sob. "I'm sorry, Delores."

"No, don't you cry now. I had a good friend, Marge, and she and I were both in the same boat. We met at a support group for infertile couples over in Kerrville. But Marge and Cal had more resources, so they adopted the boys. And honestly, they've been like mine, too, since the day they came home with Cal and Marge. You should have seen young Riggs. So suspicious of everyone. Untrusting. He wouldn't let his brothers out of his sight." She smiled fondly at the memory.

Winona thought of young Riggs and where he'd be if two kind people hadn't adopted him.

"I thought about adopting, too."

"There's a long line."

"Yes, but...I also wanted a connection to my mother. She died when I was ten. I know it's silly. All babies deserve love, but I wanted a little piece of my mother..."

"Not at all silly. How wonderful for you. After all this time. The sweetest of all things. A child."

"Riggs and I... We connected from the moment we met. You know? It all happened so fast and I didn't expect it at all. He's good to me. I'm lucky."

This was no longer a lie. After all the initial anger had dissipated, Riggs had become kinder, even if he hadn't held or touched her again since the day he'd dragged her to the midwife. She missed his touch. He had strong and capable hands that were gentle, too.

"Oh, thank the Lord. I was worried this was just Riggs doin' his honor thing. A shotgun wedding. But you two love each other!" She went hand to heart.

Winona swallowed hard. Was a lie okay if it made someone this happy? "Um. Sure, yes. We're very much in love. Can't you tell?"

"I'm relieved." She went about cleaning up the breakfast dishes. "I assume this was the real reason that Riggs took you to the doctor?"

"Yes." Winona took a breath. "I'm... We found out that we're having twins."

Delores dropped a plate and Winona bent to pick it up for her.

"I'm sorry to shock you." Winona hadn't even told Kimberly yet, thanks to the outrageously ineffective cell reception and Wi-Fi.

Delores covered her mouth and when she lowered her hand, her face had split in a smile. "Twins!"

"Yes. I always wanted a child, but *this* was certainly unexpected."

"What this home needed for a long while is the sound of little children running through the house." Delores pulled Winona into a tight hug. "I couldn't be happier for you."

But after the babies were born, she and Riggs would go their separate ways. She hoped he'd be reasonable and let her have the children most of the time. In Nashville, there were far more opportunities than in this tiny oppressed town. She didn't expect Delores to understand. Most people here wouldn't. But she'd once lived in a small town and didn't look forward to raising her children in one.

Delores pulled back. "And we're a little late with all this, since you were hitched so fast, but it's time to head into town to get your marriage quilt."

"Where do I get one of those?"

"Today, at the meeting of the ladies of SORROW." She held up air quotes. "That's the Society of Reasonable, Respectable, Orderly Women. Every new bride gets a quilt engraved with the names of the bride and groom. You also get some advice from the old biddies, but you're welcome to ignore all or most of that. Beulah Hayes runs the organization and of course she thinks she knows everything about the men of Stone Ridge. She's written the updated manual."

"There's a *manual*?"

Delores chuckled. "A manual on the men of Stone Ridge. How special they are, our history, etc. There will be gifts. Think of it as a late wedding shower. And we won't tell anyone about the babies just yet. Some of these ladies aren't as enlightened as I am."

THE LAST TIME Winona had been inside Trinity Church was on her wedding day. Now, she sat in the church basement, on a wooden chair in the center of a circle of a group of women. Most of the women, other than Delores, were strangers.

Beulah Hayes, the president, began with a history lesson. The SORROW had been founded during World War II. The women had to do something to help the war effort and they'd started by knitting baby blankets for expectant mothers. All good stuff.

The problem started when all the babies born that first year were boys. Pink blankets went unused. Once the war was over and some of the more fortunate men returned, nine months later there were more boys. And then more boys, with a lucky one or two girls born to amazed and grateful mothers.

Encouraged and searching for another way to help, the founding members put together a primer: *The Men of Stone Ridge*. They were determined for word to get out about how lucky the women of Stone Ridge were, with such handsome and plentiful men to choose from. And somehow with promises of handsome cowboys and romance, they would lure women back into town.

Winona only wished she'd known about Stone Ridge sooner. Jackson hadn't talked much about his hometown, and certainly not a word about the women-scarcity aspect.

Beulah occasionally leaned over and gazed at Winona, lips pursed, as if she were trying to weigh and measure her. She figured that if Beulah had her pulse on everything in town, as she implied, then she might know about Winona's interviews. She had to get this throwback to the fifties woman on her side, so she'd keep quiet. Forever.

"That's…truly fascinating history."

Once Winona heard where Delores would be taking her, she'd quickly changed into her country-and-western finest. She thought it might be expected of her. Today she wore full makeup complete with hair extensions. Her brown boots with white and blue inlays and a black dress that had long trails of fringe coming down both sleeves. She always felt about to take flight when she put it on, and it might not fit much longer. Already, her tummy seemed to be straining at the seams.

"The town of Stone Ridge needs some good women to join us," Maybelle, Beulah's sister, said. "It isn't fair to all the strong, dependable young men that grow up here. If we want them to stay, we need more women!"

"We can't just attract *anyone* here," Beulah said with a sniff. "I've been thinkin' that some women might just show up here without the best of intentions."

"What are you gnawing on about?" This was from Maybelle.

"Well, you know. Women dropping by looking for a *baby daddy* and nothing else," Beulah said.

Maybelle burst into peals of laughter. "Is that from one of your soap operas?"

Winona squirmed. But no, Beulah couldn't *possibly* know. Winona had been very discreet. In the next second, Winona's fears were somewhat relieved because Beulah also laughed, agreeing that would be a ridiculous situation.

"We've got a quilt?" Delores nudged Beulah.

"Now, this is probably not a big deal to someone like you," Maybelle said. "I mean, I read in *Country Style* that you spent eight hundred dollars on a pair of boots. We probably can't compete with that, and we had to sew this right quick, seein' as the weddin' did surprise us. This is just a little somethin' we love to do for all our brides."

When the ladies held up the quilt between them, displaying it in all its glory, Winona pushed back tears with the pads of her fingers. White squares covered most of the quilt but in the center was a large heart made from black curlicues and soft lines. And inside that, their names.

Winona and Riggs

September 15
Hitched

THEIR NAMES LOOKED SO PERFECT TOGETHER. ALMOST like they fit. This lie stung. A moment passed before Winona realized that the room had become eerily quiet. They were waiting for her to say something.

Anything. "I…"

A sob lodged itself in her throat because she'd rarely seen anything more beautiful or heartfelt in her life. Once one of her fans, on hearing that Winona had lost her mother young, had sent her a soft blanket with a mother and daughter quote embroidered on it. Another sent a canvas portrayal of a mother and daughter, one on earth, one in heaven watching over. Winona still had these gifts. They were the most thoughtful gifts she'd ever received.

She fought to get another word out. "It's…"

"We tried somethin' a little different for you because you're probably the most famous bride we've ever had," Beulah said. "I do hope you like it."

"Do you like it, sweetheart?" Delores asked, rubbing her back.

"It's the most beautiful…thing…I've ever seen." Then she burst into tears.

"Oh now, there, there," Beulah said. "Calm down, child."

"I think she loves it," Delores said. "Another winner!"

"It's that pattern I've been waitin' to try," Maybelle said. "You didn't want the black heart, Beulah, but I said, 'it's *elegant*.' And I was right!"

"So beautiful," Winona said, trying to compose herself.

She hadn't cried this much since she'd discovered Riggs

was a lawyer. The memory set off another avalanche of tears. Delores rubbed her back in giant soothing circles.

"What should we do?" Beulah asked.

"Just let her cry it out," Delores said and then whispered in Winona's ear. "Sugar, you're startin' to seem a tad hormonal. Might want to stop soon."

The words had the desired effect of a cold, bitter slap in the face. Winona sniffed and patted her eyes with the tissue Delores had given her. "I can't thank you ladies enough. I'm sure Riggs will love this as much as I do."

Their meeting wasn't complete without a tutorial on the men of Stone Ridge. Sort of a care-and-feeding manual which had Winona nearly doubling over with tears again. This time, from laughter.

"Never go to bed angry with each other," Beulah said, holding up an index finger.

Winona wouldn't have slept for two weeks if that were the case.

"Sometimes, you might have to let him have the last word."

In his dreams!

But in conclusion, the main idea Winona got out of the meeting was one she could accept. The men of Stone Ridge were ranchers and cowboys in the traditional sense, and she'd come up close and personal with that. They took care of their women. Who were "their" women? *Every* woman in Stone Ridge. Women were special, protected, and revered. From birth to death.

Hard to argue with that.

Afterwards, Delores wanted to take Winona to lunch. The only place in town was the Shady Grind, and Winona hadn't yet eaten inside. The Shady Burger and fries they'd sent her home with the night she performed was delicious.

Inside, Jackson stood behind the bar, as he often took a

shift as bartender. "Hey there, ladies. What can we get for ya?"

"We're just gettin' a table over here, sugar," Delores said. "Send the waitress over, will ya?"

Winona attracted a bit of attention as she walked to a table nearby. She could feel the eyes of some of the men who'd obviously heard about her interviews boring into her. One would think they would put everything together based on her quickie marriage. But still, they threw over puzzled looks and winks.

The waitress was someone Winona hadn't met. "Hi, I'm Twyla, and I'm your biggest fan. Would you autograph my apron for me?"

"Sure, sweetie." Winona took the felt tip pen offered and made her signature. It was only the second most interesting place she'd ever been asked to sign her name.

"What would you like? I bet it's on the house," Twyla said, throwing a look in Jackson's direction.

"Oh, no. I'm happy to pay." She perused the menu and stopped short of ordering everything on it. "Vanilla milk-shake for me, Shady Burger with cheese, hold the onions. Oh, yum. Let me have some of those sweet potato fries. For dessert I'll have a slice of chocolate cake. What about you, Delores?"

"I love me a woman who can put it away," said Lenny, turning to them from his bar stool.

Winona sank a little lower in her seat, still mortified that he'd shown up to interview as her "personal assistant."

Please don't say anything. Please.

Lenny slipped off his bar stool and headed toward their table. "Hey there, Miss Delores. Miss James." He nodded. "I'm sorry, I should say *Mrs.* Henderson, yeah?"

"You can just call me Winona."

He stuck hands in his Wranglers and tipped back on his

heels. "Well, well. Imagine my surprise when I heard there'd been a weddin'. *I* wasn't invited."

"No one was, Lenny," Delores said. "Winona wanted her privacy."

"Heard you were there," he said to Delores.

"'Course I was."

"That was mighty quick, you ask me," Lenny said. "One day Riggs is workin' on the patio addition, next day he's your husband. Almost sounds like a shotgun weddin'. Heh, heh, heh."

"Lenny!" Delores scolded. "Mind your manners. And no one asked you!"

Lenny held up his palms. "Take it easy. Don't mean any offense, ma'am."

"We fell in love quickly, I'll admit," Winona said, her "show" smile firmly in place. "With your incredible good looks, I'm fairly sure that's happened to you, too."

"Thank you. Yessir, it has. Yessir. Why, I remember Noelle Lee…"

Lenny went on to talk about the woman who'd stolen his heart. They'd married six weeks after meeting, which he understood must sound slow to Winona. Finally, their food arrived, and Delores glared at him long enough that he left.

"I'm sorry about him," Delores said. "He's actually a good man. Retired from the Post Office in Kerrville. He can't seem to sit still, though. He drives the ice cream truck in the summers, plays a clown at birthday parties, and is on the volunteer Fire Department."

Geez, no wonder he'd shown up for one of her interviews. Lots of energy, that one.

"He's sweet."

Winona wasn't at all sure her food would stay down, but the pregnancy hadn't reduced her appetite. She was famished so she ate fast. Still, her meal was interrupted by two more patrons wanting a selfie, today's equivalent of an autograph. Dressed in one of her showy outfits, hair extensions and makeup in place, she would be highly recognizable.

"My gosh, is it always like this for you?" Delores asked.

"Not at all. At home in Nashville, I mostly get ignored."

"That's difficult to believe."

"When they've got people like Luke Bryan and Miranda Lambert to go after, and all the new female vocalists, a woman of my age fades into the background."

She wouldn't add that she hadn't had a hit song in ages and mostly got asked on award shows to present. In country music terms, her career had faded to black. She'd had her moment, and while she'd been trying to fight her way back up the mountain range again, maybe the slow slide down could be more enjoyable than she'd ever imagined. She'd have her children now and all could be right with the world.

"Hey, Delores, is there ever a thing called a weekend on the ranch?"

She'd noticed that Riggs didn't ever stop, not even on Saturday or Sunday.

"Sunday is *supposed* to be a day of rest." Delores cradled a cup of coffee in her hands. "I go to church and take the rest of the day off."

"And Riggs?"

She shook her head. "It's tough to get the men to take the day off, even though we all know they could manage an hour. But since we tend to turn church into a half-day event with lunch afterwards and fellowship, they have a ready excuse not to go."

"You go by yourself?"

"I always have a friend or two to go with. I'm never really alone."

"I'll go with you if you'd like," Winona offered.

"Well, I just might take you up on that."

"If you don't think anyone there would mind too much." She thought of her now *four* marriages and the kind of reputation she'd earned over the years as a heavy drinker and hell-raiser.

"Honey, church is for us sinners, not saints."

I'll fit right in.

"So, I need something to do." Winona munched on a fry, then took a slurp of milkshake. "You know, during the day, while Riggs is off workin'."

"Like what?"

To offer to help Delores more than she already did might make her feel less valuable and replaceable, so Winona had been considering stuff she could do outdoors. "Can I plant a garden, maybe?"

"What kind of a garden?"

"A vegetable garden. With tomatoes, cucumbers, and maybe some basil?"

"That's a nice idea if you feel up to all the diggin' you'll have to do in our hard Hill Country ground. But you should start with winter vegetables now. Maybe squash, turnips."

"Anything is fine with me. Do you think Riggs will mind?"

"I'm sure he'll just want you to be happy."

Not so much, but Winona didn't think he'd care as long as it kept her on the ranch where he'd practically hog-tied her. She told herself he was just worried that she'd take off on him, dishonoring their agreement. He had no way of knowing that she'd never backed out of a contract in her life. She'd given him her word, and she'd stay until her babies were born.

They finished lunch and Winona paid, leaving Twyla a generous tip. On the way out, they ran into a pretty blonde who was clearly on her way inside.

"Sadie Carver, let me look at you, child!" Delores said.

"You are radiant. Do you know that? Just radiant! You're barely showing. I'd say pregnancy agrees with you."

"Thank you," Sadie said. "I had plans to come out to the Grange and say hello to y'all. And I've been dyin' to meet you, Mrs. Henderson."

Winona looked behind her to see who Sadie might be talking to. She didn't see anyone behind her, and it took her a minute to realize *she* was Mrs. Henderson.

Sadie blinked. "Oh, I'm sorry. Are you still going to go by James? I've heard that a lot of celebrities do that sort of thing. After all, that's your professional name."

"Um, no I…haven't decided." She offered her hand. "But just call me Winona, please."

"Forgive my manners," Delores said. "This is Sadie Carver, our schoolteacher."

"Yep, the only one. So far, anyway. We just started up a new school year." She patted her small belly. "I've been cravin' a Shady Burger."

"Sadie is also a newlywed. You two have so much in common." Delores turned to Sadie. "We've just been to the SORROW meeting, and Winona has her quilt. It's just gorgeous!"

"Congratulations," Sadie said. "You might not know this, but we all adore Riggs. I'm not sure the new school would have been built without his organizational efforts. He assigned men to the tasks. *Somehow* they all pay attention to him."

Winona listened to the two women go on and on about Riggs, her husband, a man she was only now getting to know. He sounded like a great guy.

Too bad he was a control freak.

Apparently, all the men in Stone Ridge had something called a "phone tree." When something went wrong, or someone needed help the phone tree was activated. And

Riggs was always one of the first to lend his neighbors a helping hand.

"He's kind of like everyone's big brother," Sadie said. "It was such luck for us all that he and his brothers were adopted into Marge and Cal's family."

"Riggs has made the best of it, even with that crazy deluded Phil who keeps comin' around," Delores said. "He doesn't have a hill to stand on and he knows it. Gettin' desperate, if you ask me."

"Who's Phil?" Winona said.

Delores waved dismissively. "Don't worry. It's nothing important."

But Sadie filled in the details. "Phil Henderson was Calvin's cousin, sort of disowned by the entire family for his drinking and gambling. He didn't take kindly to the Henderson Grange being left to what he refers to as a 'bunch of foster kids.' But the Henderson brothers were Marge and Cal's adopted sons, and they loved them like their own flesh and blood."

Winona's estimation of Marge and Cal Henderson grew another notch despite the fact that she'd never know them.

CHAPTER 15

After being shaken to the core with news of twins, Riggs settled into a routine. He'd work all day and join the family for dinner. No more random trips to the Shady Grind for a cold beer. Now that Winona was no longer sick all day, she ate everything that hadn't been nailed down.

Boxes began to arrive almost daily. They were all Winona's clothes, shipped from her home in Nashville. He didn't know one person could own so much stuff. She had his closet stuffed to overflowing. He'd finally removed what few clothes he had and let her have the entire space. Still wasn't enough. He'd swear that she had approximately six hundred pairs of shoes.

They'd had a minor disagreement when she'd redecorated his bedroom in pink and white with more pillows than a small village required. But he'd agreed that yes, he wanted her to be comfortable, and no, he didn't *know* that pink inspired calm and serene. It was temporary, he reminded himself.

Things were going well, and expectations were being met on all sides.

He just hadn't prepared for...this.

"Isn't it beautiful?" Winona held up a quilt as he walked in the door for supper.

He'd forgotten about the marriage quilts that the SORROW ladies made for every bride. They were a sentimental tradition that he could have done without and had managed to escape the first time. It was just one of the many ways that the women of Stone Ridge were made to feel special, but Winona was not *from* Stone Ridge.

Having his and Winona's names in the center of this open heart sent him into a tailspin. The expression on her face, and the way she held it tenderly to her neck. No. That was... not right. Delores beamed with pride. Suddenly this marriage felt so damn...permanent. All the air left his lungs in a rush. He'd been okay with this marriage until the moment he saw their names on a quilt, which didn't make much sense to him. He should have noticed this earlier. Their names had been together on a cake, and more importantly on their *wedding* certificate. But those were all things she'd objected to, and given him a hard time about, and this... She was *happy* about this.

"Huh...yeah. That's nice." He schooled his expression from what he assumed to be one of horror into casual indifference.

"*Nice?*" Winona said. "This is a work of art, buddy. I'm going to go put it on my bed, but I wanted you to see it first."

"You mean *our* bed," he said as Delores pulled a roast out of the oven, happily oblivious of the tornado building in Riggs's chest. He followed Winona into the bedroom and shut the door. "What are you doin'?"

She blinked. "I just told you."

"You said your bed, not *ours*. And don't you think if I were actually *sleeping* with you, I'd see the quilt more often? You're not makin' this easy!"

"What am I doing wrong?"

You're being too nice.

I'm not ready for this.

I don't want this.

I don't want to feel anything deeper for you.

All these other tender feelings that she brought to the surface were too much. He didn't love her. He didn't want to love her. Damn it, he didn't *have* to love her! That wasn't in the contract. While he realized how ridiculous that sounded, he clung to the idea. They'd spelled it all out in black and white and now she was *cheating*. Making him feel something deeper for her was not part of the deal. He wasn't even getting sex out of this, for crying out loud! Their marriage was a joke.

"You're..." He struggled for the words. "Gettin' too wrapped up in this. Don't get so good at fakin' that you start to believe the lie. That wasn't part of the deal. We're not in love. That's not happening here."

Her eyes shimmered with the spark of irritation and he welcomed *that*. This was what he understood, his comfort zone, and what he could handle from her. He could deal with her anger and hostility, but he didn't appreciate the deep sense of commitment she'd begun to inspire in him. This wasn't a real marriage and he wouldn't kid himself.

Anger had turned out to be an effective coping tool for staying away from her. For not letting his longing and desire make any decisions.

"I'm so *sorry* if I'm not straddling the line carefully enough for you. Fake it, just don't fake it *too* much. Am I right?" She threw the quilt on the bed and went hand on hip.

"No, that's not what I said."

"Gosh, then maybe you had better explain it better to poor, dumb Winona."

"Stop that," he ground out.

"What's wrong with this tradition, Riggs? Because you certainly do love *your* traditions. This one, though, might be too much for you, because I like it! And that you can't handle."

"Stop yelling!" he yelled and closed the distance between them.

Damn. She was right! He clung to tradition like he clung to this ranch and his legacy as a Henderson. He might not be blood, but he refused to give up his claim or admit deep down maybe he *wasn't* one of them. He was a foster kid whose own parents hadn't wanted him. Maybe he'd never be good enough.

But he could never allow Phil or anyone else to question he was one of the Hendersons of Stone Ridge. Keeping his legacy had become everything to him. And now he had two children on the way that raised the stakes for him. At least he liked *this* Winona, tough and challenging, not weepy and sentimental. Surely there could be nothing wrong with that preference. Because she was strong and fierce, and this was the woman he'd be proud to have as the mother of his children.

She stood below him as he dwarfed her, a small woman with the strength and force of a hurricane. Her chin tipped in defiance. Eyes shimmered with intelligence. This was not a stupid woman. She was smart and scrappy. A survivor like him.

He admired her grit more than he could say even if that courage of hers often bit him in the ass.

Raking a hand through his hair, he let out a frustrated breath. "Look, I'm sorry I yelled. That's not normally how I do things. You make me a little crazy. I don't know, I guess this is what happens when you leave the sex out of a marriage."

She snorted. "What?"

He stepped close, tweaked her nose and watched as her eyes grew warm. "Sex. We don't have sex."

"I realize that. I just didn't know *you* had a problem with it."

"Well, of course I do!" His voice rose a notch again, and he forced himself to quiet down. "That's one of the only benefits of marriage, isn't it?"

"Yes, as I recall." Her voice softer, she slid her hand up and down his arm. "I mean, it's the one thing we do well together. We made a baby, our first and only time."

"And it's not like I can get you pregnant."

"Plus, everybody already thinks we're having sex."

"There is that."

"Not to mention we're married. It's legal and everything. Moral. Upstanding."

"Yeah, that's the point." He tucked a stray hair behind her ear. "Sure."

"I don't think you like me, though."

"Don't be crazy. 'Course I like you."

"You liked me *before*. Then you found out about this crazy thing I tried to do, and you haven't really forgiven me for that."

"No. That's where you're wrong." He met her eyes. "I have."

"So, you believe me? That I didn't mean to involve you." Her eyes glimmered, so damn hopeful. It tore at his heart.

"Yeah. There were two of us that night, and we were both out of our minds with lust. At our age, that shouldn't happen. But, hell, it did. Either it's nobody's fault, or it's both of ours."

"I'd like to say it's nobody's fault. I'm gettin' babies out of this."

157

"Me too."

She bit her lower lip. "But I do miss sex. We were pretty amazing together."

"It was only a few *weeks* ago." He'd gone a lot longer than that without sex. He paused, then shook his head, fighting a smile. "And I miss it, too."

"See, we *do* have something in common."

"A lot more than you realize, actually." He took her hand and brushed a kiss across her knuckles. A question had been buzzing in his mind for weeks and he'd never bothered to ask. "I never asked you. Why *didn't* you just go with a sperm bank?"

"That's what Kim wanted me to do. But I wanted to see the father's face. My baby might look like him." She studied his face, a not-so-subtle reminder that his children might look like him.

He found himself wishing for girls who would look like their mother. Who would have that same fighting spirit that ensured no man would ever take advantage, even when he wasn't around to make sure of it.

"That doesn't sound like you. It sounds romantic and pretty sentimental."

"You have a lot to learn about me, cowboy."

"But all of your songs... They're anthems to getting drunk and having a good time."

"I didn't write those songs." She stroked his beard bristle with her thumb and sent a sliver of heat pulsating through him. "Check out some of my other stuff sometime. They're all love songs. Somehow they don't sell."

Now he felt like a Neanderthal for putting her in a little box where he imagined many others did as well. "Us having sex... It's going to complicate things even more."

"It already did." She patted her belly.

"Yeah, but—"

"Don't worry about me. I won't think that having sex has to mean something. It would be just so that we can stop being lonely and sexually frustrated. We're stuck with each other for nearly a year. After that, we'll divorce and go our separate ways."

"That *was* the plan."

"And I have no intention of changing *your* plan."

He lowered his lips to hers with a hard, deep, passionate kiss that went on for several minutes. Her hands fisted in his hair, and his lowered to her behind. He maneuvered them closer to the bed and they tumbled down on top of the soft quilt. He rolled, keeping her under him.

Ah. Sex on a bed, the way nature intended. The reminder that the first time he'd kissed her was the same night they had sex spiked through him, leaving him with a sense of regret. She deserved better. He should have courted her. Taken his time. If he'd known it would get to this point, he would have.

But then again, if he'd simply pursued her, maybe they'd have never reached this point. She might not be pregnant, and she might not be his wife, and for the first time he realized how much a small part of him would have regretted that.

Even if they were completely unsuited to each other, they had *this*.

"Dinner!" Delores's shrill voice called out, startling them both.

He pressed his forehead to hers, groaned, then braced himself above her. "I should fire her."

"Don't even joke about that."

He rolled off her, then offered her his hand. "C'mon, wife, let's go tell them about the babies."

"I thought we were going to wait."

"I'm tired of lying to my family. They're just going to have to deal with it."

"Then, I should tell you that Delores figured it out, just today. She asked me how far along I was, and I had to tell her." She looked at him from under hooded eyes.

"Guess I'm not surprised."

"I still get a little sick every morning. If you were with me, you'd know this."

He took her hand, led her to the door. "I'll see what I can do about that."

"THERE YOU ARE! I thought you forgot us," Delores said. "How does the quilt look on your bed?"

"Perfect," Winona said.

Riggs noted that Sean still appeared worried, the crease that formed between his eyes deeper than normal. Hard to believe his brother would be thirty-five this year. Still unmarried. Riggs often wondered if that had anything to do with his example. And Colton was thirty-two, never married, still in the service, having re-upped with no plans to come home anytime soon. Until now, Riggs hadn't provided much of an example to either of them for settling down. He wasn't at all sure that he was doing that now.

He pulled the chair out for Winona.

"See that, Sean?" Delores said, passing the bread basket. "That's how a good husband treats his wife."

"Uh-huh," Sean said. "Hey, Winona? When was the first moment you realized you loved my brother? Was it when he said 'hello'?"

"I guess it really was love at first sight." Her voice sounded similar to the night she'd gone up on stage and introduced her first hit.

"I don't think Riggs believes in love at first sight," Sean said, passing the mashed potatoes.

"Maybe I do now," Riggs said.

"There's nothin' more romantic," Delores said. "You wouldn't understand, Sean."

He scowled. "All I know is it took Riggs a *year* to decide on a new truck."

"Trucks are expensive," Delores said.

"Right. It's not a decision you rush into," Sean said. "This is all I'm sayin'."

"Enough," Riggs said. "We get it. You don't think we should have rushed into marriage. But I'm forty-two, and I don't see why I should have to wait another minute to be happy."

An absolute silence followed, as loud as a roar, and Sean studied his plate. "Sorry, bro. You deserve to be happy. It's been a long time."

Sean was likely thinking of Jenny. But that hadn't been on Riggs's mind so much as the fact that he'd waited too long to get married again. He might be too set in his ways now. Too unwilling to accommodate children and all that would bring into his life. Chaos. And plenty of...feelings. He didn't know that he was ready, but he would do this anyway and prepare himself the best he could.

"We have an announcement to make," Riggs said. "Winona and I found out that we're pregnant. And having twins."

Sean's fork clattered on his plate. *"Twins?"*

"I couldn't be happier for you two!" Delores said, clapping her hands.

For someone who already knew, she did a fair job of sounding surprised.

Winona turned to Sean. "I know you're worried about your brother. But I swear to you, I'll never hurt him."

He appreciated the attempt, but the words were useless. It was his job to make certain that she never hurt him.

"It's just... I'm sorry, but you've been married *a lot* of times," Sean said.

"Okay, now," Delores said. "Let's not judge someone by their past."

They ate quietly after that, the sound of forks scraping against dinner plates taking the place of conversation. Delores made small talk about the clinic, Dr. Grant, Trixie the midwife, and Sadie Carver, the town's first teacher.

"She might be teaching your children someday." Delores pointed to Riggs with her fork.

Once the dishes had been cleared, Winona headed to the bedroom, tossing one last inviting look to him. But Riggs was sidetracked, talking to Sean about plans for the new calves they'd have coming into the world soon. The vet bills would be expensive, but they also would be taking some cattle to auction soon. As long as beef prices held, they ought to be okay. He often thought his brother didn't fully understand how difficult it had become for the ranch to sustain itself.

"It might not be such a bad idea to sell some of the land to that developer that keeps asking," Sean said. "You could sure use it now. Having twins is going to be damn expensive. On the other hand, your wife is a millionaire. Maybe money isn't going to be much of an issue."

"I expect to pull my weight and support my children."

It wasn't like he hadn't thought of selling off some of their land. But though he was tempted, he'd find another way. A local dairy farmer and neighbor had asked for grazing permission recently. Riggs, of course, would let him do it for free. But maybe there was some other way he could use the land.

"Now more than ever we should hold on to this legacy.

For my children. And your children, too."

"If we can," Sean said. "But let's not kill ourselves doing it. You're going to be mighty busy with two kids. That's one for each of you."

Riggs would be lucky if that happened. Lucky to have two kids running around his ranch full time. Lucky to have to hire help because he and Winona couldn't keep up. The reality was that he would share custody with Winona, and what that meant in practicality, he had no idea. But it sure wasn't the pretty picture Sean had painted.

Even after Delores had left for the evening, and Sean retired to his room, Riggs didn't join Winona. Instead he walked with Mutt to the spare bedroom which doubled as an office, leaned back in his chair, and stared at the cracks in his ceiling. He wanted to be with Winona so much that he almost shook with the need. He knew exactly what waited for him.

A beautiful passionate woman who made him a little bit crazy. She had the ability to render him into a mute block of lust that couldn't think or reason. He'd proven that in a stellar way and would live with that consequence for the rest of his life. All he had to do was knock on the door and within minutes he'd be inside of her where he could bury every worry under a slab of cement. But he knew before he closed his eyes that he wasn't going to do any such thing. He wouldn't bury a damn thing. He would keep his worries next to him, where he could watch over them.

So yeah, he wanted her, and that raw chemistry and incredible connection between them. But he couldn't ignore the nagging certainty that sex would change everything. He couldn't simply tell himself that he was living in a temporary fake marriage until after his children were born.

No, he wasn't avoiding *sex*.

He was avoiding intimacy.

he next morning, Riggs was up early, as usual, before Winona. He told himself he wasn't really avoiding her, but just had too much to do today to also be the sweet and devoted husband. Besides, she didn't need that from him. Sex was all she wanted but she'd learn to do without. He had. What she really needed, but hadn't realized yet, was for him to give her space and rest so she could grow their babies. This is what he told himself, anyway.

He worked on the north pasture, moving some cattle to the creek and then back into their pens. Sean did some tagging of the new calves. Delores drove lunch out to them, hearty beef burritos, which they ate on the back of his tailgate. Sean didn't ask any more questions about Winona and they just made small talk. It wasn't until later in the afternoon that he spied Delores and Winona outside in the distance and to the side of the house. He squinted, wondering what on earth they were doing.

Winona was dressed in a pair of Daisy Duke cutoffs, wearing yellow boots that looked like waders, and a western hat over her long hair extensions. Delores handed her a rake, and Winona, wearing gloves, began to drag it across the hard, bitter earth.

"What now." He mounted Spur and made fast tracks back to the house.

Delores and Winona glanced up from their work, Delores giving him a shrug. Winona gave him a hard look that would scare off a bull and went back to digging.

Delores excused herself and went back into the house.

"What are you doin'?" he asked.

Exerting herself, for one. In the unforgiving Texas sun. Pregnant with his babies. Wearing what amounted to clothes probably from an online website for wealthy women who visited dude ranches for a kick.

When she ignored him, he dismounted, and came closer. "I said, what are you doin'?"

She stopped, one hand on the handle of the rake, and looked at him from underneath her thick lashes. "I thought you were a rancher. What does it look like I'm doin'? I'm taking golf lessons."

"That's hilarious. I thought you were goin' fishin', since those are waders." He pointed to the yellow boots.

"They're doing the job just fine."

"What is it you're tryin' to do here? Clear the weeds? *I'll* do that if it's bothering you."

Then he noticed the boxes leaning against the side of the house. Boxes and boxes of seeds. Green beans, peas, corn, tomatoes, strawberries, squash. Must be some of the packages that arrived nearly hourly these days. Their poor UPS guy.

"I'm *planting* a garden." She now studied him as if he was a half-wit.

"Look if you want a garden, I can get one planted for you. That's not something we do here but if it would make you happy…"

165

"You want to make me *happy?*"

"I don't want you to work too hard, that's all. It might not be good for the babies."

She held up the rake and shook it. "I'm not working too hard. What I am is bored. I want to *do* somethin' around here."

"You *are* doin' something important. Just...rest."

"I don't want to rest! I've had enough rest. I can rest all night since there's no one around to bother me. During the day I need somethin' to do."

"Fine, then. If you want to plant a garden, I see that you've already got enough seeds to start a small farm. Whatever makes you happy!" Frustration and tension sliced through him like a buck knife.

This was sheer insanity. His life was hurtling out of control, expressed right now in the form of a vegetable *garden*. He was smart enough to know that this argument wasn't about seeds. It wasn't even about her deciding that it was a good idea to dig in earth that hadn't seen a seed in decades. The issue was the two of them, trapped in a marriage because of one crazy moment. The issue was wanting her so badly his teeth hurt, but he didn't want his life to change any more than it already had.

He couldn't afford to let her have any more of him.

"You know what would make me happy? If my *husband* would have sex with me!"

Riggs turned to see that Sean was staring in their direction. Winona followed his line of vision.

"Great!" She threw down the rake and stomped up the steps and into the house.

"I'll be right damn back!" Riggs yelled to his brother and followed her inside.

He stomped through the house, ignoring Delores in the kitchen, and going straight to his bedroom. *His* bedroom even if it didn't resemble any place he'd actually live in. It was colorful and feminine. Bright and airy and he hated bright and airy! He flung the door open and slammed it shut. Locked it.

She was bent at the waist, her back to him, struggling with a wader. He swallowed at the view of her bare legs, and those creamy thighs. Then he remembered why he was here.

"Alright, Winona! You want your husband to have sex with you?" He roared. "That's what you want?"

She turned and gazed at him from under narrowed lids, still pulling on one long boot. "I wanted that last night. Now, I'd love to strangle you with my bare hands but you're too damn big."

Winona lay back on the bed, threw one leg high in the air, and struggled with all her might to get that wader off. It was plastic, and so close to her thigh it was no wonder she couldn't easily remove it. Unfortunately, her lying there, one long leg in the air, was giving him another good look at places previously hidden to him.

Because he still hadn't seen her naked.

Knowing he should help her, but unable to turn away from this display, he continued to watch. A grin tugged at his lips, but he didn't laugh. Yet.

"Stupid boots!"

"Try the other one." He crossed his arms and wished he had popcorn to fully enjoy this performance. "Maybe it will come off easier."

She actually listened to him, small miracle, and tugged on the other one. "They're defective!"

"Too bad. It's a real shame you're goin' to go through the rest of your life with waders on your feet."

"You could help me, you know." She rose up on her elbows. "We could always cut them off."

Taking pity on her, he came close. Gently, he pushed her

down and tugged on the end of one boot, then the other. They slipped off.

"It's all about the angle, princess."

She had socks on, short ones that just came to her ankles. Pink. She usually wore something pink. Today, her socks. Slowly, he peeled each one off and then brushed his thumb over the pink painted toenails. He kissed her ankle and then made his way up her leg. Her calf, the inside of her knee, her thigh. He pressed a kiss everywhere he could touch.

And she wasn't arguing with him anymore, her entire body still.

He was kissing his way up the other leg when she moaned softly, and he looked up to see she'd gone back up on her elbows. Her head was thrown back, making her look like a cross between a porn star and a really hot farmer girl. He unzipped her cutoff shorts and slowly slid them down, swallowing hard at the sight of silky black panties.

Those came off next, and this time she spoke, somewhere between a moan and a squeak. "Riggs...um..."

"Quiet. I'm going to see you naked now."

It had become an obsession. Late at night he'd lie in bed and picture what she looked like. He'd imagine the soft pink bud that he could now see and touch. She was a natural blonde with skin much softer than he remembered. He trailed wet kisses on her stomach, making his way up, tugging off her shirt. She had on a matching black bra and her fleshy breasts strained against the material. He unhooked and removed the bra and she lay before him totally bare.

"You're beautiful." His hands slid down her arms and he lowered his head to her nipples, drawing in one and then the other. "So soft."

Immediately, she bucked against him, threading her fingers through his hair, pulling.

"Get naked," she whispered. "I want to touch you everywhere."

"No. This is just about you."

He lowered his head between her thighs and didn't stop teasing her with his tongue until she shattered.

SO MUCH FOR AN ANNULMENT. Kim was going to kill Winona for this.

She found her breath and slowly came down to earth. She opened one eye and, yep, Riggs was still fully clothed. She wanted him exposed, too, helpless and bare, just like her. He rose, climbed off the bed, and simply studied her for several minutes, blazing heat turning his eyes a darker shade. A bulge in his jeans made it clear he was extremely connected to this moment. But it seemed that an internal struggle went on within him for several interminable seconds.

Last night, he'd turned her down. After teasing her, after promises, he didn't come back to bed. She told herself it was for the best, because she still wanted that annulment rather than a *fourth* divorce. Maybe he was smarter than both of them, staying away. No *maybe* about it.

Still, she'd tossed and turned all night, wondering what she'd done wrong. Wondering why he kept fighting this. She wondered if she reminded him too much of his late wife, or if he'd been paranoid that he would hurt the baby.

"Oh, the hell with it." He tore off his shirt.

His shirt and pants were discarded, flying every which way around the room, and she was rewarded with glorious male sinewy strength and muscles gleaned from hard physical labor. His taut skin was a light bronze where the sun had kissed it. This man was the real deal. A cowboy.

His hard, strong body pressed down on hers, muscles hard as marble. He smelled like leather and dust and tasted like the rich deep coffee she still craved. She wrapped her legs around him, unable to push away the sharp memory of their first time. Then the walls had been down, thinking had stopped, and she'd responded to every fleshy desire on earth. She'd wanted more of him then, wanted slow and sweet, and hoped she'd get it now. But the way they now gasped and reached for each other held that wild tinge of fierce need she'd come to recognize about the two of them.

He thrust into her, causing them both to moan, but this time he moved slowly, pumping his hips. Taking his time. She decided that if she wanted tender, if she wanted to know this man, she'd have to take charge of that on her own. Reaching for his face, she cupped his jaw and met his gaze.

"Hey, cowboy. Stay with me."

Please look at me. Please know me. Love me.

"I'm right here, baby."

He locked eyes with hers, never looking away until she was the one who closed her eyes first, as the wave of another orgasm hit her hard. Then he drove into her harder, deeper and faster, until he, too, climaxed spilling himself into her. Panting, she wondered why sex was like this between the two of them.

Hot and delicious and…rare.

He'd probably leave her now, done with his duty, and go back to his work. But instead he moved his weight off her and tucked her to his side.

He pressed a kiss against her temple. "Finally got to see you naked."

"Well, geez, all you had to do was ask."

"I'm sorry about last night. This is getting…complicated."

"I guess so. But it's what we both wanted." She rolled on top and straddled him.

"No. You didn't want this marriage. You agreed because I

had you over a barrel." He pushed a lock of sweaty hair off her face.

"Listen up. I'm only going to say this once. But...you were right."

"Yeah? I don't mind tellin' you, I like the sound of those words comin' through your lips."

She rolled off him and he pulled her into his arms.

"Don't get too used to it. But I needed this time. Back in Nashville, I wouldn't have had the kind of privacy that I have here. The media outlets would be interested in me again, but for all the wrong reasons. The tabloids would probably document every pound I gained. Every inch I grew wider. You may not realize this since it's the first time you've seen them, but my breasts are not this big. I'll need new bras soon. My waist is goin' to get wide."

"You'll be beautiful then, too."

"Maybe not, but I don't care. Whatever it takes. I just want our babies to be healthy."

Riggs quirked a brow and a smile tugged at his lips.

"What?" she said.

"That's the first time you said *our* babies. Not *your* babies."

She ducked her head to his chest in order to hide her smile. "Well, they are. I know they're *our* babies. You just have to understand that one's a girl."

"That would be my luck."

"It sure would." She tweaked his pec. "From what I've heard, Stone Ridge needs more girls. You'd be lucky to be surrounded by women. I'm going to feel so much better with Delores taking care of a little girl while you're out in the fields."

"You'd feel better if you were here, too."

But she didn't want to be here just because they had children together. Riggs would have to love her first and that wasn't likely to happen. When she didn't say anything to that, he went on.

"Do you think they're both girls?"

"We don't know if they're identical twins, so I have no idea."

"Guess it would be too perfect to have one of each."

She was quiet for a long beat, picturing raising a daughter in Nashville while Riggs raised her son in Stone Ridge.

Not going to happen.

"I will tell you that all this pink is making me feel right at home." Riggs said this in a tone dripping with sarcasm.

"I can take some of the pink out. I guess it is a *little* feminine."

"You think?"

"Alright, I was punishing you. And I'm sorry."

"No need. I gave you the bedroom."

"Do you want it back?" She waited, giving him a chance to respond. "Because if you want to move back in here, that would be okay with me."

He grinned and crossed his hands behind his neck. "You'll take some of the pink out?"

"Whatever makes you feel comfortable."

"What is it with you and *pink* anyway?"

"What do you mean?"

"Your favorite color?"

"No. *My* favorite color is blue."

"C'mon. You always wear at least one thing that's pink. Today it's your socks. From now on I'm going to guess if I don't see you wearing any pink, it's your panties."

"You notice too much."

She waited a long quiet moment, wondering if she should tell him. But right now, literally bared to him, seemed like the right time. And if he'd ever consider naming a little girl after Winona's mother, he'd have to know something about her. "It was my mother's favorite color. She was obsessed with it. She used to call me Pink because everything pink was precious and beautiful. Pinkie for short."

"You're kiddin'."

She sighed. "I wish I was. She loved music *and* the color pink."

"That's why you always wear something with pink?"

"For a long time, it helped because I felt closer to her. Sometimes, I'd forget. There were years when I didn't. But ever since..."

"I got you pregnant."

"Yeah. I think about her a lot more these days."

"Makes sense."

She held her breath, then just came out with what had been ruminating in the back of her mind.

"I've been thinking that our baby must make you think about her."

He lowered one hand to her spine and stroked gently. "Just one other time in my life when I was surprised by a baby. But other than that, everything is different. I'm ready now."

"You must have loved her...a lot." She'd tried to keep thoughts of Jenny away but found it impossible. She felt connected to her each time she thought of her baby.

At the same time, she wasn't sure she wanted to hear his answer. Of course, Riggs loved his young bride, probably his first love. His true love. And he'd lost her to a terrible accident which made Winona cringe every time she thought of it. Poor young Riggs.

"Of course." He didn't stop stroking her arm, as if he realized this would be difficult to hear. "She was my best friend."

Wife. Lover. Best friend. Mother of his child. Winona could never compete with the ghost of this woman. She sounded like a saint.

"I'm sorry you lost them both."

"It was a long time ago, Winona. I don't talk about this anymore. It's in the past and there's nothin' I can do to change it."

"It's just that I can see now why you were so worried about me and the baby."

"It's not the same."

Ouch. Of course, it wasn't the same. In one situation, he'd been young and in love. Now, they were two seasoned adults who were trapped in a marriage of convenience. For the sake of their children. Sure, they had a passionate physical connection. But if all she ever got out of him was incredible sex while she could, Winona would take it.

She couldn't be picky. Couldn't ask for too much even if she wasn't used to taking scraps from a man. She didn't think of it that way. Riggs was taking care of her the only way he knew how. Something she couldn't discount.

Riggs interrupted her thoughts. "There's something you should know, and I wish I'd told you sooner. We should talk."

Everything in her stilled. *We should talk.* That never meant anything good. She remembered Aunt Betty's words to her decades ago.

Sugar, we should talk.

Your poor mama didn't plan on goin' on to glory so soon. I want to take you with me, I really do, but I already have five children. I think it would be best if you'd stay with Leroy. He loved Mary Jo. I talked to him and he said he'll take good care of you.

Yeah, not so much.

"It's about my wife." He cleared his throat. "My first wife."

Because unlike Winona, Riggs could never say "ex." He and Jenny had never been divorced.

"Do we have to talk about her?"

"We do, because then you'll understand something about me."

Winona girded her loins, ready to hear about perfect Jenny. His true love.

"Our baby. It wasn't mine."

It took a moment for her to absorb this statement. Then all the suspicions from Riggs made a lot more sense.

"I knew all along. I told you she was my best friend, and I meant it. Maybe we were too much alike because I thought we were always better off as friends. The romance never worked like I thought it should even though we kept trying. Stubborn, I guess. Anyway, on one of our many breakups she got mixed up with another guy, got knocked up, and asked for my help. She thought I'd make a good father and we could make a go out of a real marriage. So, we got hitched. She was more than happy to let me claim the baby as my own. And I would have loved that baby like he was my own. I was halfway there when it was all ripped away from me."

"I'm so sorry. You're right, I wish you'd have told me."

"When we were sitting in that exam room with even the suggestion you might have been pregnant by someone else... all I could think was that I was about to lose this baby, too. And I don't want to lose him...or her...well, them."

"You're not going to lose them. I promise you, they're *your* children."

"That's definitely the first time you said *my* children." He brought her hand up to his lips and brushed a kiss across her knuckles. "What about you? Would you be with Jackson if he hadn't still been in love with Eve?"

The question surprised her, and she met his gaze. She would have thought he'd ask about Colby, because they'd been married the longest. Even if they'd tried to quash the gossip of the embezzlement and the affair that had gone on with her publicist, some of it had still made its way to the tabloids. But that was years ago.

"It's funny you should ask about him. Jackson was a good friend to me."

"That can't be all. You were lovers, too."

She didn't appreciate this line of questioning. She hadn't asked such personal questions about Jenny. Of course, Winona imagined that, pregnant by another man or not, marriage meant being lovers. But Jackson lived in Stone Ridge and they'd run into each other from time to time no doubt. She didn't want Riggs picturing them together, though she wasn't quite sure why it mattered.

"Sorry. Is that too personal?" Riggs reached to stroke her face.

"No. Of course not. We're both adults. Married adults. I suppose anything is fair to ask." She cleared her throat. "I didn't love Jackson other than as a good friend. We weren't in love. He came along at a difficult time in my life. I was drinkin' too much after my second divorce. Right after Jackson and I called it quits, I worked hard to clean up my life."

"Sounds like he was important to you."

Not exactly true. He *should* have been more important since she'd married him. She'd never even tried to get him back.

"No more important than you are."

Too late, she realized that sounded as though she were discounting Riggs when she'd meant that Jackson *wasn't* more important.

"Wait. I...didn't mean that to sound that way. I meant—"

"No, it's fine."

"You're both important."

Riggs rose from the bed, though he didn't look angry. Just detached.

"I should get back to work. I've wasted valuable daylight." He shrugged his shirt on.

Wasted. She probably deserved that. "Sean will no doubt be waiting."

"I'm glad to keep *him* waitin' for once." Dressed, he grabbed his hat and shoved it on. "Believe me."

She sat up and pulled her knees to her chest. "I'm sorry he heard me yelling."

He ignored that. "Okay. I'll be back for dinner."

And he was out the door without so much as a kiss.

CHAPTER 17

$\mathcal{R}$iggs would have loved to get back to work, but Sean made that impossible. He followed him out to the calving pens, making him tough to ignore when all Riggs wanted to do was sulk. Winona had him feeling like one of many and not all that special, either.

"Want to tell me what the hell is up with your wife?" Sean demanded, always the louder of his two brothers.

"She apologizes. The pregnancy hasn't been easy on her. She's been in a bad mood lately."

But he should count himself the moody one, because he'd become irrationally jealous of Jackson Carver. That made no sense at all, but just hearing his name on Winona's lips sent a hot spike of jealousy clear through him. She and Jackson were good friends even though they were now divorced. That meant they had something deeper than an amazing physical relationship. It would take more than the kind of chemistry he had with Winona for their marriage to survive the long haul. It took tenderness and affection. Friendship. Real love.

He'd be lucky if he and Winona survived the year.

Riggs opened a pen and walked inside to check on the cow who'd been in labor for a day. It wasn't her first, so it shouldn't be much longer.

Sean braced his hands on the pen's gate. "I've been mucking the stalls for the past two hours while you were havin' yourself a grand ol' time in bed, and I've had enough shit for the day. Are you goin' to tell me what in the hell that was about?"

Obviously, Sean suspected yet another woman had taken advantage of him. The same way he believed Jenny had. Sean had begged him not to marry Jenny, said that she didn't love Riggs and it would be a terrible mistake. That *he* didn't love Jenny and the baby wasn't a good enough reason for them to be together.

He had been right on all counts, but Riggs hadn't regretted his actions. Not then, not now.

Despite the similarities, the situations were starkly different. These were *his* children. He wasn't helping a friend here, but rather helping himself to his parental rights.

"What is it you want to know? You want me to admit that I screwed up? Would that make you feel better? Fine! I got her pregnant. *That's* why we got married."

"Damn, Riggs! This shouldn't be happening to you again. Are you even sure they're your kids?"

"I know you're saying this out of concern for me, so I'll let it go, but yeah, they're mine. Everything else, how this came about, is my business. But I'm not proud of how it happened."

"You didn't have to marry her! There is nothing to be ashamed of. You're a grown man and shit happens."

"Don't you think I know that? I wanted to get married."

"Why would you want to get married now? You've been single for almost twenty years. The most confirmed bachelor of Stone Ridge. We all look up to you."

"That's a *stupid* reason to look up to me."

"Not in this town. You can be proud that you don't chase after the few women we have."

"Guess it caught up to me. And hell, I didn't know that people think of me as a confirmed bachelor. I *was* married."

Riggs shut the calving pen. Sometimes quiet and privacy were needed for labor to progress.

"Not for long. Marriage and kids are going to change *everything*."

"Kids certainly will. But I won't be married for long, so if it makes you feel any better, rest assured I'll be back to my 'bachelor state.' You can be proud of me again."

Sean quirked a brow. "Going that badly already, huh?"

"This is between you and me." Riggs gestured between them. "Do not breathe a word to Delores. Winona and I have a plan to divorce after the children are born."

Understanding seemed to dawn in Sean's eyes and his shoulders visibly relaxed. "Oh, so this is one of your *legal* maneuvers?"

"We both know that she wanted a baby and she got what she wanted. She's a celebrity with a lot of money and pull, and I wanted her to realize she couldn't just take my kid away. Remember, if you let people walk all over you, they will. Being her husband when she gives birth just makes my case and rights as their father even stronger."

"I don't know why I ever worry about you." Sean gave a wide smile as he tipped his hat. "You're always two steps ahead."

"I've had to be."

"This isn't at all like what happened with Jenny, is it?"

He shook his head. Riggs had gotten along just fine with Jenny. They never fought, always solid, and were reasonable with each other. Even though they'd been young, calm conversations settled any disagreements. Other couples he'd known at the time argued passionately, breaking up every two minutes. Riggs figured he was way ahead of them all. Too smart for all of that. His marriage would last because he and Jenny were both educated, so unlike his own parents. He was far too intelligent to be reduced to fighting with angry words and ugly accusations anymore. That was his past.

"I feel better already. It's all beginning to come together and make sense to me. You don't love Winona, do you?"

"Don't ask me that question because I don't know how to answer."

"You should be able to answer that. Hell, it's simple."

"Not for me. It's more complicated than you can imagine."

"What do you mean?"

"Because I obviously liked her well enough to get her pregnant. Now, well, I care about her because she's having my kids. She's been sick every morning. Her body is changing, and it's going to keep changing. Because of what I did to her."

"It's just like you to feel guilty about that, but she wanted a kid. She *came* here to have a kid."

That was true enough, and yet the woman he'd been getting to know had a lot more layers. While initially he saw her plans as calculating and cruel, now he understood the desperation that had led her there.

So yeah, unfortunately for him, he thought he *could* love Winona. It wouldn't be all that difficult to get there. Riggs could slide right into that mess, tangling himself up in her until he was in knots. But he wouldn't do it. Loving the woman who had every plan to leave him wasn't wise. Feeling any kind of tenderness for the woman who'd tried to take away his children wasn't smart.

And he took pride in being a shrewd and educated man, far from what his biological father had been. When Calvin Henderson found that Riggs liked to fight, he'd taught him that he could also battle others with his intellect. He'd been the reason Riggs had pushed himself, had excelled academically, and eventually gone to law school.

And if there were still times when he had to prove he'd earned everything given to him, by now Riggs had proven that he'd moved on from his less-than-stellar beginnings.

"IT'S LIKE YOU'RE *TRYIN'* to fatten me up," Winona said.

"You're having twins! Twins!"

Thank goodness for Delores. A week later, Winona was still high on the news. The women of SORROW were working overtime knitting caps and blankets, two of everything. Pink and blue, with high hopes. They were doing the same for Sadie.

Delores fed Winona a big breakfast of bacon, sausage, eggs, and an oatmeal heavy on cream. There were raisins, nuts, and dried fruit, and it tasted like heaven now had its own holiday.

"That oatmeal is good for the babies. Lots of fiber. Besides, aren't you eating for three? Isn't that what they always say?"

"Sure, let's go with that."

"Can I help you in the garden today?" Delores asked.

"Thank you, but I've got this."

She'd been working on the garden a little every day, but Delores had been right about the hard Texas dirt. She'd removed every last weed, and would now start the process of creating rows and adding seeds. Winona was determined to get out there and show Riggs that those waders weren't purchased purely with a fashion statement in mind. Maybe a *little* bit of a fashion statement, because they were bright yellow and just so cute. But she meant business with this garden. She'd have tomatoes and turnips growing this winter or die trying.

"Well, if you're good, I'm going to head out to the General Store," Delores said. "Make sure you take frequent breaks to hydrate and don't exert yourself too much."

After breakfast, Winona took a shower and changed. This time, she wore a pair of Wranglers she'd ordered online, and which had arrived the same day as her seeds. They strained at her hips and waist and were still stiff, not like the soft worn pairs that hugged Riggs's amazing ass. For now, they'd have to do. She definitely wanted to fit in a little better. Even though this was all temporary, she had nearly a year to get through before she could go home to Nashville.

After dressing, she appraised herself in the mirror. A while back, she'd stopped wearing mascara every day, what with all the crying she'd done. The lipstick went the way of the mascara when she threw up so much and had to keep reapplying. Seemed a worthless pursuit. Jeans were so much more practical around the house, and the sky hadn't fallen in when Riggs had dragged her to the doctor in her jeans, wearing no makeup or hair extensions. In fact, it had been nice, this being-anonymous deal. Not Winona James, but Winona *Henderson*, and just like any other expectant wife and mother.

Sean walked in the kitchen, took one look at her, and turned around to leave again.

"Delores isn't here. She went to the store."

He turned back, stared at her for a moment. "Actually it's a good thing we're alone. A funny thing happened."

A jolt of fear zipped right through her. This was where he told her he knew everything about her plans. "What's that?"

"I was having a cold beer the other day with Jeremy Pine, and he told me what you've been doing." He held up a palm. "Don't even try to deny it."

"You don't understand."

"I don't know what you *think* you're up to here with my brother but it's not going to work. I won't let him get hurt."

"You don't have to worry about him. He takes care of himself."

"Just the idea that you thought you'd get away with this." He shook his head. "Maybe with some of the younger men you might have, but it didn't come to that. I know you're used to getting what you want, and I'm sure it hurts that you came up against someone who wouldn't roll over and play dead."

"That's... Sean, no, you don't understand."

"I think I do. You wanted to buy something from a man. My brother isn't for sale, never has been, never will be."

She wanted to protest, wanted to scream, and fight back but he was right.

"I know that."

"Want to know what I think? Riggs beat you at your own game. Now, you probably think you're stuck with him. But Riggs doesn't deserve that. He should be with a woman who loves him. So, I hope you'll actually walk away from him and leave him intact. We all rely on him around here."

"I'm sure you do." She understood why as she'd begun to heavily rely on him, too. He had a way of making himself indispensable.

"You didn't know he was a lawyer, did you?" Sean slid her a knowing grin.

"No."

"Mighty suspicious. You're in town looking for a sperm donor. Next thing you and Riggs get married and you're pregnant. I see a connection there."

"You'd be wrong about that connection. This was an accident."

"I know that even if I'm not wrong, neither one of you will admit it. But I don't appreciate the idea of you using my brother to have a baby. That might be what you think you want right now. Take a little break in the country before you go back to your glamorous life. But Riggs has been through a lot, most of which you don't know a thing about."

"I know about Jenny. But these babies *do* belong to Riggs."

"Hope you don't mind if I don't take your word for that." With a disgusted look on his face, Sean grabbed his hat and went out the back door.

Seriously? Did Sean not realize she had enough money to take care of herself? Winona James didn't need a man! Well, she did for one thing, and one thing only. But she could support herself and her baby. She'd be in Nashville right now, doing just that, but Riggs wanted to be involved.

Damn Sean for his doubts, which for the life of her she hated that she understood. That only stirred the hot fury of justified anger until she didn't know where to point it. This was all Riggs's doing, after all, forcing her to stay with him in this throwback town. She took a deep breath and closed her eyes. Always better to know her enemies rather than wonder who hid like a snake and pretended to be a friend.

At least now she had a place to vent her frustration. Normally she'd do it in a song but today she had tough soil to beat up. She'd take her energy out on the hard dirt that refused to yield. Tugging on a pair of work boots, she grabbed her hat, opened the front door, and nearly ran into an older gentleman, his hand poised in the air as if she'd caught him midknock.

"Can I help you?"

He rocked back on his heels. "Well, well, you must be Winona James. Riggs's new bride."

She offered her hand. "Nice to meet you. Are you a neighbor?"

"Not me." He chuckled. "The Cruz ranch is nearby, but the Hendersons have land for miles."

"That's right. I tend to forget. No wonder no one's come around to borrow a stick of butter." She laughed a bit nervously because something about this man gave her the creeps.

She told herself he reminded her too much of her stepfather. The leering smile. A man nearly twice her age checking her out from head to toe.

"I just wanted to welcome you to Stone Ridge. We don't have enough young, eligible ladies, not to mention pretty ones such as yourself."

"I didn't catch your name," Winona said, ignoring the compliment that gave her a shiver of the most unwelcome kind.

"Phil. Phil Henderson. I'm the deadbeat cousin nobody wants to talk about."

It had been a while, but "Winnie Lee Hoyt" had been around his type before. She'd learned to fend off the advances of her stepfather's friends first, then later the ones from the older record label executives who hit on her on a regular basis. Those took *real* finesse.

But if this man thought he'd scare her he had no idea who he would tangle with. Sean had simply warmed her up. Now, she was ready to do some damage if needed.

"I've heard about you."

"I'm sure you have, darlin'."

"You just missed Sean and I've no idea where Riggs is right now. Do you want me to leave someone a message?"

"You might want to remind Riggs that the land developer increased their offer. Not sure how much longer they'll hold out, but this could be his last chance. You hear me? They could all be filthy rich men if they'll just let this land go. Then maybe he could take care of his new bride in the style she's become accustomed to."

"I take care of myself, Mr. Henderson." She crossed her arms, sending her first message.

"That may be, but you should realize that a man like Riggs wants to take care of his woman."

"He does. We're fine and dandy." She briefly eyed the shotgun propped behind the door. Better than a fire poker any day of the week and she understood how to use both effectively.

"Well, for now. You're the blushing newlyweds. Life is good. But Riggs won't be happy as *Mr. James.*"

The words hit Winona like a slap. Riggs would never be Mr. James, but he wouldn't have to be. After their children were born, their marriage would be dissolved. She wondered if Phil was right, and Riggs would feel compelled to have as much money as she did to contribute to raising their children. Whether or not he had as much money as she did, he had a lot more to offer in the way of legacy, tradition, and homegrown values. But she wasn't at all sure that Riggs would see it that way. The idea filled her with unexplainable sadness.

Riggs was right, of course. Their convenient marriage had become *complicated* and not just because they'd slept together. So many people were involved that she'd never intended to hurt. Something so simple, having a baby, had become like walking through a minefield hoping nobody got blasted.

"I'll be sure to give him the message." Winona stepped back as if to shut the door, to send Phil her second message.

Fortunately, he stepped back and took the steps two at a time.

"Excuse me," she called out after him after realizing he was no real threat. "What do you think the developer wants to do with this land? It's out in the middle of nowhere."

He stopped at the bottom of the steps and turned. "Most

likely a dude ranch. Some place where wealthy women can visit to live out a fantasy. They pay well for that sort of thing."

A dude ranch on Henderson land. She'd only known Riggs for a short time, but her guess that the likelihood of him selling to a developer was approximately a zillion to one. She didn't know why Phil Henderson would be so interested in whether he did or not anyway. And he did seem rather attached to the idea. After all, why were the developers communicating through him?

Probably because Riggs had stopped taking their calls was her first guess. Sounded like him.

After hitting the bathroom one last time (she seemed to pee constantly these days) Winona walked to the side of the house where she'd propped the rake along with her gardening tools. There, she found a perfectly plowed and ready field. Every weed was gone, and the dirt looked watered, rich, and red.

There were neatly formed rows of small hills where she remembered the seeds would be planted. Just the way her Mama had done, but this strip of land was a lot wider than she'd ever had. No doubt these were Riggs's efforts to help, and her heart tugged. He'd done this for *her*. She went straight to work, planting the seeds in little wells at the top of each row. Using the stakes, she labeled the vegetables.

When she'd planted two rows of turnips, the sun beat down on her, and she took a swig of water. She'd take a break now and go find Riggs to thank him for his help. He was out there somewhere on the ranch, so she started strolling in the direction she'd seen him yesterday. She checked the stables first since they were closest to the house but found no one there but the beautiful horses.

"Hi, horsies! Where's your master?"

She could not interpret their replies, so she kept walking,

knowing that the exercise was good for her anyway. When she reached the first fence line, she found a pretty cow all by itself.

"Did you get lost, Bessie?"

Poor thing must have been separated from the others and she sure was a beauty, with interesting horns which Winona had never seen on a cow before. Then again, how long had it been since she'd been up close and personal with a cow? Years. Maybe it was a bison.

The cow pawed the ground, as if saying hello.

"Oh, hi. I like you, too. Can we be friends?"

She snorted and pawed the ground again. This cow really liked her. Winona had never really had a good sense of animals, wanting a dog but because of the road, she'd never been able to have one of her own.

Mutt rushed up to her and brushed his cold wet nose against Winona's leg. "Hey there, honey. I think I made a new friend."

Mutt usually followed her around the house, sleeping at her feet when she napped during the day. He started to whine, the way he did when he wanted a piece of bacon which she always happily gave him.

She bent to pet his head. He pushed her with his nose.

"What's wrong, buddy?"

In the distance she heard the thundering sound of horse's hooves and turned back to see Riggs headed toward her. She waved to him. He did not wave back, but stopped a few feet away from her, and hopped off his horse. Mutt ran to his side.

"Hey." She didn't like the serious look on his face. "I just came to thank you. For the garden."

"Don't move, Winona." It was a low, menacing tone which she did not appreciate.

"Why?" She moved.

"I said don't move. Can you just for once in your *life* follow directions?"

"O-kay."

"I know you think this is just another beautiful day at the ranch, but you have just happened upon a pissed-off bull."

And then she had no *trouble* with his directions because she froze. A pack of wolves would have trouble moving her. "That's a...bull? I-I thought you didn't have a-any bulls."

"I don't. Looks like he came through a hole in the fence that wasn't there before today." He lowered his head. "And that's the way he's goin' back."

"What are you g-goin' to do?"

She was terrified for him. Bulls gored people. Years ago, she'd seen the running of the bulls while in Spain on a world tour. This did not look like the same kind of animal to her. He looked so innocent and sweet with his cute pawing and warm brown eyes.

"First, I'm goin' to get between you and your new best friend." He walked gradually toward her while at the same time he beckoned her to take a step toward him. "Walk to me, but slowly."

"O-okay."

Her breaths came short and shallow and she could actually hear each intake when it rattled around in her chest. She took long, deliberate steps toward Riggs, soothing herself by meeting his soft gaze. He became her safe place. Her anchor. Winona didn't see a hint of fear in his gaze, but a quiet confidence. And she would trust this man with her life. Once she was closer to him, he reached for her with his long arm and tugged her behind him.

Instinctively, she hunkered behind him, his large body her shelter from the big, bad bull.

"Now, keep walkin'," he said, gently pushing her back.

"No, I can't. I don't want to leave you here."

"Go. *Now.*"

"But what if he…he…" she couldn't even finish the thought.

"He won't."

"What are you goin' to do?"

"I'll tell you what I'm *not* goin' to do. I'm not goin' to have a long discussion with you about this."

The bull started pawing again and Winona didn't know how she hadn't recognized that aggressive stance before. Blame it on baby brain. Blame it on the fact that she was a fish out of water on this ranch. The bull was going to charge. Every instinct in her wanted to stay and assist Riggs, but she had their babies to consider. Riggs could protect himself and the babies only had her.

So, she kept walking backwards, past Riggs's horse, and then a few feet more, until she was at a safe distance. Meanwhile, Riggs had backed up, too, and eventually reached his horse. And almost at the same moment the bull charged, Riggs made the loudest noise Winona had ever heard. It sounded like a war cry.

He and his horse charged the bull, which turned slightly as they did. Riggs got close enough to reach out and slap the bull hard on the back. That turned him the direction he wanted, and he and the horse crowded him until they ran him back through the hole in the fence where he'd come.

Winona slid to the ground on her knees and fought the need to clutch her chest. She watched as Riggs turned his horse and galloped back to her, jumping off when he got close. She expected him to be mad. Expected him to yell at her for being this stupid and not distinguishing a cow from a damn bull. Not that she would blame him because she was so far out of her comfort zone she might as well be on another planet.

But instead, Riggs pulled her up, his arms around her, and crushed her against his chest.

She wrapped her arms around his neck. "I'm sorry, I'm sorry. I'm really sorry."

He studied her, his gaze sliding up and down her body as his hands slid down her arms. "Are you okay?"

"I'm fine. All parts present and accounted for."

He narrowed his eyes. "I thought I told you to stay away from the livestock. Damn it, Winona, what the *hell* were you doin' out here?"

"Don't you yell at me!"

"You could have been seriously injured. I should take you over my knee for this."

"In the fun way, of course."

"In the painful way. But I won't."

"Smart." She crossed her arms. "You already know I bite."

"Yes, I do, woman." His hand wrapped around the nape of her neck. "Let's go."

"Where are we goin'?"

Instead of answering, he hauled her up on his horse as if she were simply the weight of a sack of potatoes. Then he climbed on behind her and took the reins. "Back to the house and then I'm goin' to have to fix that fence."

Winona hadn't been on a horse since…well, technically, she'd never been on a horse. In her neck of the woods, only rich people owned horses. Colby had claimed that he wanted to buy a *real* ranch and they'd looked at places with stables in Tennessee country. The owner thought it would be cute to get Winona on a horse, but she'd promptly fallen off when she tried to climb the sixteen-hand horse. She remembered exactly how many hands since that was a significant emotional event. The owner had been mortified, and fussed all over Winona, wanting to call for an ambulance, even if all that hurt was her pride.

Colby had *laughed*.

It was a heady feeling to have a man who cared to keep her safe, even if it was only to protect his unborn children.

The horse continued to gallop, and Winona felt like she was flying. On a horse. The warm wind whipped her hair in her eyes, and Riggs's strong body pressed against her back. His firm long legs were behind hers. She almost wished they'd been a little farther from the house, because she was enjoying herself, but they reached it within a few short minutes. Fortunately, Riggs didn't seem in a huge hurry to dismount.

"You didn't tell me that developers want to buy your land."

"Who told you that?"

"Phil Henderson."

"When did you see *him*?" His hands rose from her hips, lighting briefly on her waist, and finally to her shoulders. Warm and solid.

"A while ago he came by the house when both you and Sean were out. Told me to let you know they increased the offer." She swiveled in the saddle to face him. "Are you in trouble, Riggs?"

The way the straw Stetson partially shaded his face made his eyes unreadable. Short beard bristle covered a strong jawline that could probably cut glass. A pull of tenderness hit her.

No. I won't fall in love. I refuse.

The hint of a smile tugged at his sensual mouth. "Not even a little bit. You're the biggest trouble that's come my way."

"You would tell me? Maybe I can help somehow. We are married, after all."

He reached for her hand and brought it to his lips to kiss,

such an unexpectedly tender gesture that she sucked in a shuddering breath.

"Want to help me? Stay safe out there. I don't want to worry about you. I suspect that bull belongs to my closest neighbors, and he's never loose. And never wanderin' around *my* property."

"Good to know."

"You could have waited to thank me about the garden." His hands lowered to her waist. "Like tonight."

Hope thrummed through her. "You're moving back into your bedroom?"

"If you're okay with that." He cleared his throat. "And it's our bedroom."

"Yes, I'm good."

"Figured we might as well enjoy whatever time we have left."

And then he swung back to that cold and frigid tone that made her bristle. Just another reminder that she and Riggs did have an expiration date. She wished he'd stop mentioning it for a minute.

Winona always had high hopes for every man she'd ever loved. She was, as Kim called her, an eternal romantic.

Great for song writing, not so much for life.

CHAPTER 18

*R*iggs offered his hand. He brought Winona to the ground, setting her down and keeping her in the circle of his arms. Telling himself over and over again that she was safe. *Safe.* No injuries. He could start breathing again. His heart rate had only now resumed normal levels, the terror that had galloped through him like a horse on crack finally dissipating.

She could have died.

Worse, bulls didn't just wander onto his land. Fences didn't suddenly develop gaps large enough for a bull to fit through.

Riggs didn't want to believe it, but Phil *had* to have done this. A scare tactic, he presumed, and he couldn't help but think he'd meant this for Winona's sake. Maybe with his millionaire wife out of the picture, Riggs would be more inclined to rethink. But it couldn't be.

No, even Phil wasn't that stupid. He was simply trying to get Riggs's attention. Well, he had it.

Winona could take care of herself in most situations, but he wouldn't want to count on her resourcefulness. If Phil had been up to this sabotage, as Riggs more than suspected, he was little more than a crazy person. Unhinged. Maybe it would be worth making a phone call and talking to those developers whose calls he'd been ignoring for months. He'd straighten a few things out with them. He'd dealt with and understood contracts for land use, water rights, finder's fees, all of it. And people had to be able to accept no for an answer.

With Winona safely back in the house, he rode Spur back to the fence line. Someone had definitely sabotaged this fence and pried it apart. A crowbar had been left on the ground. The idiot didn't even consider removing the evidence. Riggs could see the bull in the distance, and he'd wandered further on to the southside. From here he could see that the corral pen where Wade Cruz kept his bull had been left open. This was never the case.

His closest neighbor, the family of Wade Cruz, the all-state rodeo champ, had several acres that abutted one side of Henderson Grange. They hadn't kept cattle in years, but Wade still kept the bull he'd trained on. Wade's mother, Rose, was ill with cancer, still fighting the good fight. After Jorge Cruz died, everything went to hell. Wade was gone too much to help out. Riggs and the rest of the men helped and made repairs when and where needed. The ladies of SORROW were often bringing casseroles and pies and Delores regularly stopped by to check in on Rose.

The woman would be horrified to learn their bull had nearly killed his wife. Okay, maybe he was exaggerating. But the terror he'd felt at seeing Winona standing so close to a major mauling still sent a shiver down his spine. He brought her here to his ranch to keep her safe not have her subjected to a madman who would let a bull loose.

Riggs pulled out the satellite phone he kept on him for emergencies.

"Beulah? It's Riggs Henderson. I'm gonna need some help out here fixing a fence on the Cruz property. Just need a few men."

He hung up after a few minutes. Beulah would alert the phone tree and within minutes he'd have a crew out here. There might be a shortage of women in Stone Ridge, but there was no shortage of both men and women willing to help their neighbor. He wasn't one to ask for help often but he'd like this fence fixed immediately and would need more than Sean's assistance.

Finished with that call, he dialed the land development company that had been bugging him for a year now. Within minutes, he was connected to the man he'd been dealing with on and off for months.

"Mr. Henderson." Bill Smithers cleared his throat. "You've heard our new offer. Have you reconsidered?"

"I have not. I'm not selling my land and you can tell Phil Henderson to back off. Apparently, you've offered him a finder's fee if he can talk me into selling."

"I don't think—"

"Don't even try to deny it. There's no other reason he'd be so motivated for me to sell. He's been out here to see me recently. And today, I suspect he unleashed a bull that almost killed my pregnant wife!"

"Okay, now, calm down. I can hear that you're upset. That sounds traumatic."

"You don't know the half of it. I don't appreciate scare tactics. This isn't the Old West. If he hurts my wife, in any way, I swear, you're going to be the one to pay for it."

"I can promise you those are not *our* tactics. We'll rescind our offer to him. We only thought he'd come and reason with you. Explain our new terms."

"You should have never involved yourself with someone like him."

"It does sound like he's too desperate. I apologize, we only—"

"Listen, if I change my mind, I'll contact you directly. How's that?"

"Can't argue with that."

A few minutes later, Riggs had grabbed Sean, and his crew arrived. Lincoln and Jackson Carver were together, probably having stopped whatever they were doing on their own ranch. Beau Stephens, Sadie's brother, was right behind them.

"Hey, Riggs." Lincoln slapped him on the back. "What's happenin'? You got a loose bull? Is it Wade's? He always keeps him locked up."

"Someone took a crowbar to the fence and made a gap wide enough for Wade's bull to make his way through." Riggs walked them to the fence and picked up the crowbar. "It's sabotage."

Lincoln whistled. "That Satan is one mean sucker."

"Winona happened on him, just out taking a walk." He scratched his temple, fighting a smile. "Thought he was a cow."

"Oh man, leave that to Winona!" Jackson snorted. "Fearless and clueless about ranch life."

It was Sean who first burst into laughter, and Riggs followed close behind. Then Jackson, Lincoln, Beau. Pretty soon all of Riggs's anger and fear had reduced to a slow simmer. Winona hadn't been hurt, and that was all that mattered. He could laugh about it now.

And between him and his friends, the fence was fully repaired, and the bull returned to his corral.

LIKE THEY TENDED to do after a job where they all pitched in, all four headed to the Shady Grind for a cold beer.

Levi was behind the bar. "Hey. Got the call but I couldn't leave the place unattended. Full house."

"That's alright. We got it done," Riggs said.

Levi slid over beers for all of them, as one by one they each took a stool.

"Welcome, Mr. Newlywed," Levi said to Riggs. "Haven't seen you around for a while."

"Tell me about it," Beau said. "We miss your ugly mug around here. Never thought I'd see *Riggs* get married."

"What's the big deal?" Riggs took a pull of his beer.

"You were like the George Clooney of Stone Ridge." Beau elbowed Riggs.

"By the way, George Clooney isn't even George Clooney anymore," Lincoln said.

"Stop talkin' nonsense," Sean said.

Confirmed bachelor his ass. What Riggs had confirmed now was that he'd been lonely for too many years. And every woman he'd met never held his attention for longer than a day. The younger women wanted to toy with him, and the women his age were already married. That left him with the occasional fling in Kerrville, because he hadn't exactly been a monk for twenty years.

Jackson turned to Riggs. "How are you and Winona gettin' along?"

Riggs didn't know how to answer that question. He loved having sex with her, no doubt about that. But if his feelings didn't go any deeper than that, he shouldn't have a problem talking about his wife with her former husband.

The *first* man she'd asked to be her "personal assistant."

It made sense that he *cared* about her, sure. She would be the mother of his…children. Gulp. Two of them at once for this so-called "confirmed bachelor." But today, when he'd seen her in danger, for the first time the children hadn't even been in his thoughts. His entire focus was Winona. Winona, who was trying hard to make the best of the situation he'd blackmailed her into. Planting seeds, keeping Delores happy, choosing to let a few walls down. Trying her best to acclimate.

Winona, who had just offered her help if he needed it.

"She has a way of worming her way into a man's heart."

"I wouldn't know about that. Wasn't exactly fair of me to marry her when I still loved Eve. I regret it. We both do, I guess. She's a good person, though. Don't believe her bad press. Well, I'm sure you know by now, even though yours was a pretty quick courtship."

You can say that again.

"Yeah, who knew that I'd fall for her so quickly?"

"Well, I fell for Eve the first time I saw her." Jackson took a pull of his beer. "Man, I'm glad you two fell for each other. And having a baby? I know how happy she must be. I think Winona will make a good mother. She was always reaching out to the younger musicians like me. Giving advice, mentorship, helping with an introduction to a powerful producer. She said that people helped her along the way, so she was happy to return the favor."

He'd just learned something new about her. It was good to know she'd be a good mother, though he'd already realized there was a lot more to the woman than what she presented publicly. The night when she'd referred to her transformation from Winnie Lee Hoyt to Winona James made more sense. She was a trailer-park kid, completely self-invented. Resilient. He admired that.

"You haven't heard? I thought for sure it had been all over town by now." Riggs set his beer down, readying for the onslaught of good wishes. "We're having twins."

Jackson gaped, then clapped Riggs shoulder. "I'll drink to that! Linc! Did you hear that? Riggs is having twins!"

"Better you than me," Lincoln joked. "We're having just the one, thank you very much. That's plenty."

"This is perfect," Beau said. "You never had any kids and now you're gettin' two for the price of one."

"Is Winona going back to Nashville after the babies are born?" Levi asked. "What are ya'll going to do?"

"We'll figure it out," he said, knowing that he certainly didn't want to share his plans to divorce her after the children were born.

"You should talk her into stayin', Riggs." This was from Lincoln. "I know Sadie wishes she would. Our kids will be the same age."

"That would be nice, sure."

"Well, Eve and I are working on it," Jackson said. "We'll have kids the same age, too. Don't count us out yet."

"Brother, you just keep on havin' all that fun makin' it happen," Lincoln said. "Don't rush."

There was loud raucous laughter from the gang and another round of beers.

RIGGS DROVE HOME a short time later, pretty sick of himself. He was going to be a father. Time to grow the hell up and stop wishing for things he would never have.

Winona.

Was it even worth trying to get her to stay? They could have a real marriage if she'd be willing to work with him. No need to split the children, share them, and work out a horrendous custody schedule that would work for both of them. He didn't want that, and it wasn't entirely because of the children. Winona fit here with him. He would have never dreamed it possible, but she did.

If he suggested she stay, she'd probably think he'd gone out of his mind. He hadn't made any of this easy on her, stepping all over her contract, and making his own. Rearranging her life so that she couldn't just walk away with only what she wanted from him. He wondered if, on some level, he'd taken charge because he wanted her, too. Now he had to find a way to show her that she belonged here in Stone Ridge.

By the time he got home he'd missed dinner. Delores was cleaning up when he walked in the door.

"Oh, you're in the doghouse," Delores chuckled.

"Where is she?"

"In your bedroom." Delores hooked her finger in that direction. "I warned you not to take her for granted. You can't just go drinking a cold beer with your buddies any old night like you used to do."

"I haven't been out in weeks. The men helped me with the fence this afternoon, it was the least I could do."

"Winona told me what happened. She said you saved her life."

"That's an exaggeration."

"Either way, she's mighty grateful. And so am I. That girl just is everything we needed around here, isn't she?"

And she's leaving us. But not now. She's not leaving yet. I still have time.

"Yeah." Riggs swallowed hard. "She sure is."

"Now to get those brothers of yours settled down."

"Don't hold your breath." Riggs called out as he walked down the hallway to Winona's bedroom. His bedroom.

Their bedroom. He opened the door and found her sitting on the bed, surrounded by books.

"Where have you been?"

"Got that fence fixed and the bull contained. I had some help, so we all went out for a beer." He picked up one of the books. They were all baby name books. "Already picking names?"

"It's something to do."

So, she'd been bored, and he hadn't even noticed. No wonder she'd planted the vegetable garden. It occurred to Riggs that for all he'd tried to be a good husband, he'd never actually spent much time with Winona. Never taken her on a date. He'd forgotten how to be in a relationship. If he'd ever known how to properly be in one.

She gnawed on her lower lip and wouldn't meet his eyes. "Would you mind, if one of the twins is a girl, naming her Mary Jo?"

Mary Jo Henderson.

He'd only asked for the last name, because it was so significant to him to have a child carrying Cal and Marge's last name. *His* name. He'd agreed to leave the first names to her, but she was asking him for input. She didn't have to.

"Your mother's name."

"Yes. And it's a classic."

He waited a beat, letting her think he'd really debated it, when he was going to give her anything she wanted. "I like it."

"Thank you." She went back to the books, flipping through the pages of one. "Boys' names are harder. William, James, John, Patrick. The classics. Then there are other trendier names. I don't care much for those."

"Hey, Winona?"

"Yeah." She didn't look up.

"I'm sorry, okay?"

She met his eyes. Blinked. "That wasn't your fault. You *saved* me."

"Pretty sure you would have saved yourself but that's not what I meant." He set her book down. "I'm sorry I talked you into marrying me. I forced your hand."

For the first time, she seemed speechless. "You bested my attorney. And she's still pretty pissed about that."

"I should have been kinder about it all. You didn't choose

me to have the baby you wanted, but it just happened anyway. For that, I'm really sorry. You could have picked someone better than me."

"*I'm* not sorry. And I considered asking you, Riggs. You were my *first* choice. From the moment I laid eyes on you, I wanted you to be the father of my child."

"Well, I wouldn't have done it." He chuckled.

"Of course not. Don't you think I know that? That's why I didn't even try."

"Yeah. I would have wanted more." He tucked a strand of hair behind her ear. "Right from the beginning."

"More?"

"A relationship. I would have wanted to court you, get to know you. Of course, I would have had sex with you. I think I've already proven that. But that wouldn't have ever been enough for me."

"It doesn't matter now. I realize how ridiculous my plan was. I had no right to ask so much out of any man, least of all you. But I was desperate to have a child."

"You made that clear. And I was desperate to have you." He tugged her close, meeting her gaze, hoping she'd see inside him. "And it wasn't the moment I saw you onstage, much as you like to think that's all you have to offer the world."

"Riggs…"

Then he kissed her, practically inhaled her, fully giving in to this primal need. She brought this out of him. This twisting of his heart and mind, the physical sensations that brought an intellectual man like him to his knees. He'd always believed these kinds of heightened emotions were for a different type of man. Someone given more to imagination. Fancy. Someone less grounded than he.

But she'd blindsided him with her wit, her strength, and her passion. Her obvious love for their children. He was now the kind of man who allowed his heart to make decisions for him. Dangerous.

Books were tossed aside, clothes quickly removed, and he gave in to that fiery need that had started to rule him.

She was his plan. His destiny.

He made love to her like it was the last time he'd have a chance. So that she could remember this moment and never forget him if she chose to walk away.

Afterwards, she lay in his arms. Warm as fresh-baked bread, she curled into his body. One soft leg was thrown casually over his hips.

"Hey, Winona?"

"Yeah?"

"Would you go out with me sometime?"

She gave him a beautiful smile.

CHAPTER 19

*S*ometime during the night, Winona startled awake
and bopped Riggs on the head. He didn't even
budge. He slept soundly on his stomach next to her, one arm
thrown over her waist.

She'd been dreaming of her mother again, but for the first
time in a long while, the dreams included her stepfather. All
his leering, cruelty, insults. *Whore. Slut. Tramp.* Leroy had
friends who'd come by the house and make drunken passes
at her from the time she'd been twelve. She'd managed to
fend them off, once knocking a man clear on his ass with the
help of a handy fireplace poker. But later, she learned what
men wanted from a woman. And she'd used that home-field
advantage to get her out of Leroy's house.

The memory and spirit of that young woman lived inside
of her still, and she sometimes came out, ready to brawl.
Ready to find a fireplace poker and kick someone's ass. She
wanted to see less of that woman and more of the one she
would have been had her mother lived to raise her. Riggs
would have loved that woman. She'd have been sweet and
even-tempered. A good wife and mother.

She wasn't sure what kind of mother she would be. There was always the possibility that she would royally screw this up.

Winona shifted to her side to face Riggs and played with his unruly hair. Dark and thick, it was always on the wrong side of a cut. His strong jawline was dusted with tough beard bristle.

Last night, he'd rocked her world.

Riggs was a wonderful lover but this time he'd been tender, too. Taking his time, kissing her long and hard, slowly whipping her body into a frenzy. She didn't know what had happened, what switch had been toggled. But she'd take it. She'd take him being tender, his sweet words washing over her with hope.

She imagined it had to do with the fact he could have lost a child again. This time they were his own flesh and blood and she imagined a man like Riggs would bring hellfire on anyone trying to hurt his family.

Purely by accident, she'd wound up with a good man. She couldn't have done better if she'd gone to a sperm bank and picked the best genetic qualities for a father. Riggs might not love *her*, except as a host for his children, but that didn't matter right now. Because most of all, she wanted her children to have a good father. Someone solid and responsible. This wasn't about her anymore. This was about her babies.

The next few months would be easy to get through this way. The warm rush of the body of a man sleeping next to her, making love to her, taking care of her. Winona wasn't used to a man looking out for her and when Riggs first started trying, she'd seen it purely as control. From the time he'd burst in on her throwing up in the bathroom. And maybe it had been at that time. Now it felt different. Genuine.

Hungry again, which seemed to happen way too

frequently, she shifted and tried to move his arm. The accidental bop on the head didn't wake him but trying to move his arm did. Interesting.

"Winona," he mumbled in a voice thick with sleep. "What's wrong?"

She ruffled his bed hair. "Nothing. Go back to sleep, baby. I just... I want some more of that pie."

Delores was a wonderful cook. Last night, the peach pie had been scrumptious. The crust flaky and buttery, the fresh sliced peaches caramelized. Her mouth watered.

"I'll get it."

"That's okay...I..."

But he had already rolled out of bed and tugged his jeans on. Shame. Still, she watched him and his amazing body walk out the door. Holy Grand Ole Opry, he had a great backside. A few minutes later they were both back, her pie and her man. She didn't know which made her salivate more.

"Thank you."

Half asleep, he handed it to her, pie nicely plated, fork, napkin.

"You looked tired."

"Nah, I'm good." Within seconds he was back in bed fast asleep.

Yet another man blessed with "man sleep."

Meanwhile, she'd be up for a while, both eating this slice of pie, and wondering how she got this lucky.

WHEN WINONA WOKE the next morning, Riggs was already gone. She hadn't even heard him leave.

Rubbing her eyes, she reached for her nightshirt, and pulled it back on. She found her cell on the nightstand. Once in a while, Winona would get a flurry of text messages from

Kimberly all at once, several days' worth. They were always upbeat and encouraging:

Keep the end goal in mind!
Baby,baby,baby!
You can do this!

So, it was time to give Kimberly the latest.

Finding no bars on her cell again, Winona reached for the landline kept on the nightstand and dialed Kimberly's cell. She didn't answer and it went straight to voice mail. Rather than leave one, Winona hung up and tried again.

"Yes?" Kimberly said. "Who *is* this?"

"It's me, Kim."

"Winona! Oh, I'm sorry I didn't answer my phone. That's not what I use it for."

"Out here on the ranch, I'm lucky to get a signal. I'll have to use the landline most of the time."

"Listen to you. A *landline.* The *ranch.* How quaint. How are you feeling?"

"I'm not quite as sick as I was." Winona settled back on the pillows. "You can issue the press release about my pregnancy. Everyone here already knows."

"And how did that go over with the family?"

"Delores figured it out anyway. She's very happy." Winona cleared her throat. "Are you sitting down, Kim?"

"Why? Do I have to?"

"How's your heart?" Winona winced, ready to drop the twin bomb.

"Holy popsicle, Winona, what did you *do?*"

"Oh, nothing much. I'm just having twins."

There was a long and drawn-out pause in which Winona thought she'd been disconnected. "Hello? Kim? Hello?"

A long whistle followed. "What are we going to do?"

"Be happy? I'm getting two for the price of one."

"But Winona…having twins is riskier. Recovery will take much longer. You should probably have a scheduled C-section."

"The midwife in town thinks I can do it naturally."

"Naturally?" Kimberly squeaked.

She'd been the one to beg for drugs the moment she'd felt the slightest twinge. No wonder she assumed Winona would be the same. Unfortunately, the epidural block for pain relief was one long needle in the back. Winona had watched videos. She'd almost passed out during one. That needle would never find its way into her spine. No sir.

"I know, I know. But don't worry. We'll have a doctor on standby if things go south."

"Oh, Winona. Geez. A *midwife?*"

"I'm happy, Kim. Be happy for me, okay?"

"What does cowboy lawyer say about all this?"

Winona wondered if she should mention how well she and Riggs were getting along, as in now sleeping together, but she hesitated. Kim would ruin this for her. She'd warned that an annulment would be harder to file after consummating the marriage. At this point, Winona didn't care about any of that. *She* was the one spending a long year on a ranch in the middle of nowhere. She would like to be happy for at least a little while. The fighting and arguing had become exhausting. The kissing and make-up sex were so much better.

"You let me know if you need anything. Meanwhile, I'm dealing with the business end. You were asked to present again at the CMA Awards, and I was able to put them off. I told them you were unreachable, and I'd have to get back to them."

"Tell them a big, fat no. I'm sick of them trotting me out

once a year. Anyway, I'll be as big as a house, and I don't want to travel. Too dangerous in the last trimester."

"I'm sure that cowboy wouldn't *let* you travel." She scoffed. "A few of your studio musicians are asking about you. I told them you're on a sabbatical and would call when you had work for them."

"Thanks."

The worst part of taking time off was how many musicians might only be partially employed due to her. Some of them, and their wives, were dear friends.

"I'll make a few calls, see if I can find them some other studio work for now."

"I can't *imagine* how bored you must be out there. Is it *horrible?*"

Well, she'd definitely found a fun new way of entertaining herself. She stroked the spot on the bed next to her, which still held his exhilarating scent.

"I've planted a vegetable garden. I'm working on it today after my breakfast."

"That's awesome!"

"You were right, Kim. I'm going to make it through this year and be a lot better off. I think Riggs might even like me now a little bit."

She wouldn't go so far as to saying love, but if nothing else, she hoped they would end their marriage as good friends. She'd stayed friends with Jackson, why not Riggs? Much easier to co-parent.

"See, I knew that would happen. How can anyone not *like* you?"

Winona snorted. Spoken from a best friend, but some folks seemed to do just fine.

· · ·

A WEEK LATER, on a Sunday, Delores was off to church. Too late to join her, Winona thought maybe she'd bring Riggs and Sean lunch today. She wasn't sure what they normally did on Delores's days off, but she figured Riggs would appreciate her thinking of him either way. Digging through the refrigerator, she found sandwich fixings, and prepared a lunch. Riggs often left the keys in the ignition and so she drove his truck up the hill to the pasture.

"Hey," Sean called out since he seemed closest to the gate where several cattle were locked. "What are you doin' here?"

"I brought lunch for y'all."

Sean quirked a brow, his suspicion of her thick. "Why?"

"Delores is at church. It's nothin' fancy. Just bologna and cheese sandwiches. Some chips. Water." She climbed out of the truck but before she could open the door, Sean had hauled the basket out for her.

"I haven't had bologna and cheese since I was a kid."

"Me, either." Her mama used to make these sandwiches and cut the crust off.

Riggs joined them. "What's this?"

"Your wife made lunch for us," Sean said with a bit too much snark for Winona's taste.

"Nothing fancy."

She'd seen the lunches Delores packed and wondered if she got all her recipes from The Pioneer Woman. It wasn't anything Winona would dare to attempt without help.

Another truck drove up then, driven by a beautiful blonde. "Hey, y'all! Sorry if I'm late."

Sean rushed to the truck.

"Jolette Marie usually brings us lunch when Delores has the day off," Riggs said. "I would have told you if you'd asked."

Winona deflated. "Hers looks a lot better."

Jolette Marie removed a pie, a whole cooked *chicken*, rolls, and... Winona didn't even want to watch anymore. Sean went straight to feasting on that lunch. Jolette Marie waved Riggs over, but he took his sandwich and sat on the tailgate of his truck.

"I'm good." He waved back.

Winona sat next to him, her heart squishy all over again. He had to stop behaving this way if he didn't want her to fall in love with him.

"You don't have to eat my inferior lunch."

He snaked an arm around her and the smile he gave kick-started her whole heart. "I like bologna and cheese sandwiches. You can bring them to me anytime."

Then it probably became hard for him to eat with her plastering her body against his, resting her head on his chest.

"Who is Jolette Marie? She's very pretty."

"Jo has had a rough time of it. She's made some stupid decisions and now it seems she's trying to find her way back. The Truehart family owns the horse ranch next to the Double C."

"I heard that was owned by the wealthiest man in Stone Ridge."

Riggs nodded. "Yep."

That explained the Escalade Jolette Marie drove.

Riggs finished his sandwiches and chips. Then he practically guzzled the bottle of water in two seconds and crushed it with one hand. Lord, how she loved to watch this man drink a bottle of water. She could make a day out of just that.

"I'm knocking off early this Saturday so I can take you out," Riggs said.

"Where to?" There weren't any restaurants in Stone Ridge other than the Shady Grind, but there were more options in Kerrville.

"You wouldn't believe me if I told you." He gave her a

slow smile. "This is something you're going to have to see with your own eyes."

"Really. Wow. Sounds intriguing."

"I better get back to it." He gave her a quick kiss on the lips.

She watched him as he walked back to his brother and grabbed Sean by the shirt sleeve, urging him to stop eating and get back to work.

Winona had just put up the tailgate when Jolette Marie walked over and offered her hand. "Hey, there. I don't think we've met. Not officially. Congratulations on your marriage."

"Thank you."

It didn't make sense to be jealous, but it so happened that Jolette Marie was decked out the same way Winona used to dress. This morning she hadn't bothered with makeup or hair which had become the norm. Nothing seemed to fit her right anymore and she couldn't face maternity clothes this soon. She'd taken to wearing her jeans unbuttoned at the top with blousy peasant tops. The thought of purchasing maternity clothes this soon was unthinkable.

"I can't tell you what Riggs means to me." Jolette Marie went hand to heart. "And to most everyone in town. When there's a problem anywhere, Riggs is the first one anyone calls. We have a phone tree for the men when there's help needed, and Riggs is *always* there. Not too long ago, he pitched in to help with the new school they built in town over at the old church."

"You really only have one school? What about preschool?"

"Parents do preschool at home or in little co-ops with friends. All the kids used to get bussed to school the next town over." She smiled. "That was me, all my brothers, Lincoln, Jackson, their sister, Daisy, Eve, Sadie. We grew up that way. It's nice to have a school here at least for the little ones."

"What about Riggs? Where did he go to school?"

"I heard he and his brothers only moved here when he was around thirteen?"

Yes. She remembered him telling her that he'd been a foster child when the Hendersons had taken him in.

"Did you know his wife?"

"He had a wife?" Her eyes widened. "I guess I don't know everything about him. But he is a good thirteen years older than me."

This meant Winona was ten years older than this lovely woman. She couldn't believe that Riggs hadn't ever been interested in her. Then again, maybe he had in the past. Considering the shortage of women, it might even be easier to understand him going after someone younger.

"I better get back," Winona said.

"Sorry I kept you." She crossed her arms and lowered her head. "I just... I..."

"What is it?"

Jolette Marie jumped a little. "Oh, I would like your auto-graph sometime, or maybe a selfie if you don't mind."

"Of course." Winona went straight back into showbiz mode. "Right now? I would, but I don't think anyone would recognize me without my fake lashes and hair extensions."

"Those were hair extensions? They looked so natural!"

She laughed. "You better believe it. It costs a lot of money to look that good."

For the next few minutes, Jolette Marie grilled Winona about hair products. Not surprisingly, money was no object. Jolette Marie wanted only the best.

"Do you know Twyla, the waitress at the Shady Grind?" Jolette Marie asked.

"Yes, we've met."

"I hang out at the Shady Grind a lot. There's no other place to go." She shrugged. "Twyla is your biggest fan."

"That's very sweet. I love hearing from my fans."

Party line, front and center. She never asked for privacy or to be left alone to sulk if she so felt like it. To be a celebrity in good standing, she could never have a bad day. It was exhausting.

"I was just…wonderin' if you maybe could, I don't know, help her out a little bit."

"Sure. Help her out with what?"

"Well, this is a little awkward and she'd never tell you this." Jolette Marie hesitated. "She wants to be a country music star, just like you. And she has the chops. I've heard her. Jackson lets her sing from time to time at the bar."

"If she wants to be a country music star, she has to go to Nashville."

"That's what Jackson told her."

"I'm not sure how much I can help from over here in Texas, but I'll do whatever I can."

"She'll be so excited to hear that." Jolette Marie grabbed Winona in a hug.

"I don't have the pull in Nashville that I used to. It's been a long time since I had a hit song."

"It's the same for Jackson. He'd love to help, but he's done all he can for her. And I'm thinking it's a whole different scene in Nashville for women than men."

"You've got that right."

"See, the thing is she's entering that national contest. The one where they go all over the country with a bus? They've got the crew coming to audition in Dallas, and she's going to drive on over there."

"Winning a contest is how I got out of Oklahoma. Have her call me and she can come out sometime and talk shop. Or I can come to her at the Shady Grind. All I'm doing now is growing a vegetable garden." She patted her belly. "And my babies."

"Okay, well, maybe I'll see you at the Founder's Day parade this weekend?"

"Founder's Day parade?"

"See you there." Jolette Marie climbed in her Escalade. "You don't want to miss this."

This must be where Riggs would be taking her. "I've been told."

But she'd been married in a Las Vegas drive-through by an Elvis impersonator, and once ran drunk-naked through the sprinklers in front of her mansion.

When it came to crazy stuff, the bar was set high.

CHAPTER 20

*T*he Founder's Day parade exceeded all of Winona's expectations.

And that said something.

"We probably don't have more than a thousand residents in Stone Ridge at last count, but when they all show up at once, it's a little ridiculous," Riggs said.

There were throngs of people everywhere as they walked hand in hand down Main Street. Having been to dozens of award shows with superstars of country music, old and new, Winona understood how to work a crowd. She was usually decked out in a couture gown, one that showcased "the girls" and a little bit of leg. Hair extensions, diamonds on her neck, heels, and plenty of Spanx to strap everything down and keep it there.

Today was about as similar to those events as walking on the moon.

For one, she was holding the warm, callused hand of a real cowboy, instead of a man in a designer tux, wearing his own Spanx (as Colby had). Riggs was dressed in jeans, a shirt with pearl buttons, and a black Stetson. It occurred to her that Riggs would certainly look fine in a tux, too, taking her to any one of the Nashville events she regularly attended.

Now, he was in his element and comfortable. *She* was dressed in jeans and an untucked flannel shirt, wearing her new cowgirl boots with turquoise inlays. No makeup, no hair extensions, no heels. She was beginning to fall into her new normal.

Downtown had been transformed with fairy lights strung from light posts. Everywhere there were tented booths selling everything from lemonade to knit hats made by the ladies of SORROW. But the first thing Winona noticed were the men. Everywhere. Old men. Young men. Big men, medium, small. Short hair, long hair. Dark, blond, redhead. Of course, she spied cute Jeremy Pine, but also Lenny over to the side, making balloons for the children. A group of older men were commandeering a large grill.

Off to the side, a broken-down wheel with a sign read: *Contest! Be the fastest to strap your horse to the buggy!*

Next to it, an old-fashioned broken-down buggy with a horse.

"Um, what's that about?" She pointed.

"Well, our esteemed founder Titus Ridge originally wound up settling here when his carriage broke down on his way to Gold Country."

"Yes, and...?"

"And he just stayed here. Either he was a lazy man, or he saw all the cattle and wild horses roaming free, and must have thought he'd found a different kind of gold. He put down stakes and stayed. Romantic, right?" Riggs winked.

"If you love cows." They passed a booth selling cow-shaped pastries. "Well, uh, that's certainly better than cow patties. I know what those are."

Riggs chuckled. "You know how some towns are known for growing garlic or artichokes? We're known for cattle.

The old-fashioned cattle drive is part of the Founder's Day parade." He glanced at his watch. "It should start soon. C'mon, let's find you a place to sit."

"Riggs! Over here." Eve waved and pointed to a couple of empty seats.

Oh, awkward. Winona didn't move. Riggs led them straight there, then deposited her next to Eve and said he'd be back. Self-conscious, Winona folded her hands in her lap and tried her best to enjoy the beautiful autumn day.

"Congratulations, by the way," Eve said. "Twins. Wow."

"Thank you. It was a nice surprise."

"I know how much you wanted a baby. And I'm glad it worked out with Riggs. He's a good man."

"He is."

"And also, I'm sorry."

Boy, wasn't this the week for apologies she didn't deserve.

"Why would you be sorry?"

"I was mean to you when you got to town. It's just that I…" Eve studied her own hands, flipping them over. Obviously avoiding meeting Winona's eyes. "I was jealous of you and what you'd had with Jackson. You married him. I didn't."

"I'm the one who's sorry. I asked for far too much from an ex-husband. You're the one he loved. Always. He only married me on the rebound. And…because he was drunk. We both were."

"I was his runaway bride, but I did love him. Anyway, we were both too young."

"You'll be married soon, won't you? And bet ya it will last a lot longer than three months." Winona elbowed Eve.

Eve smiled and met Winona's eyes. "And I don't plan to ever let him go again."

"There you go. Where is the silver-tongued devil?"

"He's part of the parade, of course. Beulah asked and he

delivered. Next to you, he's the biggest thing this town ever saw."

"Oh, I'm no big deal. Not anymore."

"Sure you are. Annabeth is still your biggest fan, but I hear she'll have to get in back of Twyla now. And I like your new look. It's very…natural. Real."

In celebrity circles, *real* wasn't said with admiration, but more out of concern.

I'm worried, Winona. You're looking a little...natural these days. Everything okay?

But Winona felt Eve's sincerity. She meant it as a compliment.

"Thank you. Listen. About Jackson, and all that mess. No one believes I'm insecure, because I don't let them see that side of me. But…I am."

"I know."

All I've ever wanted was to be loved for who I am.

Colby didn't.

Jackson didn't.

Sadly, Riggs was the closest she'd ever come to the real deal, and they were in a sham marriage. A marriage of convenience while doing their best to get through the year having hot sex. It was all her fault for trying to rush things before their time. She'd tried to get a child in the same way she'd clawed her way to the top of the music business. But having a baby and achieving career success weren't exactly the same things.

Speaking of Riggs, he appeared at her side with a small box full of food. In the box were French fries, a large pastry in the shape of a cow, a small carton of milk, two Shady Burgers, a milkshake, and two corn dogs.

"Thought you might be hungry."

"Thanks, but what will you have?" Winona deadpanned as she picked up the milkshake.

"The milkshake is for me." He swiped it out of her hand with a sly grin and winked.

That was some smile on her husband's face. It did things to her. Made her heart squishy and soft.

Made her wish for…everything.

Delores waved to them from behind the booth where she was selling some of the cow pastries. Sadie Carver turned in her seat near the front and waved, too. She sat next to Lillian Carver, who simply nodded her approval in their general direction. Winona felt that approval was mostly for Riggs. Many stopped by to offer their congratulations to Riggs, and her, almost as an afterthought. It would seem that she'd married a mini celebrity in Stone Ridge. An interesting and sobering turnabout. She didn't mind a partner being the center of attention for once.

But then the parade began.

It began with cows, all wearing incredible headdresses of flowers and ribbons in bright colors. They were led in a single file with a young boy on each side holding a staff. They were followed by men seated on horses. About five of those.

"See, baby, the cows have *ears*. The bulls have horns." Riggs pointed.

She snorted. "Okay."

Next came the floats. On one of them, four rodeo cowboys, whipping their lassos in the air.

Winona sensed a theme.

"That's Lincoln in the front," Rigg said. "He and Sadie are having a baby about the same time as ours."

Ours. She liked the sound of that. Not "his" and "mine." Ours.

Jackson rolled by on the second float, singing and playing his guitar through a mic and amp. He sang the old classic, "Mammas, Don't Let Your Babies Grow Up to be Cowboys" to cheers and applause. The next float had women decked out in old-fashioned western saloon dresses and parasols. Winona recognized Beulah and the ladies of SORROW.

The last float was Twyla, dressed from head to toe in western wear, including a gray Stetson. She played her guitar and sang "Cowboy Casanova" by Carrie Underwood. Damn, she was good. Great, even. What a set of pipes on that young lady.

But Winona hadn't been asked to sing on one of these floats. Maybe they hadn't been able to put enough floats together at the last minute, but she could have been with Jackson or Twyla. Were people already forgetting that she could sing, too? She told herself that she wouldn't have wanted to do it anyway. In her current condition, all of her show clothes were too tight, and she certainly didn't want to wear the hair extensions and fake lashes.

But it would have been nice to be asked.

She would have said no, but she hadn't even been *asked*. It was like she'd already been forgotten. Gone. Faded to black. A small trickle of dread slid down Winona's back. The old disconcerting sense of being ignored and tossed aside when someone fresh and young arrived. Celebrity came with the caveat that one day you could be adored and the next detested. That had been her life now for the past ten years. After her divorce from Colby, and some of the lies he'd spread about her, her popularity hit an all-time low. Then she'd briefly bounced back by associating herself with young, new up-and-coming artists like Jackson Carver.

When he'd signed on to open for her act a few years ago, it had helped his career. He'd bolstered *her* career by demonstrating she was still relevant among younger people. The record label and Winona's new publicists had then floated a few rumors that they were engaged. That may have been one of the reasons they'd married in Las Vegas on a whim.

Believing their own press. Always a bad idea. She'd always assumed that going back to Nashville was the only answer for her.

Because slinking away quietly was definitely not her style. Once, she'd been asked to judge one of those national singing contests on TV. But Winona always thought her time better spent writing songs and singing. That was her first love. But Jackson, and others, had been grateful in the past for the so-called star power she'd lent to them.

If only performing were something one could do "on the side" instead of committing one-hundred and ten percent. Performing and touring from city to city had been exhausting and took so much out of her. She had to think of her children now.

She might not want that life anymore, but she also couldn't let go of her attachment to the city that had made something out of her. Nashville had taken her in, accepted her, and turned her into a star. She couldn't walk away from all that history because she owed Nashville, and not the other way around.

"Are you okay?" Riggs squeezed her hand. "You're not eating."

"Give me that." Winona pulled the milkshake out of his burly hands and took a big slurp. "For the babies."

He smiled and let her have it. Smart man.

After the parade, people milled around the town square eating and talking. Riggs and Winona were separated when a few of the men grabbed him for some assistance with the cattle.

Annabeth Dantzer, Eve's partner at the vet clinic, found Winona. "Congratulations, I guess."

That seemed rather half-hearted. "Thanks. Now I have an *excuse* for my clothes being too tight. It isn't just the cookies."

"Seriously, though, you are going to keep making music. Right?" Annabeth crossed her arms. "Don't flake out on me."

"Of course. I can't let children stop me. Right? They'll just slow me down a bit."

"Oh, whew. Because I'm getting a little tired of all the syrupy sweet ballads on my Spotify. I need some more of your older angsty stuff. Like the one about your cheatin' ex."

"I'll see what I can do," Winona said, even if she was far from the woman who'd written *that* tune.

Which wasn't a bad thing at all.

"Winona?"

She turned and the tiny voice behind her did not seem to match the powerhouse vocals that Winona heard from the float.

"Hey, there, Twyla. You sounded amazing today, honey."

"Oh my gosh, really? You think so?"

"Of course! And "Cowboy Casanova" was a great choice. I think Carrie would be proud."

"Well, all the songs were supposed to be about cowboys."

"I did notice the theme."

"Honestly? I can't *wait* to get out of this town."

"I felt that way about Oklahoma."

"You won a contest, too, and that started your career."

"It definitely helped. I made a lot of contacts. Would you like to come up sometime and talk shop?"

"Yes! Thank you so much! I didn't really want to bother you. I mean, I know you're busy and all with….um, with the babies." She briefly glanced at Winona's belly, which to be fair was almost nonexistent to anyone else.

Still, Twyla looked a little horrified.

"They're not taking up much of my time at the moment, seeing as they're still baking."

"Sure, but I guess you're going back to Nashville after

they're born? I mean, lots of moms do it all, right? You can always hire a nanny."

Winona swallowed. "Yes, sure. That happens all the time."

She wondered what these folks thought Riggs would do in that case. Stay behind? Come with her to Nashville and be Mr. Mom? She didn't see that happening.

"It would be so great if when I move to Nashville, I already know someone. Not that I would expect you to hang out with me or anything. You have your people, I know. Jackson said I should move there, like he did, but he already had a band. They all went together. Right now, it's just me. And my guitar."

Winona studied young Twyla and the sparkle in her eyes and wondered if at one time she'd looked the same. She didn't think so. To Winona, singing was a way to get out of Oklahoma. Having been raised by her stepfather, she'd no reservations about striking out on her own. She'd been alone since age ten. She could tell it was different for Twyla, who had probably been sheltered all of her life in Stone Ridge.

Winona should tell her to toughen up right quick. That she should be prepared to move to Nashville on her own if required, because she shouldn't ever count on anyone besides herself. A reminder she would also heed.

Riggs was the father of her children, but he didn't love her. She'd have to make her own decisions without relying on him. Without counting on him.

But she could support Twyla and get her strong enough to leave for Nashville on her own.

"Sure, honey. When I get back to Nashville, I'll be sure to introduce you to some people."

CHAPTER 21

*R*iggs drove home wondering where and when things had gone south today. He thought the date had gone well until he overheard Winona make plans to meet Twyla when she got back to Nashville. After the babies were born.

But that had been their plan all along.

You're an idiot. It's going to take more than one great date to keep her here. To convince her she belongs.

But the problem was Riggs didn't know *what* it would take. It might be something he didn't have. In that case he'd be sunk like a rock because he no longer wanted to return to his previous existence BW. Before Winona.

Because after he'd almost lost her, he'd come to a stunning realization. He was in love with Winona James, and the thought pierced him.

It might well be the stupidest thing he'd ever done.

"Why are you so quiet?" Winona asked now.

"Did you have a good time today?" He kept driving, attempting to keep his focus on the road.

"You know I did. If I eat any more, I'll explode."

"I'm not talkin' about the *food*."

"What else is there?" She snorted then elbowed him. "Okay, that was supposed to be a joke. You should be laughing now."

"I noticed what happened when Jackson and Twyla went by on their floats. It doesn't take a genius to see that you miss that. You're jealous."

"That's not true. I just wondered why I hadn't been asked. I would have said no but still. It's nice to be *asked*, Riggs."

"Right. Same way I would have liked to be asked to interview as your personal assistant." He made air quotes. "I wouldn't have done it, but you *could* have asked."

"You're not making any sense. I didn't ask because I *knew* you would say no. I should have asked just so you could refuse me?"

When she put it that way, he had no idea what he was thinking. He had zero experience feeling this way. Out of control. Desperate. Thinking with his heart instead of his head for the first time in his life.

"Guess I'm not making any sense."

"Well, you said it. I didn't. Hey. Just because I offered to help Twyla get to Nashville doesn't mean that I'm not enjoying myself here. And I'll keep doing so. Every night."

She gave him a flirtatious smile that hit him square in the solar plexus.

"Good." At least he had *that* going for him. He kept her satisfied in bed. Yay him. "I don't know how to do this, Winona."

"What do you mean? You're doing fine."

"No, I'm not. You don't get it. I'm not getting my message across."

"You are, loud and clear. We're getting along, for the sake of our children. I appreciate what you're doing. The time is going to pass a lot faster this way, us getting along."

"And then what?"

"Then, we… You said we would get a divorce." Her voice was quiet and so help him, quivering. One quick glance from the road and he caught her staring at her hands.

"Is that what you want?" His own voice sounded thick with something he couldn't even name.

It might be fear.

"Why does it matter anymore? This isn't what I wanted at all, but we agreed. Kimberly and I agreed to your contract. Remember?"

Riggs pulled over on the side of the road. His state of mind was such that he couldn't even focus on the two-lane country road ahead of him. Not much of a challenge on any other given day.

His concentration was shot.

"Why are we pulling over?"

"Look at me."

She turned in her seat, frustration lacing her tone. "I *am* looking at you! I asked why we pulled over. Are you going to tell me?"

"If you shut up, I will." He growled and reached for her hand. "There are some things you need to know about me and my past. My parents thought getting their next high was more important than their own children. From the time I was twelve, I was raising my brothers. Keeping us together, fed, and going to school. Keeping us safe from an unpredictable father who'd just as soon hug us one day, knock us down the next."

He thought his throat might close off and shut off his airway. His breaths were slow and ragged.

"You don't have to—"

"I want to, so you understand me and why I did what I did to you. To us. When Cal and Marge Henderson took us all in, it meant my brothers and I could stay together. They gave us more than a family. A legacy. This land was passed down from generations of Hendersons. I'm now a part of that, even if not by blood. That's why I can't ever leave Stone Ridge, nor would I ever want to."

"I know." She bent her head.

"It's also why it meant so much to me to be able to be a father to my children. I know I shouldn't have pushed you into marrying me. But here's the thing: I don't want a divorce. I want you to stay."

"What did you say?" she whispered after a long beat of silence.

How about that, he'd shocked her. Well, he was about to do a whole lot worse.

"You told me you couldn't get married because you wanted your next marriage to be the last one. *That's* what I want. You're it for me. Everything. I love you, Winona." Now that he'd choked those tough words out, the others were coming a lot faster out of him. Flowing easier. "I love that you're a fighter and I love that you idolized your mother so much you still wear pink to honor her. I love that you go after what you want even when it's crazy. And I know you'll make a great mother to my children. Our children."

"Wh-when?" Her voice sounded shaky, breathless. Soft as a sigh.

"When *what?*"

"When did you fall in love with me?"

He'd spent several nights thinking about this so he had the answer, strange as it might be.

"I thought it was the moment I thought I might lose you to a pissed-off bull. But now that I'm really thinking this over more, I think it was the day I saw you trying to plant a garden wearing yellow waders."

"You're a strange one, Riggs." She smiled at him from under lowered lashes.

"Yup. Well, takes one to know one." He cleared his throat. "I wanted you so much I couldn't see straight. It was easier to stay mad. I didn't avoid *sex*. I avoided commitment. You scared me. I thought my life would never be the same again. And I was right."

She didn't say a word but simply gaped at him, giving him the sense that he was doing this all wrong. But even at his age, this was the first time he'd fallen head over heels like in one of those love songs he hated listening to. Call him a late bloomer but he'd have never thought this kind of intensity was possible for a man who thought with his head instead of his heart.

"You don't have to love me. But I would like you to consider whether you could. Maybe one day. I shouldn't have pushed you into this situation the way I did, and I'm not surprised if you can't love me. At least you don't hate me anymore, and I can work with that."

"When you fell asleep watching me. That's the moment that I started falling in love with you."

It was his turn to be speechless as he simply stared at her. She was beautiful, and she was his. His wife. After all these years, he'd finally found someone who suited him. Someone worth fighting for.

She unbuckled and crawled into his lap.

"I used to sing 'Cross My Heart' when I performed at weddings. And I'd imagine myself waltzing with my handsome husband someday. That's why I was so angry with you. I wanted this to be real."

"I'm sorry I put you through that."

"I've been through a lot worse. Even when you were trying to be mean, you couldn't quite pull it off. After my mother died, my stepfather let his friends try to come after me from the time that I was thirteen. Before long, I knew how to defend myself. So, you married a girl from the trailer park. Does that shock you?"

"I wouldn't have it any other way."

When she removed his hat and threaded her fingers through his hair, he nearly groaned in pleasure.

She pressed her forehead to his. "You sure are a handsome cuss."

He palmed her neck and brought her lips to his to kiss that pouty mouth. Then he went long and deep and ravaged her lips. His hands were under her loose flannel shirt, searching and tweaking her rosy pink nipples. She pushed back and reached to unbuckle his belt. It always felt like the first time with her. He'd never wanted crazy before but when it came to Winona, sign him up.

A knock came at the driver's side door. They'd fogged up the windows like a couple of teenagers.

"Shit fire!"

Winona jumped and probably would have fallen off his lap, had she not been sandwiched between him and the steering wheel. Riggs push the button to roll down the window because he didn't think he had a choice.

It was Lenny, and he wouldn't go away.

"Well, damn, Riggs. I thought you broke down! Here I was, tryin' to do a good deed. And then I happen upon *this*."

"Yeah, I'm sorry. We weren't—"

"Clearly, y'all weren't *thinkin'*. Not much traffic here, granted, but holy biscuit eater, y'all don't want to get caught by the pastor, do ya?"

Riggs was about to remind Lenny that he was a forty-two-year-old grown-ass man who could also fix his *own* damn truck when he realized something far more important.

"We're married."

"That's right." Winona, still in his lap, wrapped her hands around his neck. "And we're newlyweds, very much in love, so that's what happens. We just can't keep our hands off each other. The ride back to the ranch is too long."

Riggs tightened his hold around her and probably smiled like a buffoon. He didn't care.

"Well. Guess it's a free country. Carry on, then."

Lenny wasn't gone long, but back rapping on the window within seconds. "Y'all want me to be the lookout? I could honk my horn if another car's comin'."

"No *thanks*, Lenny."

He waved and was off at last.

"Boy, the people in this town really will do anything for you, won't they?"

"Not just me. For each other. And now that includes you, too." He tugged on her bottom lip with his teeth.

"I love you, Riggs."

"Love you back."

"But...how are we going to do this?" She buried her face in his neck, whispering the words. "I have a career. After the children, I don't think I can completely give that up."

"I wouldn't want you to. That's what you love, and I wouldn't ask you to give it up."

They would figure something out. He had an analytical brain, after all.

Except occasionally and when it came to Winona.

"But I love you also. It won't be easy to just go back on the road the way I used to."

"I don't know how we'll do this, but it's something to think about. We can figure it out. Right now, let me just enjoy that you love me."

FOR THE NEXT TWO MONTHS, Winona grew larger, passed the first trimester, and her life was a constant honeymoon. She was head over heels in love. They'd start and end the day together, usually tangled in each other's arms after a round of sweaty amazing sex. This time, Winona was the one sending uplifting text messages to Kimberly. She might not be getting any of them, but when she did, Winona hoped it would be of some relief.

Good morning! It's a beautiful day in Hill Country.

Can't decide if I should find out the sex of my babies or be surprised. Riggs says up to me, but he wants to be surprised.

It really doesn't smell bad on the ranch, you kind of get used to it.

I baked an apple pie yesterday! Riggs said it was the best he'd ever tasted. He might be lying.

No longer counting days she had left on the ranch, she started to get up at dawn with Riggs, simply to spend more time with him. Later, she took a shower, helped Delores cook, and checked on her garden. She read more baby books, tried her hand at a few songs, and had been mentoring Twyla off and on.

"Delores is going to teach me how to bake peach strudel and Twyla is coming by later," Winona said to Riggs one morning in the kitchen. "I've also got a doctor's appointment in the afternoon."

"Do you want me to take you?"

"I can take her, Riggs," Delores said.

"Nah, I'm fine."

"Seriously, I can knock off early and take you." Riggs finished the rest of his coffee and grabbed his hat. "I don't mind."

"Don't worry, if they take another ultrasound I won't ask if one of them has a pecker."

Riggs winked. "I told ya, you can find out if you want. Just don't tell me about it."

"It's better to be surprised!" Delores said.

"I'll bet neither one of you were the type to sneak an early peek at your Christmas presents." Winona waved them both away dismissively.

She gave Riggs one last kiss and watched from the front facing window as he strode down the porch steps and toward the stables. She enjoyed this view because boy howdy, what a backside her husband had.

"You never used to watch him leave," Delores said when Winona walked back into the kitchen. "Is it possible you're even more in love with him than before?"

"That's *entirely* possible."

"Well, sometimes a baby really does bring two people closer together."

You have no idea how true that is in our case.

They passed the morning peeling and boiling peaches, chatting about the baby, and how they'd have to fix up the spare room Riggs sometimes used as an office.

"Though Sean plans on moving out soon so there'll be plenty of room in this house."

The news rattled Winona. Sean detested her. If he thought she was kicking him out, she'd probably grown horns and a tail in his estimation.

"I didn't know that. Why would he move out? This is his home, too. I don't want to displace him. I—"

"Don't worry, sugar. He and Colton both long had plans to build cabins here for a while. Sean has been working on his cabin off and on and he's up there today. It's just time to spread his wings a little. This is no longer a bachelor pad, after all."

"Maybe we can remodel the house. I'll talk to Kimberly about moving some of my funds around."

"What about your home in Nashville?"

She and Riggs hadn't talked about that much. Mostly, she got the impression that they were both tiptoeing around anything remotely having to do with any more changes other than the ones they were already experiencing. But she'd have to sell her Nashville mansion sooner rather than later. She'd just have Stone Ridge be her home base instead of Nashville. It didn't mean she'd have to give up her career entirely.

Which meant soon she'd have to tell Kimberly.

Never mind the annulment, there would be no divorce, either.

"I'll have to sell. It shouldn't be a problem."

"Or you could keep it, as a vacation house." Delores smiled. "I'd love to visit Nashville."

But her home was worth millions, which would be a nice nest egg for her children. Considering they would also inherit a legacy of rich Texas soil, between her money and the Henderson land, their children would never want for anything.

CHAPTER 22

*T*wyla arrived just as Winona was going through a box of some of her old "show" clothes.

"I wore this to the Grammys one year." Winona held up the glittery gold gown that fit her only weeks ago. "Why don't you try it on?"

"Really? Oh my gosh, what a thrill! I remember seeing you that night, presenting with Tim McGraw."

"He's *wonderful*, so handsome, and very down to earth. A real southern gentleman."

Like Riggs.

That award presentation had been the last year she'd been married to Colby, and he and her publicist had come separately. This was to give Winona the "time and space" to arrive alone, and really shine. She still wondered what they'd been doing instead, though she had a few good ideas. But for the first time, the memory didn't cause her a ripple of pain.

Winona sat on the edge of her bed and watched as Twyla twirled around in the dress.

"You look amazing!" Better than Winona had ever looked

in that dress. "I imagine I'll be handing these down, but some I'll want to keep for memories."

"I'd hang on to *all* of them. Are you kidding me? Besides, I'm sure you'll fit back in your old dress size after the babies are born."

Winona was quiet for a moment. "Well. I'm not going back."

"Wh-what?" Twyla turned, jaw gaping.

"You're going to have to move to Nashville on your own, sweetie, but I'll put you in touch with good people. First Kimberly, my manager, and the person I trust most in the world."

"I thought you'd be going back."

"How would that work? Riggs is not going to move to Nashville."

"Oh. Yeah." Twyla sagged as the knowledge of that truth hit her.

"Besides, I really like it here and my family is going to be my focus from now on. It doesn't mean I'll be completely out of the business, of course. After the twins are older, I can probably still tour occasionally and record a little, but Stone Ridge will be my base."

"So, you're going to be like Garth Brooks."

Winona laughed. "Yes, I'll be *just* like Garth, without the millions of records sold."

They spent time talking about music, Twyla playing her guitar and singing while Winona gave helpful critiques. She had so much she wanted to tell Twyla about the business that she didn't know where to begin. A beautiful girl, she'd be bound to come up with plenty of propositions from less-than-scrupulous players. Winona wished she could accompany her, as a big sister, to guard and protect her.

"Never let anyone take your dignity," Winona said. "And

they *will* try. Just work hard and you'll get to the top eventually. Your time will come. Don't be in a big rush. Okay?"

Advice Winona wished she could go back and give young Winona. That young lady had wanted so much. Too quickly. She'd rarely given herself time to think but just plunged headfirst into everything. Taken risk after risk, blessed that most had worked out in her favor.

"Can I come back soon? Or maybe you could come down to the Shady Grind next time I sing."

"I'd love to drop by sometime. My husband owes me a date night." Winona glanced at the time. "Oh, we lost track of time. I'm late for my doctor's appointment! I've got to go. I'm sorry."

"Can I drive you?"

"No, I've got the truck. Just need to find Riggs's keys." But she dug in the dish by the door and didn't find them.

Delores was also absent, probably off to the big box store in Kerrville since Winona hadn't needed her help this afternoon. Finding Riggs somewhere on the ranch would take her too long.

"If you could give me a lift into town, that'd be great. I don't want to waste any more time looking for the stupid keys."

She grabbed her purse and was out the door within minutes. Thirty more minutes or so later they arrived at the clinic where Trixie, the midwife, was waiting.

"I was about to give up on you," Trixie said. "Come on in."

"I'm so sorry," Winona said and followed into the exam room. "I lost track of time."

Winona set her purse down and glanced in the mirror on her way to climb up on the exam table.

And what she saw there shocked her.

Other than her shower this morning, she'd done nothing to her face. No makeup, her hair gathered in a high ponytail.

She looked like every other married woman in Stone Ridge, having blended in somewhere along the line when she wasn't paying attention. It had all happened so gradually, that she hadn't even noticed her complete transformation. No wonder she was never approached anymore. No one recognized her. She was back to her old self, Winnie Lee Hoyt. But she felt as if she'd slipped into another woman's skin.

She'd always been told by neighbors and family that she favored her mother. But when she left her stepfather's home, it had been without a single photo of Mary Jo. She'd forgotten that she'd often been called the "spittin' image" of her mother. Others had said it was the reason Leroy resented her for the constant reminder of Mary Jo. Winona hadn't purposely wiped her mother away, but Mary Jo's look hadn't fit into her new Nashville world. She hadn't ever been one to dress up and didn't care about clothes. Her beauty was simple and understated.

Oh, my word, I'm turning into my mother.

Fortunately for Winona, this would not be a bad thing.

"Looks good. No ultrasound today," Trixie said, snapping Winona back to the present. "But we can listen to their heartbeats."

"I love listening to their little hearts." The *whoosh-whoosh* sound was comforting, knowing that it indicated beating hearts.

After a few more minutes, Winona dressed and met Twyla in the waiting room, which had filled in the interim. There sat Sadie Carver, looking bright and pretty as usual. She always wore a dress and looked every bit a little boy's first teacher crush.

Winona and Sadie embraced. They kept running into each other at these appointments. Small-town life.

"Sadie, we're ready for you," Trixie said.

Winona turned to Twyla. "Can you take me back to the

ranch? I know it's asking a lot."

"Of course."

Winona bounced down the steps toward the street and saw Kimberly walking toward the clinic.

Kimberly. How about that? Two shocks in the space of thirty minutes.

"Excuse me, miss," Kimberly said and brushed right by Winona on her way up the steps.

"Kimberly!" Winona called out with a laugh.

Kimberly turned back, did a double-take, and her neck swiveled back chicken-style. *"Winona?"*

Winona laughed and went to grab Kimberly in a hug. "I've missed you. What are you doin' here?"

"I was just over at the Grange place. And one of the men there told me you'd probably gone to the clinic." Kimberly continued to stare at Winona. "Wow. You look so...so..."

"Relaxed?"

"Yes, that's just what I was going to say." Kimberly blinked, giving Winona the idea that she was going to say something far different.

Possibly how very "real" Winona looked today.

"You look younger, actually. I almost didn't recognize you."

"Almost? You walked right by me, lady." Winona elbowed her.

She introduced Twyla and Kimberly. "This girl has the most amazing talent. I wanted to put you two in touch. But for now, how about you and I head over to the Shady Grind for a burger?"

"The shady what?" Kimberly wrinkled her nose.

"The only place in town to get a good meal." Winona turned to Twyla. "Honey, I'll get Kim to drive me back. You go on ahead and I'll be in touch."

"Oh, Kim. I've missed you." Winona threaded her arm

through Kimberly's and walked her across the street and down the block to the bar. "How long are you stayin'?"

"Well, um, I'm not sure. I...just didn't quite expect this, you know."

"What? Me, with the 'natural' look?" She held up air quotes. "I get it. Hey, I just had a minor shock myself when I looked in the mirror at the doctor's office. Do you know this is almost exactly how my *mother* looked?"

Inside the Shady Grind, she found the usual lunchtime crowd. There was Lenny sitting at the bar eating with his brother-in-law Brad. Both were volunteer firefighters.

"Hey, Lenny!"

"Hey there, Winona. What's doin'?"

It seemed a lifetime ago that Lenny sat in the living room of her rental while she hid from him in the bedroom. Good times. Jeremy Pine was sitting in a corner booth with a pretty redhead, and Levi was wiping the bar and chatting with Lenny and Brad. Beulah and her husband were sitting at another booth. Everyone waved hello and said "hey" because they all knew each other in one way or another.

"Where do we sit?" Kimberly stood near the entrance.

"Anywhere we want." Winona walked to a booth with a window giving her a street view.

Not that there was much to look at, but occasionally Winona would let her imagination run and picture an old western ghost town. Plus, she wanted to wave to anyone she caught walking down the street.

Winona ordered for both of them, but Kimberly claimed she'd stopped eating red meat.

"I'll have a salad."

"The protein is good for the babies," Winona said, as if she had to excuse going back to her meat-eating roots.

"I remember that." Kimberly smiled, and reached across the booth to pat Winona's hand. "I've been so worried about you. Those text messages… I mean, is that all *real*? You sounded so happy. I'd get them days later, and I was afraid to respond. Was he monitoring your cell?"

Winona laughed. "Monitoring my phone?"

She spied Jackson and Eve coming out of the vet clinic across the street and waved. They waved back, smiling happily.

"I'm glad you're here, Kim. Things have changed."

Kimberly rolled her eyes. "Well, I can see *that.*"

"Oh, that. I stopped wearing makeup when I was crying and throwing up all the time. The hair extensions went next and dressing up in my eight-hundred-dollar designer boots just isn't practical on the ranch. I like being comfortable."

"About that. I'd hoped Riggs would be kind when you were so sick. I remember how insufferable he was when you kept falling asleep during negotiations." Kimberly puckered her lips in a grimace.

Winona *should* have kept in better touch with Kimberly, even by phone, email, or…carrier pigeon. "He's been so good to me."

"*Really?*"

"Yes. He's a good man. You don't know him."

"I know that he made you miserable when he forced you to stay here for the entire pregnancy. He hasn't insisted you…*you* know." She leaned in to whisper. "Consummate the marriage. Because remember, if you don't, it might still be possible to get an annulment."

This would be harder than Winona expected. No wonder, since it had happened so quickly. With Wi-Fi reception so spotty, Winona had eventually stopped texting or even emailing Kimberly. But truthfully, she'd been avoiding this moment because she knew what to expect. Kim had been with her through the contentious divorce with Colby, and then the easier one with Jackson.

She'd once affectionately called Winona a woman "in love with the idea of love."

"No, he didn't insist." Winona studied her nails, in dire need of a manicure. "I pretty much did. That's half the fun of a marriage."

Kimberly didn't look surprised as she picked up her fork. "Oh, honey. I told you that would make it so much more difficult to get an annulment. It might be impossible now."

No time like the present.

"But that's okay. I don't want one. Or a divorce." Then she took a bite of her juicy Shady Burger and dipped a sweet potato fry in ketchup.

Kimberly dropped her fork. "That was the *agreement*. And why would you want to stay married to him, anyway?"

Winona met Kimberly's eyes, enough for her to see and know everything.

"I was afraid of this. I can see I should have come sooner. There are some things you need to know about Riggs. You don't know everything about the man you've obviously fallen in love with so easily."

"I know what you're thinking: there goes Winona, falling in love with love again."

"I never said that!"

"You were right. Maybe I never knew what real love was before this, but now I do. I've gotten to know him. And he's *so* much like me."

"No, he's not like you."

"We're two of a kind in a lot of ways. He had a rough start in life, a foster kid, until he got adopted by the Hendersons."

"Yes, I know *all* about the Hendersons."

"What do you mean?"

"Phil Henderson. He was a first cousin of Cal Henderson's and he didn't take kindly to being cut out of his estate completely."

"I know that man. He came by the house the day a bull was found on our land."

"What?"

"Calm down. Riggs saved me. The thing is, I'm embarrassed to say I didn't realize he was a bull. I thought he was a cow."

Winona went on the explain it all.

"Winona, you could have died!" Kimberly's hand flew up over her mouth.

"No, I don't think so. I would have taken him down."

"A *bull*, Winona? He's not a two-hundred-pound man and I'm guessing you weren't carrying a fireplace poker with you."

"Or a rifle." She shrugged. "I don't know why you're gettin' so upset. You can plainly see that I'm fine and dandy."

Kimberly went narrowed eyes. *"Dandy?* Since when do you say 'dandy'?"

"My mama used to say dandy all the time. It's a *word.*"

"You hardly even look like Winona anymore. And you don't belong here in this small town."

"I think that maybe that I do."

"I see what's happening here. You're acclimating, which is what you do. It's why you're such a survivor. And you've been forced into this unbearable situation."

Unbearable? Hardly. The nights were her favorite time, and now early mornings, too.

"I blame myself," Kimberly continued. "I should have fought harder for you."

"You tried. I don't blame *you* for what happened. It was my stupid fault for thinking that I could ask so much from any man. You were right. If that's all I wanted, I *should* have gone to the sperm bank."

That's not what I wanted.

She'd wanted it all: love, marriage, babies. But getting all

245

she'd ever wanted took a transformation back to who she'd been in the first place. Mary Jo's daughter. Removing the outward armor had been the start. Her heart went next because her husband was a man who loved a woman with more than his body.

"It's just like you to give me a pass. When I got back, I took it upon myself to dig all the dirt up I could on Riggs Henderson."

Winona froze midway to another bite of her burger. *"Why?"*

"Why? Why? Do you remember what he did? I've been working on this all along in my spare time. You shouldn't have to stay here for the *entire* pregnancy. It's a ridiculous requirement and I always intended to fight back on it. You could always come back to Stone Ridge in the last trimester, maybe, while still safe to travel. Then have the baby here, as he wanted. But the man wouldn't give an inch!"

"I don't see why you're still stuck on this." Winona put down her burger, having lost her appetite. "And what dirt?"

"I always wondered why he so easily signed the prenup. Then I found the court documents."

"Court documents?"

"He's been fighting this Henderson cousin for years. He finally won, as you might imagine. No doubt he's long ago become accustomed to winning. Apparently, the cousin had a contract he produced after his brother had died. Well, Riggs shot holes through that contract just as he did with mine. Still, the ranch hasn't exactly done well. He's more of a lawyer than a rancher. Now, there's a corporation that wants to buy their land, and has offered him a substantial amount of money for it. But like so many cattle ranchers, all *he* wants is to hang on to that land."

"The legacy."

"Exactly! Even if the ranch has had some lean years, to say

the least. He's going to have trouble hanging on to it. Without you." Kimberly, who hadn't even taken a bite of her salad, did so now and chewed slowly as if she wanted to give *Winona*, not Winnie Lee, time to digest. "Don't you see? It works best for him to *stay* married to you. That way he can keep the ranch."

"That…no. No. I-I can't believe that."

"I believe he planned to pretend to fall in love with you all along, so that he could talk you into staying with him. Have his child nearby *and* your money, too. You were the best thing to ever happen to him, accidental pregnancy or not."

"No. You don't understand. He'd never do that. Riggs is… He's just too honest. And too proud. He disliked me at first, and I don't blame him. I had no right to ask him to sign away his rights. Are you saying that he'd *stay* married to someone he detested just for the money?"

"Stranger things have happened, and you and I both know it."

But not here. Not Riggs. Not in Stone Ridge where the men took such pride in their honor. Their traditions. Riggs would never hurt her, or *any* woman purposely. He had too much male pride to even admit he might *need* her money, much less find a way to take it.

But why hadn't he told her any of this? She hadn't kept any secrets from him.

The timing was at the least suspect. He'd had such a quick turnaround when he'd confessed that he loved her. She was the one to fall in love easily, and she had, but Riggs definitely didn't seem the type to fall in love quickly.

"H-he said he loves me."

"And in the next breath, did he ask you to stay?"

She didn't want to believe it, but what if this was true? Riggs hadn't even liked her much until shortly after the bull incident. He loved having sex with her, but not much else.

She could say the same thing herself. But she'd grown to appreciate the man who did everything he could to be a good husband even if his heart wasn't in it at the beginning.

Winona trusted Kimberly more than she did anyone else in the world. She doled out the truth, good or bad. Even when Winona didn't want to hear it. As Kim said, it was better to be hurt sooner rather than later.

Colby won't go away until you give him the settlement.

You want him out of your life, don't you?

He doesn't deserve you.

He's only using you.

And Winona's world began to cave in, as she realized that Kimberly could be right.

About everything.

CHAPTER 23

*R*iggs had been in the office for over an hour going over the books looking for funds. The only local dairy farmer in Stone Ridge had not too long ago asked to lease some Henderson land for grazing rights. Riggs didn't have any objection to this, but he'd rather offer his land to a neighbor in need. At this point, however, he'd be the father of two, and he'd have to stop being so generous. There was no way he'd allow Winona to be the sole support of their children, no matter how much money she might have.

Despite a rough couple of years where cattle prices took a nosedive, the Grange had done well, and their bottom line remained newly promising. The prized-bull sperm he'd leased on contract had come through with some promising new heifers. Cattle prices were close to their highest level in over a decade. He could sell now and get ahead.

Exhausted from lack of sleep, he ran a hand down his face and listened again for the sounds of a vehicle coming up the dirt road. Nothing.

He hadn't really been able to think clearly since Sean had informed him that Kimberly was in town. She'd stopped by looking for Winona. Left no message. Nothing. Went looking for her at the clinic, he guessed, and they still weren't back. He told himself they were probably catching up. He heard Delores in the kitchen, unloading from her monthly trip to the big box grocery store in Kerrville. Unable to focus anymore, he got up and joined her, putting away big bags of flour, dry cereal, and cans of soup and tomato sauce.

"Don't worry, she'll be here any minute," Delores said, taking a can from him when he'd been about to put it in the refrigerator.

Damn.

"Worried?" He snorted. "What makes you think I'm *worried?*"

"I'm sure she and her manager are having a late lunch at the Shady Grind and she's showing her around town a bit."

"Yeah, I'm sure."

But Delores wasn't privy to the "contract negotiations" he'd been through with Kimberly. The fact that he'd found holes in her contract the size of Texas had not been appreciated. He'd sensed her embarrassment at having lost the battle but at the time he hadn't thought it would matter. Now it did, because Kimberly was Winona's good friend and confidante, as well as being her manager.

What she had to say about the two of them, and their changing relationship, would matter. Too much.

"Riggs, *honey.* You're not going to lose her or these babies." Delores voice was soft. Kind. "I have a good feeling about this."

"You're right. It's all different this time around."

"How is it different?"

These are my children.

But Delores did not know everything about Jenny, nor did he want to burden her. She had all the information needed: he'd lost a wife and baby in one clean break. At the time, that's certainly how it had felt. He'd carried grief the same as if the child had been his own flesh and blood. Now, he was terrified to lose his wife *and* children.

Because he had everything invested in Winona. His entire heart.

"Winona is very different, for one thing."

"You love her more than you ever loved Jenny, don't you?"

"What makes you say that? Jenny was my best friend."

"I think you're older and you understand more about the nature of love. You aren't as confused as you were then. There are different types of love, and *this* type of love...well, it's overwhelming. I've seen you fighting it since the moment you said, 'I do.' When you give in to what you're feeling, when you realize she's your one and only, it will only get easier."

One and only?

Did he even believe in that sort of thing? It didn't seem logical to his left-brain way of thinking, and yet...

"I don't think anything about this will ever be *easy*." He ran a hand through his hair.

"Well, maybe easy is overrated." Delores chuckled. "Don't hang on to her too tightly. I know you already can't live without her, but you're going to have to trust her. I can see it in the way she looks at you. She's deeply in love and that's not just going to fall away with a few problems here and there."

Ha! A *few* problems here and there. But he'd started their relationship by almost literally pushing her into a corner. Putting on the metaphorical shackles. Punishing her for trying to even suggest he'd give away his baby. He was lucky that she'd forgiven him at all, but had she done so because she wanted the year to pass by easier, or because she'd fallen in love with him? It was his own fault that he had no idea, and no way now he'd ever know for certain.

Until after the children were born, that is. By then, she might as well rip his heart out of his chest by the ventricles.

When he heard the sound of a vehicle, he looked out the kitchen window.

"There she is," Delores said happily.

It was a sedan rental, and as it pulled in front of the house, Winona hopped out. She didn't wait for Kimberly but ran toward the house. The door flew open, but instead of stopping in the kitchen, she kept going down the hallway toward the bedrooms.

Great.

"Fried chicken for dinner!" Delores called out, and then to Riggs, "She probably has to hit the bathroom."

Yeah, well, he didn't think this was about having to empty her bladder. Every well-honed instinct in him went on high alert. He considered running outside to stop Kimberly from leaving and asking her what she'd done or said to Winona. But he'd face his wife instead. She'd tell him everything he had to know.

He watched the rental sedan back out and drive off. "Be right back."

"Take your time and do what you have to do." Delores cupped her ear. "Did I mention I'm a little hard of hearing these days?"

"Uh-huh. Hilarious."

He found Winona sitting on the edge of the bed, facing the door. But she didn't meet his eyes when he walked in and shut it.

"I take it Kimberly didn't want to stay for dinner," he said, heavy on the sarcasm.

"I didn't ask her. She's staying at a hotel in Kerrville."

"How long is she stayin'?"

"I don't know." She did meet his eyes then and after a long beat, spoke. "Riggs. Do you love me?"

"You *know* I do. Why? What did she tell you?"

"It's just that…this wouldn't be the first time a man used me for what he could get out of me."

"What's that supposed to mean?"

"Phil. You had a lot of lawsuits with him over this land. You never told me about any of that."

"Because that doesn't have anything to do with you. With us. It's in the past. He lost. And he never cared about this land. It's all about money to him."

"How am I supposed to believe you? I know that he also had a contract. Did you play target with it, too?"

"It wasn't a *contract.* Phil put together a fake document and forged Cal's and Marge's signatures. He thought he'd get it by me, the estate, and an entire court system. He always thinks he's smarter than everyone else in the room. I'm not that great of a lawyer, no matter what Kimberly thinks. His forged document was useless. Phil had been estranged from the family for years."

"I know it takes a lot of money to keep up with a ranch this size. Kimberly thinks that you had a plan to pretend to fall in love with me all along. So that I would stay. That's *why* you signed a prenup. You never *intended* to divorce me."

Heat and anger pulsed through him at the realization that Kimberly was trying to come between him and Winona. Just as he'd suspected. He wouldn't mind being wrong every once in a while, when it came to stuff like this. But people rarely surprised him.

"She's wrong. Whatever she's filling your head with, don't listen to it."

"You would say that! But Kimberly is the one person I trust most in the world. She would never steer me wrong."

With that, she went right by him and out of the room toward the front door.

Wait. Was she leaving him?

For now, he would ignore the poison dagger she'd just thrown at his chest with amazing precision. *Kimberly* was the person she trusted most.

Riggs followed Winona, stopping to see Delores in the kitchen first. "This is going to take longer than I thought."

He found Winona in her garden. She was going at weeds with a hoe, getting all her frustrations out on the red dirt.

"*She's* the person you trust the most? It should be your husband. We're in this together, you and me. We're a family."

She stopped hoeing long enough to glare at him. "Kimberly has always tried to protect me from men who want to take advantage. Who want either my fame or my money. Not *me*."

Riggs took the hoe from her and threw it to the side, earning him a death-stare. Too bad, he needed her undivided attention.

"Why is it so hard for her to believe that someone could want you for who you are? I don't want your stinking money, Winona. All I wanted from you was our child. And now, I want you, too. Because I fell in love."

He wanted to touch her, pull her into his arms and kiss her till she forgot they'd been having an argument, but held himself back.

They had to get through this and if she didn't trust him, well, he couldn't blame it *all* on Kimberly.

She crossed her arms. "If we weren't married, would you have to sell some of your land off?"

"I never have had to consider that and never will. Granted, I'd probably be a multimillionaire if I sold. But I intend to pull my half when it comes to the children. You're not going to be the sole provider."

"What are you going to do? Kimberly told me that your ranch has struggled for years."

"Did she." He cleared his throat and took her hand. With

one finger, he stroked her palm. "That's probably because she can't put it into perspective. Most folks don't understand ranch life. We had lean years but we're doing fine now. And because I want to contribute more for our children, I decided that I'm going to lease some of our land to the local dairy farmer. Normally, I would give him grazing rights for free because that's what we do around here for neighbors. But I have to think about my family."

Her lower lip trembled. "I want to believe you love me like you loved Jenny."

"No, I can't. That's entirely different."

He heard her breath hitch and in that moment, he realized that *Winona* felt vulnerable. Even before learning about Phil and how he'd tried to take this land.

Maybe even threatened by the memory of the so-called perfect wife. Jenny. And after all, how could she ever compete with a ghost? She might believe that he'd idealized Jenny because she'd been gone so many years.

She had no idea how wrong she was. No one else had ever or would ever be in competition with Winona. Not with Winnie Lee Hoyt, the real Winona, a woman he loved with his whole heart.

"Sometimes I'm an idiot." He brought her hand to his lips. "Seriously, woman, I'm forty-two and you make me feel like a teenager with his first crush. It isn't the same because I wasn't in love with *her*. There's a reason I keep saying she was my best friend. It was a different kind of love, baby. A different kind of closeness. Not like with you. I'm not sure that I've ever felt this way before. I didn't know that I could. This is new to me even if I've been around for over four decades. I never thought I'd be committed to anyone again and then I saw you for the first time."

She started to smile, but a hesitancy in her eyes nearly broke his heart.

"Don't you believe anyone could love you and *only* you? Because I do."

"I want to believe but I've heard it all before. Those are the words a woman likes to hear. How am I ever supposed to know for sure?" A single tear rolled down her cheek.

"Because they're not just words to me."

He'd always been a man of action.

Show, don't tell.

Taking her hand, he pulled her up the steps and back into the house. Riggs led Winona to the office, opened the door, and dug through the desk drawer for the manila envelope. Removing the contents, he tore their contract in half from top to bottom. She could walk away now, take his children with her. Take his heart. Take everything. This was a risk, possibly greater than any he'd ever taken.

He'd have to trust and there was nothing tougher for him than leaving his future in someone else's hands.

"Our agreement is over. You stay with me only if you want to stay. Love me only if you do."

CHAPTER 24

$\mathcal{W}$inona stared at the ripped agreement. It felt like forever since they'd entered this marriage of convenience for the sake of their baby. Now, they were having two babies, and she couldn't imagine walking out that door and leaving Riggs behind. Never. But he'd torn up their contract and he wasn't lording anything over her anymore. Even if he'd "won" he didn't care anymore. Their marriage, their agreement, had to be her *choice*.

She could walk away now without repercussions.

But she still couldn't leave him. This experience had changed her, for better or for worse. And he was right. She had to *trust* him, despite how they'd wound up here. Despite their less-than-traditional beginning. Because every little thing had changed. She'd always trusted Kimberly and her advice. But she couldn't know it all. And this time, she was wrong. Winona knew it with every single beat of her heart.

Because she finally trusted the person she should have trusted all along. Herself.

"Thank you." She stood and took a step toward him. "I

love you, Riggs. I will always love you. You gave me everything. Even gave me back myself."

"No, baby, you did that." His warm hands curled around
her waist. "You remembered who you are. Mary Jo's daughter, Pink."

She smiled at the memory, personal and intimate.

"I couldn't have done it without you. I'm not going
anywhere, husband. You are stuck with me for life."

"I've never been happier to be stuck." He bent to kiss her
on the lips, a tender caress that wound its way deep inside
her heart.

That same heart that she hadn't believed had room left
for anyone but her babies. She'd made a lot of mistakes in the
past while she desperately searched to regain the sense of
family she'd once felt. Looking for someone to love her.
Someone to be her family. This time she hadn't even been
trying to find forever and she'd found the one man with
whom she wanted to spend the rest of her life.

And even though the fried chicken smelled deliciously
enticing and she *was* constantly hungry these days, she led
him back to their bedroom.

"Lock the door."

She didn't want to think about anyone or anything else
for the next couple of hours. She wanted to give herself to
Riggs, every last piece that she'd held back out of fear. A fear
that he'd change his mind about loving her. A baseless but
terrible fear that once the babies were born, he'd realize that
she wasn't such a great mother and try to take them away.
Gone now. She'd pushed those terrors away.

Slowly, she unbuttoned her shirt and then pulled off the
tank top she wore underneath. Next her jeans. Each piece of
clothing felt like another layer of skin she removed. She was
tough and didn't fold easily when trapped in a corner. But
Riggs was unlike any man she'd ever met. He didn't back

away or give up easily, either. And he wouldn't give up on her.

He licked his lips when she unclasped her bra and slipped off her panties. Then he swept her up in his arms like he'd done their very first night, touching and tasting.

He carried her to bed. A sense of desperation clawed at her heart with a wonderful intense desire. A magnetic heat and passion she sensed would never wane.

This was everything.

Afterwards, they lay sated and entwined, his head resting on her belly while she played with that wonderful head of thick hair.

"I hope they have hair like yours." She ruffled his hair and a moment later her thoughts went to where they were so often lately. "I know I say this all the time, but I'm hungry."

"Do you want me to go get you some fried chicken and bring it to bed like that other time?"

"You didn't get *me* fried chicken, you got yourself some, and fell asleep watching me."

He rose above her, arms braced on either side of her body, wearing a full smile and nothing else. "That's what I let you think."

"Sure." She swatted him playfully on the butt. "Okay, go get your fat wife some fried chicken."

"Don't forget old." He winked.

"I don't feel old at all anymore." She stretched like a cat under him. "I feel young and restless."

"And knocked up." He rolled out of bed and pulled on a pair of jeans commando. "Be right back."

She went up on one elbow and watched him walk out the door. Her cowboy, her man.

For once, having it all wasn't a lie.

. . .

When Riggs emerged from the bedroom, the sun had set. In the kitchen, he found two place settings by candlelight, rolls, mashed potatoes, and a plate of fried chicken in the middle of it all.

He was going to give Delores a raise. And also thank her for having such faith in him. For a moment, *he* wasn't so certain he'd be able to reassure Winona. To keep her. But if she wanted a grand gesture, he hoped that torn contract would do. Maybe he'd have it framed someday.

Riggs decided it would be easier just to pick up the whole spread of food and take it with him into the bedroom. He blew out the candles, grabbed a couple of water bottles from the refrigerator, and at that moment a streak of brown outside caught his eye.

What in the...? He looked closer from the window. Spur had somehow gone loose from the stables. Riggs pulled on a nearby jacket from the coatrack. He tugged on a pair of boots in the mud room, briefly considered taking his rifle, but instead just headed outside.

And found Spur chewing on Winona's vegetable garden. Great.

"Oh, she's going to love you for that." Grabbing him by the bridle, Riggs walked him back toward the stables. "How did you get out, anyway?"

It could have been Sean but he was never this careless when it came to the horses. What he saw when he came around to the stables sent a chill straight through him. Every single horse had been let out of the stables. In the distance, he saw flashes of white and brown roaming freely through the pastures.

"Shit fire!"

"Imagine how I feel," came a voice from a dark corner of the stable.

Riggs's head jerked in that direction. Phil Henderson walked out of the darkness, pointing a handgun.

Riggs immediately began to list his regrets. He should have realized sooner that Phil had become desperate. *Never be a sore winner*, one of his law professors had advised. Riggs took for granted that he was safe in this town, where they all had each other's backs. All the men were like his brothers. Which meant he should have shared more of his concerns about Phil. He should have asked for more help.

And he should have brought that rifle with him.

Riggs held up his palms. "Put the gun down, Phil. Let's talk."

"I'm done talkin'! Damn you and your fancy law degree. Always thought you were better than me. Better than anyone. I should have had this land. I'm a Henderson by blood, not you and your brothers."

He had to keep Phil talking. As Riggs tried to figure out a way out of this mess, he would commiserate. Hell, he'd even promise to sell. Anything to get that gun off him. Because even if he'd grown up with biological parents who brought home unsavory, gun-toting characters from time to time, he'd never been as terrified as in this moment. He had a wife inside waiting for him. If she walked out and found him and Phil here, *she* could get hurt. He prayed she'd fall asleep waiting for him.

"Yeah, I get it. It was unfair."

"You don't know the half of it. Cal was another one who always thought he was better than me. Do-gooder, trying to help all those foster kids over the years. Never shared a damn thing with me, though. And then he *adopted* you boys. If you think that makes you a Henderson, you'll always be wrong."

"I know it doesn't. I'll never be a Henderson, Phil." Riggs slowly lowered his hands as he spied the shovel only a foot away from him.

Just a little room. A slight diversion and he'd knock him out with that shovel.

In order to talk a madman down, give him what he wants.

Truthfully, Riggs wondered why he'd tried for so long to distance himself from his biological family. From his humble beginnings which had made him the man he was today. Maybe he should have accepted all along that he wasn't a Henderson, and that was fine. It didn't mean he'd loved Cal and Marge any less for everything they had given him. But he was a scrapper down deep just like Winona. Cal and Marge had been decent people who would have never hurt anyone. They'd encouraged him to go to law school so he could fight with his brain and the law when his first inclination had always been to fight with his fists.

But whether or not Cal and Marge would approve, Riggs would kill this man with his bare hands if that's what it took to protect his family.

He was a survivor.

"You finally admit it. Where's your lovely wife, anyway? I'd love her to hear this." He waved his gun. "I want her to know how you weaseled your way into Cal and Marge's life, just so you could get this land."

"She's not here," Riggs lied. "She had to go see her manager in Kerrville."

"Just my luck. I wanted this to be nice and dramatic, with the terrified multimillionaire at gunpoint. She's an entitled celebrity bitch."

Riggs's jaw went tight as granite, but he nodded in agreement. Snorted. "Tell me about it."

"Regret marrying her already, huh?" Phil sneered.

"Yeah. She doesn't want me to keep this land." Riggs shook his head, defeated. "I think you were right all along. We should sell. I don't know the first thing about cattle."

And now he'd gone too far. He sensed with deep regret that the jig was up. Phil narrowed his eyes. He didn't buy it.

"I don't believe you." He pointed the gun at Riggs and took a step closer. "You're just tellin' me what I want to hear right now."

All Riggs had to do was reach for that shovel or allow Phil to get close enough to punch him. Right now, he seemed to enjoy keeping a reasonable distance.

"This isn't smart," Riggs said. "You're not going to get what you want out of this."

"I already have what I want. Seein' a terrified look in your arrogant eyes. You feel helpless, don't ya? Trapped? Now you know how I feel!" he roared. "You just had to take away the last chance I had of making a buck off this land. You should have never called those people, and left well enough alone. You have no proof I let that bull loose. Whatever happened to innocent until proven guilty?"

Riggs heard the sound of a rifle being cocked and turned to see his greatest fear materialized.

"Mister, if you want to keep that gun you had better stop pointing it at my husband." Winona stood at the front of the stables, aiming that rifle as if she knew what she was doing.

Riggs didn't know whether she did or not, but either way he broke out in a cold sweat.

"Well, well. If it isn't the beautiful celebrity come to save her husband."

"Phil, put the gun down. You don't know what she's capable of."

I don't even know.

"Listen to him. My stepfather wasn't good for much, but he did teach me how to hit a target. And I can hit a copperhead at twenty feet. Don't make me prove it." Winona spoke slowly, that rifle set on her shoulder as she aimed at Phil.

He'd learned a few things about the woman who was now his wife. She rarely backed down. Riggs reacted with what he now believed his only real option. It might not be the most intelligent thing to do, but he was a smart man caught in an impossible situation. He was back down to his roots in a trailer park where he would protect his brothers or die in the effort.

"Winona, get out of here!" Riggs yelled.

"I'm not leaving you."

Of course, she wouldn't listen to him. Why start now? She mistakenly thought she would save him from this crazy man. Riggs would have been willing to talk all night just to keep Winona away from this. But now she'd inserted herself right in the middle of danger. Enough. Riggs made an executive decision. Reaching for the shovel when Phil briefly glanced in Winona's direction, he swung the short distance between them, and knocked the older man out cold.

Riggs watched Phil fall back, and the gun went off, the blast splitting the quiet night.

Winona didn't make much of a sound as she slid to the floor.

No, no, no, no! Cursing, Riggs went to her. Thank God, her eyes were wide open.

"Damn that old man." She held her left shoulder, blood oozing through her nightgown. "He *shot* me."

"It's okay, it's okay, you're going to be okay."

Riggs just said this over and over as he tore off his jacket and stanched her blood. He told himself it wasn't bad, that it just couldn't be. It had just been a surface hit, that's all, but there was *so much* blood. His mind had trouble accepting the situation. Everything around him turned to muted shades of gray.

Panic. Sheer unbridled panic rose in him like bile. This couldn't be happening. He wouldn't survive losing *her*. He didn't know how long Sean had been shouting when Riggs finally heard him.

"What the hell *happened here?*"

Sean stood at the opening of the stable, his shotgun poised. The sound of the shot would have sent him running.

"Is that...Phil?" Sean moved to the old man's side and poked him with his boot. He bent to check his pulse. "Out cold."

"He had a gun on me, and Winona pulled the rifle on him. She was trying to help me."

"You have got to be kidding me." Sean quirked an eyebrow and then bent beside Riggs. "Damn it, Winona."

Delores showed up and he couldn't help but wish that she could fix this. She wanted to. It was in her eyes, the look he would have paid a million dollars never to see again. Pity. Shock.

This couldn't be happening to him again. Who would be *this* unlucky?

"Oh, Riggs!" she covered her mouth. "No. *No.*"

"Help me," he said, and gathered Winona in his arms. "Get my keys. I'm driving her to get help. I won't sit here and wait for anyone."

"I'm okay," Winona said, but she sounded weaker. "I did a stupid thing."

"Please don't talk," Riggs said. "You're losing too much blood."

"I'm sorry. I didn't listen to you."

"That's okay."

"My babies. I don't want to lose the babies."

I don't want to lose you.

I can't. I won't.

Delores returned with his keys. "Take her to the clinic. I called Dr. Grant and alerted the phone tree."

But Riggs didn't want to take her to the local clinic. He

wanted a first-rate hospital with cutting-edge equipment, but he also needed the bleeding to stop. Immediately. Kerrville would take too long and surely the GP in Stone Ridge could handle stitches. He could hope it would be that simple.

"You drive." Riggs threw his keys to Delores.

He grabbed the first aid kit he kept in the truck. Meant for minor cuts and injuries while hunting or fishing, it wouldn't do much for a bullet wound, but he had to do *something*. He couldn't just helplessly watch her continue to lose blood. With Winona spread over his lap, he ripped off a piece of rolled gauze with his teeth and used it to tape the wound.

He told himself it wasn't bad, but a gunshot wound was still a damn gunshot wound.

Winona moaned. "I'm already a bad mother. I should have thought of our children."

"You were thinking about me." He ripped off another piece of gauze. "Total badass. I would marry you all over again."

"I should have shot him," Winona said. "I swear I could have had him. He was in my scope. Must be gettin' soft in my old age."

"Stop talkin' about being old before I spank you."

She smiled and her eyes fluttered closed. "I don't even know if you realize how cute you are."

"Delores, can't you drive any faster?" Riggs shouted.

"I love you," Winona said weakly. "Don't forget it."

And then, because he didn't know what else to do, Riggs put his palm on her shoulder to apply pressure.

He held her against him while he told her he loved her over and over again.

CHAPTER 25

*W*inona was dreaming of her mother again.

Dancing around the kitchen to "Sweet Home Alabama," Mama swung a pretty dress in the air.

"Look what I bought you." The dress was Easter egg–blue for a change. "You're the best girl in the whole wide world. I love you so much. You're going to have to be strong for me. Just one last time. It's really important. Okay?"

"Sure, Mama. I can do it. What do I have to do?"

Live.

Winona woke with a startle, gasping for breath. But breathing, it turned out, wasn't the problem. That honor would go to the ripping pain in her shoulder, like someone had tried to tear off her arm at the joint.

And all because she'd hesitated. She'd had that madman in her scope, and he'd be the one bleeding right now if only she hadn't waited.

"Riggs," she spoke through the haze of pain.

"I'm right here, baby."

"Don't leave me. I'm scared."

"I won't ever leave you."

His large callused hand pressed on her shoulder, causing pain, but also felt like he was holding her together. And good thing because she needed someone to piece her back together right now. While Riggs pressed down on her shoulder, she pressed on her belly, keeping them inside. She'd rather die than lose her children. Maybe she could manage to hold them, but a shock like this could very well bring on a miscarriage. There would be no saving her twins, even with all the advanced medical equipment in the country.

When Riggs hadn't returned to her in the bedroom after several minutes, she'd called out to him. No response, and also no sounds of him rattling around in the kitchen. She'd thrown some clothes on and went to the kitchen. Not only was he not there any longer, the refrigerator door had been left open. The spread of food still sat on the table. Curiosity more than fear seized her. Because she'd grown up in Welch, Oklahoma, she grabbed the shotgun by the door before walking outside.

Winona was more afraid of copperheads than she was of cattle. Snakes would lie low and strike when you least expected it. She'd learned how to shoot because Leroy didn't know what else to do with her after Mama died. So, he'd taught her how to shoot cans and, later, rattlesnakes. And she was ready to take down that awful man rather than watch him shoot her husband.

But she'd hesitated.

While Phil's attention had been briefly on Winona, Riggs was the one to take action and knock Phil out with a shovel. And Winona had thought: *that's it. Over. Thank the Lord.* Until she'd heard the shot ring out that somehow made its way to her. She hadn't even realized she'd been hit until she slid to the ground, a burst of red on her nightgown. What were the odds? A few inches higher and it could have missed her. Then again, the odds of an orphan from Oklahoma making the big time had also been long. She'd always believed that much of her success had been tied purely to good luck.

And she'd had about as many blessings in the music industry as lack of them in romance. Then, she'd gotten herself knocked up quite by accident by the best man she'd ever met. It worked out that he was everything she'd ever wanted. Smart as a whip and educated. Kind and compassionate. Handsome as all get-out. Now, she was in love with him to boot, topping off the cherry on this salted caramel sundae.

So, maybe her many blessings had officially run out.

Maybe she'd been greedy. Asking to be someone's mother had been asking for a little too much.

"We're here," Delores said, shutting off the truck. "Everyone's already here."

"Everyone?" Winona murmured.

She hoped that didn't mean press or media. She'd been lying low for months and this wasn't the kind of news she'd liked leaked.

But Delores meant something else by "everyone." Winona saw that when Riggs hauled her out of the truck and carried her inside the doors of the clinic. Past sunset, the town had closed up for the night, but there were trucks everywhere outside the clinic parking lot. She recognized Lincoln, Jackson, Lenny, and a bunch of other men with them.

"What are all these people doing here?" Winona asked.

"They want to help," Delores said. "Before we left, I alerted the phone tree. Beau Stephens went to the Grange to help Sean. The County Sheriff's deputy is on the way but that could take a while. They'll hold him there."

"Don't worry," Riggs growled. "He's *not* gettin' away with this."

"Right this way into the exam room," a man indicated.

She assumed this man had to be Dr. Judson Grant, the

one who'd started the clinic in town. Lord, he looked so *young*. How much experience could he realistically have? The midwife, Trixie, followed all three of them in as Riggs gently laid her down on the bed in the birthing room.

"I don't want to be in this room," she wailed. "It's not time yet."

"You'll be more comfortable in here," Trixie said. "Don't worry about the babies right now."

"She has a gunshot wound," Riggs said. "It was a 9-millimeter handgun."

"You know your guns," Dr. Grant said.

"I hope you do, too," Riggs said, stealing Winona's thoughts.

She squeezed his hand. His dark leather jacket was stained with her blood and he hadn't let go of her since he picked her up off the floor of the stables.

The doctor put on plastic gloves. "Not that I ever expected to use any of this in Stone Ridge, but I did a trauma rotation in Los Angeles during my internship. I have definitely dealt with my share of gunshot wounds."

"I don't want to lose my babies," Winona said, biting her lower lip against the pain. "Don't do anything that could hurt my babies."

"I was going to suggest a little Lidocaine to numb the area," Dr. Grant said, looking to Trixie. "Looks like I might have some stitching to do. I'm afraid if we need more than cleaning and stitching, we're going to have to transfer to Kerrville."

"Riggs, if you'll just step outside, I'll assist Dr. Grant."

"No!" Winona cried, grabbing his wrist.

"She needs me."

"Alright," Dr. Grant said. "But *I'm* going to need you to let go of her hand and let me work."

"I'm not going anywhere." Riggs let go of Winona's hand and stepped back.

Winona sobbed when Dr. Grant peeled off the gauze and went to cleaning the wound. The pain was unlike any she'd experienced, counting the time she'd fallen off a stage in Albuquerque, drunk off her ass. Back then, the alcohol had dulled the pain.

Under the bright lights of the birthing room, Winona closed her eyes and pictured her smiling babies.

Two identical sons, both the image of their father.

RIGGS WISHED he could be anywhere but in this room utterly helpless as the doctor and Trixie worked on Winona. He knew he should be grateful because in any other hospital they'd have shoved him out without asking any questions. Busy and focused, Dr. Grant seemed to barely tolerate Riggs's presence, but the man was too polite to put him in his place.

Outside, he heard others assembling to help. Someone would be tasked to get some clothes for Winona and Riggs, in case they would need to go on to Kerrville. He should be out there, too, directing them. It was what he did. Lead and organize the men. There were things to be done, he was sure, but he couldn't really think of anything right now. He needed a clear head.

Someone should probably call Kimberly.

After a while, Winona had stopped whimpering and Riggs figured she'd probably passed out from the pain. He tried not to listen to the doctor and midwife as they worked.

Blood loss.

Check for signs of fetal distress.

He didn't want to lose the babies, either, but Winona was more important. The irony of that was not lost on him. Such a short time ago, his main concern had only been for his child. For protecting him or her from a selfish mother. He hadn't wanted to be cut out of his child's life like nothing more than a sperm donor. The *child* had been his entire focus. But the pendulum had swung heavily and if he lost Winona, he'd lose everything that mattered to him.

His entire future.

"She wouldn't take anything for the pain. I think she's worn herself out," the midwife turned to say. "That's why she's sleeping. Her vitals are stable."

"What about the babies?" he asked.

"I'll do a quick check but there are no signs of distress."

And then the words he didn't even want to voice, "Is she going to be okay?"

Dr. Grant turned to face him. "Yes, she's going to be just fine. It was mostly tearing of skin which is never fatal but definitely bleeds a great deal. I've cleaned and dressed the wound."

Riggs nodded. "Can I use your phone? I need to make a call."

Dr. Grant led him to the landline and Riggs dialed Kimberly's cell phone. He'd had it practically memorized during all the negotiations they'd had a few short weeks ago. At the time he remembered thinking Kimberly was the reasonable one. She had the law degree and he'd preferred to deal with her. For him, at the time Winona had simply been the painful realization that he didn't have the control over his emotions like he'd always believed. She'd pushed him to his limits.

"Kimberly, it's Riggs Henderson." He spoke into the phone. "You should know that Winona's been hurt. But she's okay."

After giving her the directions on how to get to the clinic, he hung up and went to the waiting room. It was filled to capacity. Nearly everyone he knew was seated in a chair, wearing creased brows and tight lips. Sadie and Lincoln; Eve and Jackson; Hank, Lincoln and Jackson's father, and Brenda, Eve's mother; Lenny, Jeremy, Levi, Jolette Marie. Beulah and Lloyd Hayes. Twyla, of course. Mrs. Carver, sitting with Delores, holding her hand.

"Is she okay?" Delores stood.

"Yeah, she's fine." He felt ready to collapse himself, but there were things to do. Phil, for instance. He was going to pay for this and pay dearly. "What about Phil?"

"No one's heard yet." Lincoln stood. "But you know it takes the Sheriff a while to get out here."

"Eve and I will head back to the Grange and find out for you," Jackson offered. "And we'll get you and Winona a change of clothes. You probably want to stay here tonight with her."

"Yeah, thanks. I'm not going anywhere." He clapped Jackson on the back as he and Eve walked by on their way out. "I feel like I should do something."

"Your job is to stay here with her," Delores said.

Jolette Marie came to his side. "What can I do, Riggs? How can I help?"

"I don't know, Jo." He dragged a hand through his hair. "I can barely think right now. Her manager is heading on over here now and she'll probably have stuff for us all to do."

"That's true. Winona is a public figure, and this will get out."

"I'm not sure there's much we can do about that."

He knew that in this room everyone would respect their privacy as they had all along. No phone camera at the ready trying to film something to post to social media. No one waiting to go viral. There were some advantages to poor Wi-Fi. But the crime, and Phil's arrest, would be public record. If Winona still had any plans to return to her career after the children were born, this could put a dent in them. He imagined Kimberly would want to do some damage control.

"Riggs," Dr. Grant said as he walked out and scanned the crowd. "Oh, hello, everyone. The last time I saw this many people in our waiting room was our grand opening."

"Now, don't take offense, Judson," Mrs. Carver said. "I'm very healthy or I would stop by more often."

"No offense taken." Dr. Grant mopped his brow. "And please, people, no more gunshot wounds. I may have to start taking blood pressure meds after tonight."

"We do like to entertain you, doctor," said Delores.

The doctor turned to him. "I would prefer if she took a ride into the Kerrville Hospital to spend the night. Out of an overabundance of caution."

"Great!" Lenny stood. "I'll go get the Hummer. I've been dying to drive that baby."

"Is she awake yet?" Riggs asked.

"Yes, and she's asking for you."

"Well, why didn't you say so, man." Riggs rushed to the room.

Winona was awake, propped up on pillows, her shoulder bandaged. She gave him a weak smile. "There's my handsome husband."

"You're okay." He came to her side, took the seat next to the bed, and held her hand.

Winona seemed relaxed. "We just heard their heartbeats. They're fine in there."

"A couple of real badasses just like their mother."

"And their father."

He hooked his thumb toward the waiting room. "You should see how many people are out there. For you."

"For *us*."

"Everyone loves you. They may not have understood you at first, but you're one of us now." He took her hand. "I phoned Kimberly and told her what happened. She's on her way. Figured she'd want to see you, and you might want to see her, too."

"Oh, gosh. Kimberly." Winona covered her face. "She's going to kill me."

"You mean when she finds out that you pulled a shotgun on a crazy man?"

"Um, yes." She lowered her hand and looked sheepish.

He winced. "Probably not the image you want to project to your fans?"

"Kimberly won't think so. But my fans will understand. I did what I had to do."

"I wasn't happy with you, either, but your heart is always in the right place." He brushed a kiss across her knuckles. "For a minute there, I worried I might lose you."

"I'm sorry." She cupped his jaw. "First the bull, and now this. I bet I've given you another gray hair."

"Never a dull moment around you."

He climbed on the bed, gathered her into his arms, and before long, they were both fast asleep.

CHAPTER 26

"*W*here is she?"

The piercing sounds of Kimberly's voice woke Winona out of her cozy nap. They also woke Riggs, who grumbled and shifted his weight on the twin bed obviously meant for one.

Kimberly's face appeared in the doorway, face ashen, eyes wide.

"Hey, there. Calm down, I'm fine."

"Fine? Fine? Oh, good, you're fine! My God, is that…" She slumped on the chair. "Blood?"

"Need me to get the doctor for you, Kim?" Riggs asked, carefully disentangling himself. "I'll be back."

Before he shut the door, he gave her a sly wink. For the love of Twinkies, she was so in love with this man she could hardly breathe.

"I'm sorry to scare you, but really, I'm fine. It's a flesh gunshot wound. An evulsion or some such thing. They bleed a lot but are never fatal."

"Gunshot wound…tend to bleed a lot. Are you hearing yourself?" Kimberly looked horrified and hooked her finger in the direction of the waiting room. "Everyone out there is acting like you're the second coming of Annie Oakley."

Winona chuckled. "Hardly. I should have had him, though. I lost my focus. He was in my scope and a hell of a lot bigger than a copperhead."

"A copperhead. In. Your. Scope." Kimberly spoke as if repeating foreign words in another language.

"Yes, the shotgun scope."

"You mean it's all true? No small-town exaggeration or colloquialism? You pointed a *shotgun* at a man?"

"I had no choice. He pulled a gun on Riggs."

Kimberly closed her eyes, and pinched the bridge of her nose, but didn't say another word.

"Wondering what to say in the press release?"

"Among other things."

"Make something up. No one here is going to say otherwise."

"Let me see if I understand this. After our talk, you went home and fended off an intruder. And here I thought you were going to tell Riggs that you know all about the lawsuits. I thought you were going to tell him that it's over and you won't be fooled any longer."

Winona took a deep breath. "I have to apologize to you."

"No, you don't! You've just been shot for the love of Pete. And all because I let you go with this man. I don't even *recognize* you anymore. I should have never allowed you into this travesty of a marriage!"

"No, listen. Please. You're not the one who made that decision. You're not responsible for me, Kim. You've been such a good friend, not just a business partner. You took care of me. But somewhere along the line, I relied on you too much. It got to where I trusted myself so little with men, with everything, that I let you make some important decisions for me. I gave up on love. You decided when I should divorce Colby *and* Jackson. You worked all that out for me."

"And I was happy to do it. Honey, men have always taken advantage of you."

"Not all men. Not Jackson. And certainly not Riggs."

"You still believe that?"

"He's not *that* good of an actor. You should have seen the look on his face when he saw I'd been shot. He was terrified. And he hasn't let go of me since he carried me in here."

"He *should* feel guilty."

"Maybe there's some guilt, but it's a lot more than that. Believe me, I know what it was like when he didn't like me very much, and I know what it's like now. You need to trust me like I trust myself. You weren't here with us so you can't know what we've been through. I'm sorry I relied on you so much for all these years. I don't expect you to understand this but...I belong here in Stone Ridge."

"What about Nashville?"

"I might go back someday but not for a while. It's time for me to think about myself and what I want. And I want to be a wife, a mother, and nothing else for a while."

"Well, I certainly was right about one thing. I said he'd get to know you, and then grow to like you. Didn't I? But it's a lot more than that, isn't it?"

"Yes."

"Winona, it's an awfully big risk."

"Maybe, but it's mine to take and I've never felt surer about anything in my life. This isn't me just jumping in and hoping for the best. I know him, and I know me. I've never loved anyone like this before."

"I guess that's something."

"No. It's everything."

A few minutes later, Jackson and Eve returned from the house with a change of clothes for both Winona and Riggs.

"As we were leaving, the deputy sheriff arrived. Phil was awake, and claimed he'd been assaulted. I'm sure you'll have to get your stories straight at some point," Jackson said with an eye roll.

"Expect we will," Riggs said.

"Y'all ready to ride to Kerrville?" said Lenny from the doorway. "Got the Hummer waitin' outside, all gassed up."

"Kerrville?" Winona said. "Why can't I just go home?"

"I'd like you to go to the hospital to get checked out. Maybe stay for the night to be safe. You lost a lot of blood. There's no way for me to tell how much, but I don't like the pallor of your skin at the moment," Dr. Grant said. "You might need a night in the hospital with an IV to get your fluid levels back to normal."

"I'll follow you back," Kimberly said. "I'll have some damage control to do."

Riggs picked Winona up again and carried her to the Hummer.

"I can walk, you know," Winona said, tousling his hair. He still had bed hair from earlier tonight and wasn't wearing his ever-present hat.

"Just humor me."

"Don't worry," Lenny said as he drove away. "This is on the down low. We'll tell everyone you had a gardening accident."

Winona and Riggs burst out laughing because they both realized how true that could be.

WINONA WAS RELEASED from the hospital the next day. Kimberly worked her magic and no one from the media managed to get an inch past security. Winona had been registered under her married name, which provided extra anonymity even if due to the marriage announcement, many had figured it out. Kimberly issued a press release with news of Winona's hospitalization for "exhaustion" and a somewhat difficult late-in-life pregnancy.

In other news, Phil Henderson was arrested after a deputy sheriff interviewed both Riggs and Winona in the hospital. Separately. Thankfully, while in the hospital, another ultrasound showed that their babies had weathered just fine, even if their mother was a little dehydrated.

And Riggs? He spent the night in a chair by her hospital bed, reminding her again of the night at the Grange when he'd fallen asleep watching her. The night she'd started to fall for the cowboy.

Lenny waited curbside in the Hummer. According to Riggs, the vehicle had been purchased after years of ladies of SORROW fundraisers and served, for now, as the town's ambulance. Lenny had been itching to take someone to the hospital in it for months.

"I can't wait to get home and actually get a good night's rest," Winona said as she stretched out in the roomy back.

"It's good to hear you say 'home.'" Riggs squeezed her thigh.

And it was true. She felt as if Stone Ridge and all its quirky residents and sometimes over-the-top ladies of SORROW were her new tribe. Her family. But especially the handsome cowboy beside her, the one who'd never left her side.

"When I first drove you out to the Grange on our wedding day, I worried you'd think the place was a dump."

"Well, you were wrong."

"About that, and a lot of other stuff."

"It's true that I didn't want to marry you *because* I wanted my next marriage to be my last. Little did I know."

As they passed the open gate, Winona noticed all the

trucks and vehicles lining the road. People were coming in and out of the barn and spilling out of the main house.

"Are we having a party or something?"

"We are," said Riggs. "It's a welcome-home party."

"Ain't that somethin'. I sure hope there's cold beer," Lenny said, pulling up to the barn.

"We were gone one day."

"Yeah. You know Delores," Riggs said.

"Did she warn you?"

"Of course. She wanted to make sure we didn't stop by the Shady Grind first and ruin our appetites."

"Well, looks like the entire town is here anyway. Is the Shady Grind even open?" Winona asked.

She recognized so many residents and friends milling around, carrying ice coolers, picnic baskets, large covered platters. There were tables covered in red-and-white checkered cloths set outside underneath temporary awnings.

"It does look like a big crowd." Riggs climbed out first, offering his hand.

This was familiar to the times she'd been on the red carpet at the Grammys when one of her dates for the evening would do the honors. Or Colby, in those earlier years when he might have actually loved her. Funny how she'd once imagined that Riggs would have looked mighty fine in a tux at one of her award-show events. She'd worn couture gowns to those, and today was dressed in the clothes brought by Eve and Jackson to the clinic. Her too-tight Wranglers, and a tankini covered by a western shirt and boots. Her hair was pulled into a high ponytail and as usual these days, she wore no makeup.

But accepting the hand of the man holding it out for her now felt like she'd already won every award she'd ever been short-listed for.

Riggs pulled her into his arms and pressed a kiss to her temple. "Have fun today because this is all for you."

Kimberly ran up to them wearing her tan pantsuit. "This is my first hoedown. I'm sorry I don't have the clothes for it."

"You look great." Winona gave Riggs a smile and then took Kimberly's arm. "Walk with me."

"Winona, could you ever have imagined this would happen?" She waved her hand. "This is all for you. They're still calling you Annie Oakley, but they've added the 'singing Annie Oakley from Stone Ridge.'"

Winona wrinkled her nose. "Who's calling me that?"

"Um, almost everyone."

Somehow, she would lay the blame of that new title on Lenny, but it could be almost any one of her new friends. Maybe even Sean, she hoped, because she had a lot to do still to win him over.

"There's someone I want you to meet." Winona led Kimberly in the direction where Twyla stood near Jackson.

They'd put up a mock stage in the middle of a field, which means she'd get to enjoy some music today, too.

"Twyla, this is Kimberly Foster, my manager and dear friend." She gestured to Kim. "Kim, I want you to meet the next big thing in country music. Twyla has a powerhouse voice that reminds me a lot of a young Carrie Underwood. And she's just as sweet."

"Nice to meet you, Twyla." Kimberly offered her hand. "We should talk. Plenty of opportunities in Nashville."

"You'll get to hear her sing in a few minutes," Jackson said. "And I can vouch for that voice."

It occurred to Winona that she and Jackson hadn't collaborated on a song in a long while, and this might be a good time to start. They could write a song for Twyla and give her a good start. Send her on the way. After that, it would be up to her and how hard she wanted to work. How much she would be willing to give up.

Hopefully not nearly as much as Winona had.

Winona left them chatting and walked up to Sean, manning the grill along with some of the other men.

"Was it you, Sean? You're the one who started calling me Annie Oakley?"

"Maybe." He took a pull of his beer, smiling. "I can't believe you were ready to shoot a man for Riggs."

"I should have taken that shot."

He shook his head. "That might have made everything a whole lot worse."

"I'm sorry. I know you didn't trust me at first, and you had good reason not to."

"I was worried about my brother. But it's clear to me now that I had no reason to be. You've been in love with him all along, haven't you?"

"Am I that obvious?"

"I can't deny that I'm shocked because I never believed in love at first sight." He flipped a burger. "But hell, there's a first time for everything."

"There sure is."

"Winona, dear, excuse me?" This was from Beulah, coming up to Winona.

"Hi, Beulah. Did you help organize this shindig?" Winona went hands on hips.

"I had a hand in it." She tipped her chin. "We ladies of SORROW have a hand in *everything* that happens in Stone Ridge."

"I don't doubt it."

"Sugar, your situation got me to thinkin'. How many single women of childbearing age are out there in the world looking for a *fine* specimen of a man, such as our Riggs Henderson?"

Winona wasn't sure she liked where this conversation seemed to be headed. "Um, a lot?"

"Exactly. I think that together, we can find a way to bring more women here, in order that everyone might have a chance at their own happily ever after. With a man of Stone Ridge, of course. Because as you well know, we have plenty." She winked, and that's when Winona realized that Beulah had known of the initial plan all along. *And kept it to herself.* "What do you think?"

"I couldn't agree more."

"Then let's you and I talk sometime."

Jackson interrupted them. "We're going to get started with a little entertainment, and I'd like you to come up whenever, and *if* you feel up to it. I'm sure we'd all like a song, but no pressure, Annie Oakley."

"Okay, smartass. I think I can manage a song if you or Twyla play guitar for me. My shoulder isn't quite up to holding a strap." She met his gaze. "And hey, thanks for asking."

She would have said no, because she actually wanted to just kick back and enjoy the show with her husband, but she didn't want to let Jackson down.

Winona found the rocking chair on the wraparound porch, one that would face the mock stage, and settled in. Around her, the sounds of the rushing river in the distance buoyed her spirits. People chatting and laughing, waving at her, embracing each other. Lincoln was walking Sadie to a seat and went back to get some food. Eve was in the food line with Brenda and Hank. Apparently those two were newly dating, if one were to go by the shy looks they gave each other, and all of the hand-holding they were doing.

Lots of solid couples everywhere she glanced, but also a large group of men and a small group of women. Such a darn shame. Then again, there was Jolette Marie surrounded by four cowboys. She waved to Winona.

Someone didn't seem to mind all the attention.

Riggs took a seat next to Winona. "I heard what you're doing for Twyla. You're going to make a good mother, you know? Already helping someone younger than you find their way."

She squeezed his hand. The words touched her in a way she'd never imagined. Because he was right. She'd be a great mother because she'd had the world's best example even if only for the first ten years of her life. And at this point she didn't care if she had boys or girls, though something told her Beulah Hayes would prefer girls.

Winona felt something move inside her, so slight it would be almost undetectable to someone who hadn't waited years for this moment.

My babies!

"What is it?" Riggs reached for her. "What's wrong?"

"Nothing at all. Something kind of wonderful," she said, taking his hand and putting it on her belly. "Feel that."

A moment later, another soft flutter, and Riggs's eyebrow quirked in surprise.

And the smile on her husband's lips took over his whole face.

EPILOGUE

*L*ittle Joe Henderson fussed from his crib, and Riggs bent to pick up his son.

"There, there, little buddy." He rubbed Joey's back. "I'm sure you want your mama. But she's with your brother right now. Only one of you she can feed at a time."

No surprise to anyone born and bred in Stone Ridge, Winona gave birth to fraternal twin boys. Joe, named after Mary Jo, looked a lot like Riggs, with hair darker than his brother's golden curls. Both boys had blue eyes like their mother and would likely be breaking hearts for years to come.

Riggs inhaled the sweet smell of his baby boy. He swore he'd be able to identify them each simply by their scent. Joe smelled of baby powder and fresh-cut grass. And Calvin, born two minutes after his brother, like sunshine and strawberries.

Swaying Joe in his arms as he walked, Riggs went out the front door where he found Winona in the rocking chair with Calvin.

"Look who's up," he said.

She smiled lazily, her hair tousled and disheveled as she nursed Calvin, a blanket thrown around her shoulders covering them both. Dawn broke over the horizon bathing her in soft rays of light, and if possible, Winona looked even more beautiful than she had yesterday.

"Wait your turn, little guy," she said. "Cal is almost done here."

Her shoulder had fully healed in time for the birth, but the doctor claimed there might always be a residual weakness. In every other way, she was still the strong woman he fell in love with. And more generous than he would have ever dreamed. Winona sold everything she owned in Nashville, and some of her money would go to update both the clinic and school. The clinic had plans for a women's birthing center named after Mary Jo. And the school was working on hiring a staff of teachers who would be moved to a larger building once construction was complete. Riggs was involved in that project along with the rest of the men. They could have hired and paid for an entire crew but chose to save money on manual labor. There always seemed to be plenty of that in Stone Ridge.

Holding Joey, Riggs leaned against the porch railing. "When are we going to give them a bottle so I can help?"

"Soon," she said, leaning her head back. "I promise."

Her long hair cascaded down her back and he was struck with a wave of love so deep and wide that he nearly lost his balance. She'd been an amazing mother, wearing herself out breastfeeding both boys. But she also realized how much Riggs wanted to help.

Joey kicked and waved his angry little fists.

Me! Me! Me! Riggs imagined he said.

"This one is just like his daddy." Riggs grabbed Joey's fist and kissed it. "He wants you. Now."

She put Calvin to her shoulder and patted his back a few

times, then accepted Joe. For a moment she cuddled both babies, one on each shoulder, her face buried in their heads' soft fuzz. Then Riggs reached and took Cal from her. They'd become quite skilled at passing the twins, taking turns, and managing routines. Delores, of course, was always more than willing to rock a baby. Winona had all the help she needed, but Riggs was her only middle-of-the-night assistance. They took turns getting up, and Riggs hadn't been this bone-deep tired since his years in law school.

But it was a good kind of exhaustion. There were times in the middle of the night when he swore they'd simply catch each other in a shared thought: *I can't believe this is our life.*

They were two late-in-life parents and appreciated their children even more so than most. Riggs never thought he'd have this, a family of his own, and had given up long ago. Winona, fighter that she was, *never* gave up. And even if an unintentional event brought them to this place, it was the happiest unplanned time of his life.

And today was the day they'd christen their sons at Trinity Chapel.

Winona finished nursing Joe and took Riggs's hand to help her up. The irony of all this, and something they hadn't yet announced to their friends, was that Winona was pregnant. Again. Life would be crazy for some time, with actual twins, and what came down to Irish twins. Or would that be triplets? Riggs had no idea. What he did know *now*, however, was that a mother was sometimes still fertile while nursing.

This they'd both learned the hard way.

Together they laid both babies down in their side-by-side cribs.

"You get ready first," Riggs said. "It takes longer."

She cupped his chin. "If I was a handsome cuss like you, it wouldn't take half as long."

"Get out of here." He slapped her butt as she walked away. "You're beautiful and you know it."

Most days she walked around the house barefoot, without a stitch of makeup, her grown-out long hair wavy and wild. But today there would be photos, many of which would be released to media outlets by Kimberly, who now managed Winona's official "leave of absence" from performing.

The community of Nashville had reacted strongly to the news that Winona gave up performing and recording for an indefinite period of time. She helped her band members find other work. While some fans feigned outrage that she'd leave them in the lurch without all the promised new recordings, most were far more understanding, including her hero, Dolly Parton, who issued a tweet saying she supported and encouraged Winona's decision to put her family first.

And Winona's protégé, Twyla, was doing her best to pick up the slack in Nashville.

For his part, Riggs still didn't want Winona to give up the career that she loved. But she assured him, every time he asked, that *he* and their children were what she loved.

A few hours later, Riggs, Winona, Sean, and Delores arrived at the chapel on time. A small miracle. It always took forever to make a trip into town, and this time was no different. Riggs remained *astounded* as to how much effort it took them to leave the house, and no longer questioned why Winona chose to stay home most days. There were *at least* two of everything: car seats, strollers, playpens, pacifiers, wipes. Soon they'd add bottles to the mix. It took a while to pack the truck and they were usually late everywhere.

The twins had also demonstrated, on the few rides to the clinic for checkups, that they were not fond of being strapped down into car seats. This meant a two-part harmony of wailing most times, though Winona's voice soothed them.

"Hey, Riggs!" Jackson clapped Riggs on the back as he made his way up the steps of the chapel. "You hear the latest on Phil? Can you believe it?"

"Yep, sounds like we won't have to worry about *him* anymore."

Phil had served a few months for trespassing and assault, narrowly evading charges of attempted murder. But Riggs kept careful tabs on the man, never willing to risk underestimating him again. He'd moved to Las Vegas, where through some random chance, he'd met and recently married a showgirl. With any luck, he'd never be through Texas again. But in case he did, he was on the radar of every man in Stone Ridge. He wouldn't get far.

Eve walked next to Jackson, beaming because she was newly pregnant. Riggs marveled at how his third baby would arrive close to Eve and Jackson's. Now each of his children would be close in age with one of the Carver boys. Life in a small town.

"There he is!" Winona squealed, catching sight of Lincoln and Sadie's baby.

Yep, *another* boy.

Seemed there was definitely something in the water.

Sadie called Samuel "Sammy" Carver the image of his father, with deep blue eyes and matching dimples. "Are you kidding? We wouldn't miss this."

Sadie carried her bundle, Lincoln right behind her. Holding Cal, his usual charge, Riggs turned to see that nearly everyone in town must have decided they also couldn't miss this. People were spilling out of the chapel, not an empty seat to be had.

A far cry from their unhappy wedding day.

Riggs and Winona stood at the altar, each holding a child to be blessed by Pastor June. But face it, his sons already had a great beginning born to a mother like theirs, in a town where everyone looked out for one another.

As the pastor spoke and welcomed everyone, Riggs reached for Winona's hand. She smiled up at him and squeezed his hand.

"I love you," she mouthed.

No doubt about it, he was the luckiest man alive.

A RECIPE FOR SOUTHERN FRIED
CHICKEN BY DELORES

Ingredients:
    2 tablespoons paprika
    2 tablespoons freshly ground black pepper
    2 teaspoons garlic powder
    2 teaspoons dried oregano
    1/2 teaspoon cayenne pepper
    2 cups of flour
    1/3 cup of cornstarch
    1/2 teaspoon baking powder
    1 cup of buttermilk
    1 large egg
    Salt
    1 whole chicken, cut in pieces

Combine the paprika, black pepper, garlic powder, oregano, and cayenne in a small bowl and mix thoroughly with a fork.

Whisk the buttermilk, egg, 1 tablespoon salt, and 2 tablespoons of the spice mixture in a large bowl. Add the chicken pieces and toss and turn to coat. Transfer the contents of the bowl to a gallon-sized zipper-lock freezer bag and refrigerate for at least 4 hours, and up to overnight, flipping the bag occasionally to redistribute the contents and coat the chicken evenly.

Whisk together the flour, cornstarch, baking powder, 2 teaspoons salt, and the remaining spice mixture in a large bowl. Add 3 tablespoons of the marinade from the zipper-lock bag and work it into the flour mixture with your finger-tips. Remove one piece of chicken from the bag, allowing excess marinade to drip off, drop the chicken into the flour mixture, and toss to coat. Continue adding chicken pieces to the flour mixture one at a time until they are all in the bowl. Toss the chicken until every piece is thoroughly coated, pressing with your hands to get the flour mixture to adhere in a thick layer.

Adjust an oven rack to the middle position and preheat the oven to 350°F. Heat the shortening or oil to 425°F in a 12-inch straight-sided cast-iron chicken fryer or a large wok over medium-high heat. Adjust the heat as necessary to maintain the temperature, being careful not to let the fat get any hotter.

One piece at a time, transfer the coated chicken to a fine-mesh strainer and shake to remove excess flour. Transfer to a wire rack set on a rimmed baking sheet. Once all the chicken pieces are coated, place skin side down in the pan. The temperature should drop to 300°F; adjust the heat to main-tain the temperature at 300°F for the duration of the cook-ing. Fry the chicken until it's a deep golden brown on the first side, about 6 minutes; do not move the chicken or start checking for doneness until it has fried for at least 3 minutes, or you may knock off the coating. Carefully flip the chicken pieces with tongs and cook until the second side is golden brown, about 4 minutes longer.

Transfer chicken to a clean wire rack set in a rimmed baking sheet, season lightly with salt, and place in the oven.

Bake until thickest part of breast pieces register 150°F (65.5°C) on an instant-read thermometer, and thigh/drumstick pieces register 165°F (74°C), 5 to 10 minutes; remove chicken pieces as they reach their target temperature, and transfer to a second wire rack set in a rimmed baking sheet, or a paper towel–lined plate. Season with salt to taste. Serve immediately—or, for extra-crunchy fried chicken:

Place the plate of cooked chicken in the refrigerator for at least 1 hour, and up to overnight. When ready to serve, reheat the oil to 400°F. Add the chicken pieces and cook, flipping them once halfway through cooking, until completely crisp, about 5 minutes. Transfer to a wire rack set on a rimmed baking sheet to drain, then serve immediately.

Enjoy!

ABOUT THE AUTHOR

Born in Tuscaloosa, Alabama Heatherly lost her accent by the time she was two. Her grandmother, Mima, kept both the accent and spirit of the southern woman alive for decades.

After leaving Alabama, Heatherly lived with her family in Puerto Rico and Maryland before being transplanted kicking and screaming to the California Bay Area. She now loves it here, she swears. Except the traffic.

She lives with her family in Northern California.